The Avengers

* * *

by

Georgette Sable

A previously-published title authored by
Georgette Sable

Murder on M99

ISBN: 1-4392-4540-1
ISBN-13: 9781439245408

Visit www.booksurge.com to order additional copies

Chapter One

Liz unlocked the front door of her flat, going in and throwing her bag onto the settee. She felt like emulating the bag, throwing herself onto the settee and lying there. She had not done anything that day that was particularly tiring, but she had had to put up with another round of male chauvinism on the part of her boss, Detective Chief Inspector Lawrence. The thing that made it difficult for her was the fact that for the most part Simon Lawrence was such a nice man. It was just that he had a blind spot when it came to dealing with the opposite sex. He treated all of them as though they were feeble creatures, adept only at those skills undertaken by women down through the centuries. He had never actually said it, at least not in Liz's presence, but he acted as though he thought that policing was not a job that should be undertaken by women.

That day the DCI had assigned the newest arrival at the Mile End police station, Detective Constable Ken Ribak, to a new investigation that was just commencing. It was one that involved a criminal gang that was operating in the East End of London. Liz thought that undoubtedly DC Ribak had been chosen because of the nature of the crimes being committed by the gang, but she didn't see any reason why she couldn't have contributed to the case just as well as her male colleague. The DCI appeared to have ignored the fact that Liz was not working on anything except some relatively-unimportant routine enquiries. On the other hand, he had taken DC Ribak off a drug investigation so that he could work on the new one.

Once at home, Liz was tempted to 'drown her sorrows' in a couple of glasses of wine, but she couldn't take the time.

She had to eat something and then catch the tube to go to choir practice at a church in central London. She had been looking forward to the monthly choir practice because it was her opportunity to get together with one of the few friends she had. It was Lydia Mussett, a detective sergeant at New Scotland Yard. It was Lydia who had convinced Liz to join the Metropolitan Police.

Despite being members of the same police force, about the only time that Liz got to see Lydia was at choir practice. In fact the opportunity to meet with her friend was the main reason Liz continued her participation in that particular choir. The journey into central London and back by underground was not very convenient, especially after spending a full day at the police station.

Because he liked to have his weekends free, the choir director always held practice sessions on weekday evenings. This particular practice was on a Friday evening, so Liz was hoping that Lydia would invite her to her flat in West Hampstead. There were topics that she wished to discuss with Lydia. Also, perhaps, the two of them might enjoy some moments of intimacy like those they'd had before Lydia decided that as serving police officers they could not risk such a relationship being discovered.

It was obvious that Liz had arrived quite early at the choir practice, but London's underground system had become so unreliable over the previous few years that she had left her flat allowing plenty of time. As it was, she had got a train almost at once and, amazingly, there had been no delays between Plaistow, the location of her flat, and central London. She was disappointed to see that Lydia was not there, but her attention was taken up at once by the choir director, who told her that he would like to speak to her.

He said that the choir's next performance would feature a series of classical and semi-classical themes. It would feature an item in which a soprano and a mezzo soprano sang a duet to an orchestral accompaniment. "I was hoping that you would agree to sing the mezzo part, and Lydia Mussett would agree to do the other. My assistant has informed me that someone from the Metropolitan Police rang in just before I got here tonight. They said that Miss Mussett sent her regrets, but she will miss the rehearsal; she had to go up north someplace on police duties. If you are in touch with her regularly perhaps you could discuss it with her. I will give you the music containing the parts I want you and Miss Mussett to sing, so you can pass her bits on to her."

Liz was disappointed that Lydia would not be there that evening, but she welcomed the opportunity that discussing the idea of the two of them singing together would give.

On her way back to her flat, Liz made up her mind that she would take advantage of having made no plans for the weekend to visit her mum in Cambridge. It had been quite some time since she had visited Cambridge; maybe she could even arrange a get-together with her friend of long standing, Patricia Nesmith. She would ring Pat after she telephoned her mum.

After a prolonged period of ringing, Liz found herself saying to herself, "c'mon, mum, be there. Don't be out to the pub getting pissed." She let it ring for a short while longer and then rang off. She had to admit to herself that the lack of an answer was somewhat of a relief. Although she knew that her mum always was pleased to hear from her, the woman seemed incapable of speaking to Liz without reminding the supposed miscreant of her misdeeds. In this case those misdeeds would be the usual: "why must you ring me late at night?" That would be followed by: "why has it been so long since you last visited 'your poor, old mother'?" Sometimes, especially if her mum had been drinking, Liz would hear a shortened version of a story that she had been hearing all of her life, either from her mum or, when she was alive, her Nan. "Your mother has sacrificed everything for you, Elisabeth; rather than marry again after your father died, she decided to devote her life to you."

That story had been continued even after it had been established that the dead father part of it was a fabrication. When she had applied to join the police, Liz had had to submit a copy of her birth certificate with the application form. Much to her surprise, the certified copy of the certificate sent by the Registrar of Deaths and Births had written in the space reserved for the name of the father the word: "unknown." Most likely Liz's mum had chosen to remain single for her own purposes not because of the reason she announced to her daughter and the world in general: that she was a grieving widow who never could get over the loss of a devoted husband.

After Liz had rung off, she looked at her watch; it was almost midnight. She wondered where her mother could be. Her first thought was to cancel the trip to Cambridge, but then she changed her mind again. She really did wish to see Pat, and it was unlikely that her mum would be away. Besides, she had a key to the house, so even if no one was home she at least would have a place to stay. She toyed briefly with the idea of ringing Pat, but she knew that it would be likely that she would awaken Pat's mum who would not be pleased. No, she would wait until she got to Cambridge before trying to contact her friend.

* * *

On a Sunday the train journey from Cambridge to London's Liverpool Street station was a slow one, taking almost an hour and a half. However, Liz always enjoyed the trip because the carriages never were very full. She could engage in an activity that never failed to give her comfort: daydreaming. On this trip, returning from visiting her mum, she had much to think about. First of all she had learned that Audrey had been home when Liz had telephoned on Friday night. However, what it had boiled down to was the fact that the women had been too drunk to be able to answer the telephone.

Liz had discovered the problem when she had spoken to the next-door neighbours during her visit. She had gone to the neighbours, Rose and Fred Paltry to say "hello." At that time, Fred had expressed his concern that Liz's mum was drinking far too much. He said, "we go to the pub with her fairly often, but she never wants to come home until closing time. Last night, for example, Rose and me saw that she had had too much to drink, so we waited until she was ready to be tossed out of the pub and we helped her to get home. I don't think that she would have made it otherwise. Rose and me helped Audrey into her house and I got her up the stairs to her bedroom. As far as I know she probably collapsed onto her bed and passed out. I just left her there. I don't suppose there's much that you can do, Elisabeth, but it might help if you had a word. She'll probably be mad at us for saying anything, but Rose and me are really worried." Liz had said nothing to her mum; she knew that it would only precipitate another argument.

Then Liz thought of the long conversation that she had had with her friend, Pat. That had seemed rather strange. Pat seemed depressed, which was not her usual state of mind. She said that her job was going well and that she was expecting to be promoted. However, her relationship with her boyfriend, Roger Moffatt, was not going well. Pat admitted that in part the difficulty with Roger was her fault. "He wants to marry, have a family and settle down to a nice, middle-class existence. I want to continue to live a little. Occasionally, I have thoughts of giving up the bank and becoming an artist. Then I would go to far off places and paint and draw." Liz started to say something, but Pat held up her hand: "oh, I know, I've got to be practical. Unlike some, I wasn't born with a silver spoon in my mouth. And to add to my worries I've missed a period! God, Liz, I hope I haven't screwed myself! I know what will happen. If Roger has made me pregnant he will insist that we marry, and my mum will be with him one-hundred percent."

"I know it shouldn't feel that way, but the thought of marriage depresses me. If you weren't so damned hooked on that police career of yours I would gladly live with you. We could be so happy together. Oh, Liz, you should see the look that came on your face when I said that. That tells me everything I have to know." At that point, Pat burst into tears and Liz took her in her arms, repeating words she had spoken before: she wished that they could be together, but it was not possible as long as Liz was a member of the police.

As she thought of the minutes when she held Pat in her arms Liz felt a moistening around her eyes. She purposefully blinked and looked out of the train window at the passing landscape. It had been obvious for a very long time that her relationship with Pat was going to be a sad point in her life. She believed that she loved Pat like she loved no one else in the world, but she was sure such a relationship between them could not be sustained.

Back at her flat after the rather long journey by tube; the excuse given being "repairs on the Central Line between Liverpool Street and Mile End." She had more or less decided that if, when she got to Mile End tube station, there were delays on the District Line to Plaistow, she would forget about the bloody public transport and take a taxi! She was getting tired of continual delays and, almost as bad, having to travel in carriages laden with litter and whose windows were covered with spray-painted graffiti!

Fortunately, everything appeared to be running smoothly on the District Line so she got home very quickly, even if the carriage in which she sat looked like a pig-sty. When she got to her flat, the first thing she did after unpacking her overnight bag was to open a bottle of wine that she had bought a few days earlier. She was going to have a couple glasses of wine, a microwave supper, a hot bath and then retire to bed. She was looking forward to an activity in bed which, she sometimes felt, guiltily, had become a habit with her.

Liz was just finishing her first glass of wine when she got a telephone call from Lydia, who wished to know all about what had happened at the choir rehearsal. When Liz told her about the director's wish that they sing a duet together, Lydia said, "oh, I'd love to Liz, but I won't be able to do it, I'm afraid. I'm going to be away on secondment for the next two or, possibly, three months. I suppose that I had better ring the director and explain. Anyway, what I wanted to ask you was whether or not we could get together before I go away, which is the end of next week. I tried to ring you yesterday, but no luck." Liz explained why she had been away over Saturday night and saying that she would be delighted to get together with Lydia whenever and wherever she liked.

A short time later Liz put down the 'phone. She was pleased that she was going to stay overnight with Lydia on the following Wednesday evening. Her friend was going to cook them a meal for which Liz would supply the wine. She hoped that she and Lydia would be able to do more to-gether than just eat and drink. She rationalised her desire to have sex with Lydia by telling herself that their relationship never could be permanent. On the other hand, were she to have such a relationship with Pat there would be all kinds of complications because of the permanency it implied.

* * *

Chapter Two

Liz arrived back at the detectives' room very pleased that at last she had been assigned to something that showed promise of being interesting. Chief Inspector Lawrence had asked her to come to see him during the morning, and she had to admit that he had been rather charming; there was no sign of his male chauvinism. He said, "the super has been approached by the principal of Queen Mary and Westfield College, a Professor Mortlock, who said that he was worried about one of his staff. He said that the staff member, a woman lecturer in the School of Biological Sciences, Dr Anita Brinton, was in some danger. He wanted to know if there was anything the police could do."

"Professor Mortlock said that the threats had begun with a letter, unsigned, telling Dr Brinton that she must cease being cruel to animals or there would be 'consequences'. She had ignored that and, in fact, threw away the letter, thinking that it was a practical joke by a colleague in her department who did that sort of thing...practical jokes, that is. A short time later, there had been a telephone call which she ignored also. However, when she received a second telephone call she began to worry, so she told her head of department who informed the principal. When the principal questioned her about the incidents she said that the calls had been made to her flat during the day and had been recorded on her telephone-answering machine. However, unfortunately, she had recorded other messages over those from the person making the threats."

"The principal told Dr Brinton that he thought that there was little that the police could do unless they had some evidence that would help them find the caller. She said that if the person called again she would be certain to save the message that he left. A few days after speaking to the principal she received a third call. She saved a recording of that, and the crime lab is in the process of analysing the voice patterns of the caller who issued the threat. Of course before that analysis will be useful we shall have to have a suspect. That will be your job, Liz. Doctor Brinton did say that the voice was muffled somewhat, but she was fairly certain that the caller was a man. That narrows it down to only about half the population of London!"

The chief inspector continued, "two nights ago the threats became more specific and serious. An object that turned out to be a form of petrol bomb was pushed through the mail slot in the front door of the flat in which Dr Brinton lives with her partner." The DCI held up a plastic evidence bag in which was a small, flat bottle that was closed by what looked like a wad of cotton wool. He said, "originally the bottle contained petrol, but that has been removed. Forensics thinks that although the 'bomb' could have wreaked havoc, it may have been meant only as a warning. Whoever pushed the device through the mail slot had lit it first, but then they rang the doorbell. Very likely they wanted to make certain that someone would come to the door and discover the bomb before a fire had really taken hold. The idea that the bomb served as a warning was more or less confirmed an hour or so after the device was put through the door. Someone telephoned her saying, 'now that you know what might happen, Dr Brinton, perhaps you will take us more seriously'."

"Anyway, investigations that have been carried out so far have thrown up some interesting possibilities. Normally petrol bombs are made from glass bottles into which a quantity of petrol is placed and the open end is closed with a cloth or some flammable material. In use, the material that closes the mouth of the bottle is set alight and the bomb is thrown, the glass shattering upon impact with some solid object. The result usually is a wide area of fire. The bomb put through Dr Brinton's letterbox was quite patently different, being constructed of a relatively-unbreakable plastic. Doctor Brinton said that she recognised the type of bottle as the kind that is used in biological research to culture various kinds of organisms and tissues. Doctor Brinton said that she had no idea how widely available the containers were, but she'd try to find out."

"Anyway, Liz, I would like you to go have a word with the principal of Queen Mary. Here's his secretary's number; she's expecting a call from you. To be honest, I don't know that there is anything we can do, but maybe the principal has something in mind that might be helpful. He did ask the super if there were any young coppers who had attended university so might know their way around a college campus."

Despite the fact that she walked by the campus of Queen Mary and Westfield College on her way to and from the Mile End underground station, Liz knew very little about the school. She knew that it was part of the University of London; she had met students from there when she was doing her undergraduate work at King's College.

When she reached the campus she asked one of several people who passed her to direct her to where she would find the principal's office. That way she found herself entering a two-story building that faced on the Mile End Road. It was part of the main administration block.

When she made enquiries at a desk labelled, RECEPTION, she was told to wait for a few moments whilst the man seated there said that he would contact the principal's secretary. He said that getting to the principal's office was complicated, so he'd ask someone to come fetch her.

A short time later Liz was being shown into an office where a bald, middle-aged man rose from his desk to come forward and shake her hand. He introduced himself as Lawrence Mortlock. Liz was taken with the man, who seemed quite informal and friendly.

The principal said that he would explain more fully later, but what he had in mind would be greatly aided if the person involved had spent some time recently as a university undergraduate. "Your superintendent seems to think that you will 'fit the bill'. I have discussed the way forward with the head of the School of Biological Sciences and the four members of staff there, including Dr Brinton, who work with laboratory animals. Three of them only work with tissues. However, Dr Brinton is doing work with living, intact animals; possibly that is the reason that only she has attracted the attention of the animal-right's extremists; at least so far."

"A few years ago, when the activities of the animal-rights people began to become more widely publicised they seemed to be concentrating their activities on the quarters in which animals were kept. For that reason when we set up such quarters they were placed in a fairly inaccessible place at the top of the then new biological sciences block. Entry to the animal quarters is restricted to only a few people and even they must go through a fairly rigorous security screen. It is possible that Dr Brinton has been threatened and attacked personally because of the extremists' failure to get at the animal quarters."

It looked as if the principal was at least pausing in his narrative, so Liz asked what it was that he thought the police could do to help. He said, "my colleagues and I discussed that point, and we came to the conclusion that probably it was not very practical to mount a 24-hour guard on Dr Brinton.

After all, very likely that would tie up a lot of policemen for a long time, and the extremists might just move on to some other target. The head of biological sciences said that one of the academic staff in the school had told him that one of his tutees had told him, in confidence, that she was fairly certain that a Queen Mary undergraduate was involved. The staff member said that all he had been able to find out from the student was that a friend had told her about a member of the animal-rights movement at QMW. The student said that she didn't know the name of the person, but she thought that it was one of the undergraduate physicists."

"It was that information from the head of biological sciences that gave me the idea that it might prove to be useful and productive were a police officer to become an undergraduate at QMW. Possibly, such a person could gather evidence that might be helpful in positively identifying the animal-rights person and, with luck, the people with whom he or she associates. I must say, I find it difficult to believe that one of our undergraduates would be an extremist, so it is likely that his or her associates hold the answer to what happened to Dr Brinton."

"The head of the school of biological sciences offered to help with an attempt to find out more about the physics student, but I told him to wait until I discovered what the police had to say. When I spoke to your Superintendent Cleary a few days ago he seemed keen on the idea of putting someone undercover. He was not so keen on mounting a 24-hour surveillance of Dr Brinton. He said that he would discuss it with a colleague and get back to me, which he did and the result is that you are here today."

"Let me tell you my idea for what you can do; you can tell me if it seems feasible to you. I have to take guidance from you on this because, after all, you will be the person on the 'firing line' so to speak. I have had a word with the head of the physics department, Professor Edwards, who, in fact, thinks he knows who the undergraduate in question may be. However, I'll let him discuss that with you. He told me that he is certain there would be no difficulty in arranging to accommodate someone undercover. Apparently there is quite a lot of interchange between physics departments, particularly within the University of London. He said that the main problem would be to make the undercover police officer believable as an undergraduate in physics. I told him that the officer that Superintendent Cleary had in mind was a recent graduate in mathematics from King's College London. He told me that a sound knowledge of mathematics would help, but he would have to discuss it with the police officer nominated."

As an aside the principal said that he and the head of the mathematics department at Kings, Professor Martin, were good friends. Liz said that she had been very fond of Professor Martin. "He was the one to introduce me to Gilbert & Sullivan." The principal said, "oh, you sing also? You have many talents. I used to take part in such activities; in fact, that's where I met Tony Martin. Unfortunately, I don't have the time, or, for that matter, the voice for such things these days."

* * *

As Liz walked back to the police station she thought over what it was that she was to do at QMW. She had had a long conversation with Professor Edwards who suggested a 'scenario' that would account for her being a visitor to his department. He said that the department had developed an expertise in an area of astrophysics which often attracted visitors. He said that she was perhaps a little younger than most such visitors, but he was confident that together they could dream up a plausible cover story.

With respect to the undergraduate who, he suspected, might be involved in the animal-rights movement, Professor Edwards showed her a photograph. He said that the young man concerned was a third-year student named Barry Goff. He said that the young man had been one of his advisees as a second year, so that he had got to know him reasonably well. "During that year he performed very well in all of his academic work, and his exam marks were always first class. He's a personable and well-mannered young man. I don't recall that he ever expressed opinions that would indicate that he was an extremist of any kind or even that he was a follower of the animal-rights movement. Nevertheless, shortly after the start of the present term I was attending a meeting at the Senate House, you know, the central administration building for the University of London in Bloomsbury. About halfway through the deliberations a tremendous ruckus was set up outside. The volume of the noise was aided by the fact that it was a warm day and all of the windows of the room I was in had been opened fully to give us some ventilation. When we looked out of the windows we could see that the forecourt area outside the front entrance to Senate House was filled with young people who were carrying placards and chanting slogans such as, 'say no to animal cruelty', 'no to research on monkeys' and 'Bertrand, out, out, out'!"

"We were all puzzled why such a thing should happen at that particular time until one of our colleagues explained: during that same afternoon a committee headed by the Vice Chancellor of the University, Lord Bertrand, was meeting. The committee was supposed to decide whether or not a primate research centre should be established at Silwood Park, southwest of London, under the auspices of Imperial College."

"The demonstrators were making so much noise that the chairman of our committee decided that we had best call it a day; he adjourned our meeting. However most of us continued to watch out of the windows to see what was going to happen. It was then that I saw Barry Goff. He was standing near the middle of the crowd of protesters and was carrying one of the placards. I must confess that I didn't think much of it at the time because I just thought that the kids were a harmless bunch who enjoyed making a fuss. However, if he is involved with the sorts of things that have been happening to Dr Brinton, I can have no sympathy for him."

Professor Edwards then told Liz, "getting back to you, constable, my main concern, I'm afraid, is whether or not you have the background to convince a genuine physicist that you have had training in the science. The principal told me that you have a first-class degree in maths from King's College, so that should be a big help. Tell me something about the areas of maths with which you are most familiar." Liz had been expecting such a question. During a recent trip to her home in Cambridge she had 'dug' out all of her old revision materials and brought them down to London. She then recited for Professor Edwards the main areas of the lectures and tutorials during her three years as an undergraduate in mathematics at King's College. She said that during her final year she had had quite a lot of exposure to the mathematics of wave theory, which, she believed, was fairly central to astrophysics.

Professor Edwards went on to say, "you pursued a splendidly broad course in your three years at Kings, some of which will stand you in good stead with respect to our physics course here. Of course the mathematics of wave theory will be most helpful to you whilst you are with us. May I ask if you are familiar with other than the purely mathematical aspects of the theory; structures such as electrons and quarks? I can give you some references to read that will bring you up to date on the purely astrophysical aspects of the theory. Would you like that? You will be exposed to that whilst you're here, but your lecturers will assume that since you are in their courses you have an adequate background. It might be easier for you should you read some references that will help you with that background." Liz thanked the professor, telling him that she would very much appreciate having the list of references.

Professor Edwards then said that he thought that the best course of action would be to welcome Liz to the department as an undergraduate visitor. "We could say that you are here to profit from our expertise in astrophysics; a subject not well covered by the department at which you are doing your undergraduate work." The professor then asked if Liz was familiar with any university or college location other than Kings. When she told him that she was borne and reared in Cambridge he said, "ah, perhaps that wouldn't be appropriate. Cambridge is rather well known in astrophysics, and it would be unlikely that someone from there would be coming to visit us on a long-term basis." He said that a good friend of his was the head of the physics department in York; had she ever been there? She said that she had not.

Finally, they had decided that Liz would be a visitor from Durham University. At least Liz had visited there whilst she was a sixth former and knew something about the city and the university. Also, it was far enough away from London that it was unlikely that anyone she would meet at QMW would have a friend or friends there.

Liz came away from speaking with Professor Edwards with his agreement that, her superiors willing, she would begin her duties at QMW about a week later. The professor said that he would look out the references he mentioned and send a list of them to her. "All of them will be in the College library, so once we've got you set up here as a student, you should have no trouble gaining access to them."

* * *

Liz outlined to Detective Chief Inspector Lawrence the plan that Professor Edwards had suggested: "the professor said that he would speak with a Dr Sangstrom. He is one of the astrophysics team in the department and, also, acts as an advisor to Barry Goff, the young man the professor thinks may be involved in the animal-right's movement. Professor Edwards told me that he thought it best not to say anything to Dr Sangstrom about the true purpose of my being at QMW; just that I was a visitor from Durham University, there for the experience. The professor also is going to suggest to Goff's advisor that it would be helpful if one of his advisees could help me to settle in. He will suggest further that he thinks that Barry Goff would be a good candidate. Hopefully, with Professor Edwards help I will have a more-or-less automatic entry to Goff's acquaintance without arousing suspicion."

At first the DCI was very sceptical about the plan that Professor Edwards had proposed, and told Liz that he would have a think about it and get back to her. In any event he would have to discuss it with Superintendent Cleary. "After all, it will be the super who will attract the blame if it all goes wrong or if we end up spending too much time and money on a futile investigation."

Liz was just at the point of leaving the station to go home when the 'phone on her desk rang. In response to her answer with "DC Andresen" the voice of the DCI said, "he thinks it's a great idea, Liz. He's told me to supply you with anything you need, and he wants you to keep in touch on a daily basis. He'll be ringing the principal of Queen Mary and Westfield to let him know that he has approved what you will be doing."

* * *

Chapter Three

During the first week of her 'stint' at QMW Liz 'buried' herself in the library. She found that most of the references Professor Edwards had suggested were very heavy going, even though the mathematics was explicable. She remembered that the O-level chemistry course she had taken at school had gone into detail on the structure of atoms, but the term, "wave theory" had been missing entirely from the explanation. Now she was beginning to see that wave theory was central to an understanding of atomic structure. After 'slogging' her way through all of the references she had become quite enthusiastic about the theory, concluding that it was a wonderful unifying theme for the whole of the natural universe. She was dying to discuss some of her findings with someone, but at that stage of her stay at QMW, there was no one. Perhaps, when she got to know him better, Barry Goff would be such a person.

Liz had met Barry Goff, briefly, just after arriving. The man who was to act as her undergraduate advisor, Dr Sangstrom had arranged a meeting between himself, her and Barry Goff. At that meeting Goff had said that he would be pleased to help Liz settle in and hoped that she would enjoy her stay at QMW. Liz's first impression of the young man was that he had a pleasing personality and was well mannered. However, by then she had had enough experience in the police not to rely too firmly on first impressions.

Once Liz abandoned the library and got into the mainstream of student life, she found it difficult pretending to be a student again. Most of the youngsters; and that's all they were, seemed to have little idea about the world outside. She didn't think that in the short time since she had been in their position her ideas had changed. However, finally, she had to agree to herself that being more-or-less on her own in the world had made her grow up. Most of the undergraduates she had met at QMW had still to undergo that process.

She had attended several lectures, discovering to her chagrin that she really was not well prepared to be an undergraduate in physics. However, the fact that she found herself struggling with the material of her lectures served as a good excuse to form a relationship with Barry Goff. He was proving to be most helpful to her academically, and, of late, she had detected signs that he wished them to meet under non-academic circumstances. She was waiting for the opportunity to introduce the topic of animal rights into their conversation, but an appropriate moment had not arisen.

That situation changed on the weekend following Liz's second week at QMW. Doctor Anita Brinton was injured in an automobile crash, sustaining facial lacerations and considerable bruising of her thoracic region. She realised afterward that had she not been wearing a seatbelt her injuries could have been very much worse. She was held overnight in the Accident and Emergency Department of a hospital near the scene of the crash and then released, after being interviewed by the police.

In her statement to the police she said that she had no idea what had happened. "I was driving at about seventy on the M 11 motorway. Suddenly ahead of me was a sea of red brake lights, so I slammed on the brakes and nothing happened. I ploughed straight into the back of another car. Fortunately, there was only a single person in the car that I ran in to, and he was also wearing his seatbelt. He was relatively uninjured, but both of our cars are write offs."

Inspection by the police revealed that the brakes of Dr Brinton's automobile had been tampered with. A small hole had been drilled into the walls of the metal lines filled with brake fluid that transmit the pressure applied to the brake master cylinder to the two fronts wheels of her car. The hole had been closed by wrapping electrician's tape around the brake line. According to a police technician, it was very likely that the brakes would have been functional for several applications of the brake pedal. However, finally the pressure within the brake line would have fallen to a level where it was inevitable that the brakes would fail. The exact cause of the crash in which Dr Brinton was injured was not revealed in reports of the incident that were made public.

That the incident involving Dr Brinton was the responsibility of an animal rights group was shown by two messages received after the crash. The first had been telephoned to the offices of a London tabloid newspaper, the Daily Mail, almost an hour before the time of Dr Brinton's crash. The caller, a male who had disguised his voice, said "very shortly an infamous vivisectionist will meet a well-deserved fate. Let what will happen to that person serve as a warning to all of those who continue to inflict pain and misery on our fellow creatures." It had taken the paper three days to discover the identity of the so-called 'infamous vivisectionist'.

When Dr Brinton arrived home after being released from hospital she found a partner who was frantic with worry. After he had listened to a recorded message on the tape of the answer phone in the flat he shared with Dr Brinton, he had rung the police and several London hospitals. At that time no one was able to tell him anything. After a time, when her partner's excitement had subsided,

Dr Brinton listened to the message from the animal-rights extremist that had been recorded on the telephone-answering machine. She said that the voice was identical to that of the male caller who had rung after the petrol bomb had been put through the door of her flat. It was a rather long-winded diatribe that had been directed toward Dr Brinton's partner. The monologue assumed that Dr Brinton was dead. The caller went on to say that at least for her the suffering was brief unlike that that she had inflicted upon the victims of her research.

Once the newspaper that had received the call about the incident involving Dr Brinton discovered her identity they contacted her, asking for an interview. At first she refused, saying that the sooner the whole matter was forgotten the better. However, the reporter who spoke to her convinced her that it was unlikely that the animal rights people would soon be forgetting the matter. "Besides, Dr Brinton, I assume you are not doing what you do to animals because you enjoy inflicting pain. Would it not be to your benefit to say why it is you are using animals in your research? To do otherwise would be to concede victory to extremists. I'm sure you wouldn't want that."

Liz was happy to see the article about Dr Brinton that appeared in the Daily Mail. She thought that the person who wrote the article had been quite skilful in presenting the arguments. She discovered that Dr Brinton's work was concerned primarily with attempts to get parts of the rat nervous system to regenerate. The research was important to a very large number of people in the world who have been invalided by spinal injuries.

Doctor Brinton had admitted freely that her work necessitated purposefully damaging the spinal cords of the experimental animals. Although that was done painlessly, she realised that the injury would be permanent and would handicap the animals. She was quoted as saying, "I can see no other way to do the research. It is aimed at restoration of function in a whole animal and, I'm afraid, that necessitates using whole animals."

Liz's ideas on animal experimentation were not fully formed. She liked animals and never would mistreat any of them. She even had no objection to the presence of wasps. When she was a girl her mum and Nan used to get upset with her because when a wasp got trapped in the house she would insist on opening a window or door and releasing it, rather than killing it. She held the same regard for all of the insects, crustaceans and molluscs that attacked the plants of her mother's garden. Because of her ideas about animals she thought that she would not find it difficult to sympathise with many of the goals of the so-called animal-rights movement

The opportunity to discuss animal rights with Barry Goff came on the same day that the article containing the interview of Dr Brinton appeared in the Daily Mail. As they exited one of the lectures that she and Barry Goff both had attended, he asked her if she had the time to go to the Junior Common Room for coffee. She had been hoping for just such an invitation, but had been waiting for him to ask. They had got on together quite well on the professional level. She had spent considerable time studying in an effort to avoid giving Goff any grounds for suspecting that her claim to be an undergraduate in physics was not genuine. It had been obvious from time to time that he had recognised shortcomings during their conversations on the subject of physics. However, usually he, himself, would cover up for her by saying that he expected that the courses at Durham and Queen Mary didn't emphasise the same topics.

Immediately across from the place where Liz and Barry Goff were queuing in the JCR were some racks on which rested daily newspapers that were for sale. The headline of one of them read:"ANIMAL EXTREMIST CRACKDOWN." Liz made no comment when she saw it. However, Barry Goff asked her to hold his place and went over to the racks, removing a copy of the paper with the animal extremist headline. As he rejoined the queue he asked her if she had read about what had happened to a lecturer in biology at QMW. She feigned ignorance, so he résuméed the story as they collected their coffees and found a place to seat themselves. As he spoke he gave no indication as to where his sympathies lay, with Dr Brinton or the persons who were responsible for what had happened to her.

As they talked in the JCR Liz gently made Barry Goff aware of the point of view that she had decided that she would adopt if and when she discussed the topic with him. She said that she could not agree with inflicting cruelty on animals. "I reckon that if some drug company wants to know how effective their drug will be to combat some disease they should pay human volunteers to try it. Nobody asks the poor animals; they have no say in the matter. I saw a terrible film on the telly once: a poor little baby monkey was taken away from its mother just to see what would happen. After a time, all the poor little beggar would do was huddle in the corner of its cage, frightened of everyone that came near it. When I saw it I didn't understand what the point of the research was and I still don't! However, that is not to say that I agree with what has been done to Dr Brinton. That is going too far. I understand that some people get frustrated when the government won't listen to them, but there is such a thing as going too far."

Liz watched Barry Goff as she was speaking, seeing that he was nodding his head in agreement and had a slight smile on his face. When she finished she said, "I'm sorry for going on like that, Barry, but I'm afraid I get rather wound up when the subject of inflicting cruelty on animals comes up."

"Oh, don't apologise, Liz; I feel the same way. I think some of the things that are done to animals in the name of so-called science are horrible. However, I'm not sure that I can agree entirely with you about what has happened to Dr Brinton. I haven't read the article in this paper yet, but someone told me that she had had a crash, and it was thought to have happened because animal-rights extremists tampered with her car. I wouldn't want to see her die or be injured seriously, but I hope she takes it as a clear message that she shouldn't be doing what she's doing."

That afternoon, as Liz walked toward the Mile End underground station to get her train home she felt very pleased with the day's accomplishment. At last, she would have something positive to report to DCI Lawrence when she rang him that evening.

Finally, she had had a conversation with Barry Goff that was relevant to her reason for being at QMW. It was apparent that he had accepted her for what she appeared to be: a third-year in physics visiting from Durham University. Also, he seemed pleased to know that the two of them appeared to have many of the same ideas about animal experimentation. He had not gone into any detail, but it was obvious that he did not condemn violence in support of the animal-rights campaign. She wondered if that position on his part indicated that he would be willing to take part in such violence, or if, indeed, he already had taken part in such violence. However, what was hopeful about their meeting was the fact that Barry Goff and she had made a date to go out together. She hoped that a more personal relationship with him would give her entry to the animal-rights movement, and, hopefully, an opportunity to identify extreme elements within that movement.

* * *

Chapter Four

On their first date Liz had met Barry Goff in a pub that he had recommended. Liz had been worried about their meeting place because it was not very far from the police station at which she worked. There was a possibility that she might encounter one of her police colleagues in or around the pub. However, Barry had wanted to meet there because he had been several times and knew that the food served there was better than the usual 'pub grub'.

The food was everything that Barry had said, but the red wine that the pub served by the glass to go with it was very disappointing. Liz had offered to pay for her own food, but Barry insisted that he had asked her so that it was his treat.

Just after a young woman had delivered their meals and they had begun to eat, two men entered the pub and came over to where Liz and Barry were seated, greeting him by name. Barry introduced Liz to the two men, calling them Richard and George. The two men stood by the table for a few minutes to chat and then excused themselves, George saying that they would leave Barry and Liz to enjoy their meal. The two men went to the bar, got themselves each a pint of beer, and then took seats.

Liz had tried to discern from their conversation with Barry in what way the three men knew each other, but from that viewpoint what they had to say provided no information. Liz did not recognise either of the two men as anyone she had seen on the QMW campus; in fact George, clearly, was in his thirties. She hoped to get Barry to talk about them by saying to him, "your two friends seem to be quite nice; are they at Queen Mary?" The question seemed to amuse him. He replied, "no, George is a bit long in the tooth to be a student, and Richard left school as soon as they'd let him. He's bright enough but anything but academic." That was the only information that Barry seemed prepared to give about his two friends, so Liz had to leave it there. However, for the remainder of the evening surreptitiously she kept them under observation.

After they had finished eating, Liz suggested to Barry that she wouldn't mind if he would like for the two of them to join George and Richard. However, Barry said that he saw enough of them at other times. "I'd rather that this evening be for just the two of us." Liz was disappointed. She had hoped that during further conversations between the three men one or another of them would reveal information about the nature of their relationship.

Unfortunately for Liz, for the remainder of the evening the conversation between her and Barry did not touch upon animal rights. He seemed more concerned to learn about her background and how she was enjoying her time in London. She hoped that she had not been stupid in telling him the truth: that she had lived most of her life in Cambridge prior to going to university. Also, he was happy that he had not asked too many questions about Durham.

She was surprised to learn that he was a product of the East End of London and had gone to local state schools, which, he said, "are not as bad as everyone makes out. My parents kept encouraging me to leave London to go to university elsewhere, but I like it here. I even like the East End. I was lucky enough to find a bed-sit in a house that is only a 15 minute walk from QMW. The room is fairly large and it has a sink and microwave. I bought myself a small fridge so I can keep milk and that sort of stuff. I was thinking that after we leave here we could go there and have a cup of coffee or something." Barry had just said finished speaking when his two friends rose from where they were seated and again approached their table. George said, "we're just off, Barry; we'll see you tomorrow night?" Barry and Liz said, "good-night," and Barry added, "yeh, I'll see you tomorrow, George, Richard."

Shortly after arriving at Barry Goff's room, Liz was worried that she had made an error of judgement. She had accepted his invitation to go to his 'digs' for a cup of coffee hoping that it would give her further opportunity to learn more about his involvement with animal-rights activists. However, their time together had turned into a rather passionate love-making session.

Once they had entered his room there was no further mention made of coffee. She had not objected, in fact she fully accepted when first he attempted to kiss her. That had occurred almost immediately upon their arrival at the bed-sit. She had tried to stop him when he pulled her blouse free from her skirt and fondled a breast. However, her attempts to object verbally were blocked because his tongue was occupying most of her mouth. Almost before she knew what he was doing he had his hand between her legs and was manipulating the most sensitive part of her genitalia with considerable expertise. He was sufficiently good that Liz forgot for a time that she must not let him continue. She relaxed resting her body against him.

It was obvious that he took her action to indicate that he had overcome her resistance; he suggested that they would be more comfortable if they seated themselves on the settee. She started to agree, then she said, "no, Barry; really, I must be getting home. Perhaps we can do this another time, but I hardly feel that I know you well enough." She couldn't help it, she giggled when his reply to that was, "well, it would be one sure way for us to get to know each other better!" Nevertheless, the pause afforded by their exchange allowed her to escape from a situation that she, as a police officer investigating him, could not allow.

Liz finally arrived back at her flat in Plaistow, having just managed to catch the last underground train from the Mile End station. Barry had insisted upon walking with her to the tube station, and she was happy to have him with her. He had wanted her to spend the night with him, even promising that he would behave himself. However, she had argued using the excuse that their relationship had not yet progressed to that point. Reluctantly, he had accepted that excuse.

When Liz made her report to DCI Lawrence the morning after her pub evening with Barry Goff, she summarised her findings during the almost three weeks she had been undercover at QMW. She said that she had found no evidence to link Barry Goff with extremist activities. "To the contrary; he certainly sympathises with the goals of the movement, but so far, at least, he has said nothing to me that would indicate that he is sympathetic to the more extreme methods used by some of them."

Then she told her boss about the two men she had met when she and Barry went to the pub. She said that it was only a guess, but it was possible that they were linked to an animal-rights group. "I understood from Barry Goff that the two men are regulars at the pub which we visited. Do you think it would be a good idea to attempt to discover who they are and then investigate their backgrounds. I think that it might raise suspicions if I question Goff about them any more, but I can give you a good description of them. Maybe you can persuade one of the lads to spend a few evenings in that pub until they appear." Instead of saying that he thought Liz's idea was a good one, the DCI said, "yes; I was just thinking that myself."

Despite the fact that Liz had developed a friendship with Barry Goff she knew no more about his animal rights activities than the fact that he sympathised with the motives of the movement. She had hoped that he would invite her to go to meetings with him, but if there had been such meetings since they met, she had heard nothing about them.

The only aspect of their relationship that had proved helpful to her investigation was the fact that she had been instrumental in allowing the police to identify George and Richard. She had met Barry Goff in the usual pub a few times since their original date; each time Liz had alerted DCI Lawrence to the fact that she was going there, and each time he had sent DC Chris Houghton to spend the evening there. On the second such occasion George and Richard were in the pub when Liz and Barry Goff arrived. Liz looked around the pub, seeing DC Houghton seated at the bar talking to the landlord. Liz said quickly, "I think it is time that I bought the first round, Barry; the usual?" He replied, "you sure, Liz? OK, I'll have my usual." He then went to the table where his two friends were seated whilst Liz went to the bar.

Neither Liz nor Chris Houghton made any sign of recognition when Liz approached the bar, but whilst the landlord was at the other end of the bar getting the drinks that she had ordered Liz whispered to him that the subjects he was there to see were seated at a table on the far wall near the darts board. "The bloke with whom I came into the pub is talking to them." All DC Houghton said was, "gotcha!"

* * *

Liz smiled at the station sergeant when he greeted her with, "welcome stranger; where have you been?" Liz replied, "oh, here and there." He said, "ah, secret mission, eh?" Tapping his forefinger on the side of his nose he said, "say no mo-ah! Anyway, Liz, the DCI is waiting for you in his office."

When she got to the DCI's office, Liz was waved at to enter. She noted that DC Houghton and another man were there already. "Ah, Liz, we were just talking about you. You know Chris Houghton, of course, but this is PC Bob Lenihan; he's helping the CID out on this one." Liz nodded at Chris Houghton and shook hands with PC Lenihan before seating herself. The DCI continued, "we just want to bring you up to date on those two men you pointed out to Chris in the pub. We have found out quite a lot about them, but it's not been overly helpful, I'm afraid. The man known as 'George', George Baird, that is, is a known animal-rights agitator. He has a record of arrests for creating disturbances outside of animal-breeding establishments and university labs, although there has been nothing in the past few years. The other one, Richard Cowling, is cut from the same mould as Baird, but he has been arrested only once and that was for assaulting a police officer. That occurred during a demonstration about six months ago. Unknown to them we have recorded their voices whilst they were talking in the pub. The speech patterns do not match those of the voices recorded on her answering machine by Dr Brinton. That's true also of the voice recorded by the Daily Mail."

"Chris and Bob have been nosing around into the background of your friend, Barry Goff. As we know, he has no police record, but as far as we can see he's completely clean. We haven't been able to see if his voice fits any of the patterns on Dr Brinton's machine because the damn woman wiped the tapes. For some reason she's not been very co-operative of late. She keeps saying that she just wants to forget that the whole episode occurred. Unfortunately we can't do that. The only thing that seems to link Barry Goff to the animal rights movement is the statement by Professor Edwards and, of course, the fact that he appears to be friendly with Baird and Cowling. We're wondering if, perhaps, you couldn't be more proactive in your relationship with Goff. Although he and his two friends may not be involved in extremist activities, it is possible that there are elements of extremism in the group that they belong to. Therefore, it definitely would be worthwhile for you to try to get Goff to introduce you into that group."

Liz said nothing for a short time as she thought: "what in hell do you think I have been doing during the past four weeks! I have tried every subtle way I know to discover who his associates in the animal-rights movement are. So far I've had no success!" Instead of saying what she thought, Liz said, "yes, sir; I shall try harder to do just that!"

* * *

Chapter Five

Liz felt herself somewhat caught on the horns of a dilemma. She was coming under increasing pressure from her boss to get results; he was certain that Barry Goff was the key to her infiltration of the animal-rights group that, in all probability, was responsible for the attempt to murder Dr Brinton and other incidents involving her. During one of her telephoned reports to him Liz had got quite upset at a suggestion that he had made: "ah, c'mon, Liz. You and I both know that if you only applied your womanly wiles, he'd be putty in your hands."

Although she had said nothing at the time, for several minutes after talking to the man she had fumed: she resented the implication. That resentment was not just based on the fact that for her to prostitute herself was contrary to police procedures and would be counter productive; no prosecution could be successful that was based on evidence obtained in that way. She had felt like telling him, "presumably you would give the same advice to one of your male colleagues; you would tell him to get himself buggered in order to gather evidence!"

Despite the fact that she intended to continue to resist taking the shortcuts that her boss had suggested, Liz did realise that she would have to do something to make events move more rapidly than they had so far. The end of the first semester of teaching at QMW was approaching, and the cover story had indicated that she would be returning to Durham at that time.

Almost always when they had been to the pub together, Barry Goff had invited Liz to return with him to his room afterwards. After what happened the first time, she had always invented a reason why she could not go. She knew that recently he had moved into a new flat, so perhaps she could use that as an excuse to accept his invitation the next time he made it. She wasn't too sure what she would do if he attempted another seduction scene, but she would adjust to that possibility should it arise.

Barry Goff rarely had more than two pints of bitter when they were in the pub together. However, Liz had noticed on an occasion when he had had more than that to drink he had become rather loquacious. That had happened only once, whilst they were in the bar in the Junior Common Room at Queen Mary. Unfortunately, at that time the two of them were amongst several undergraduate friends and it had been impossible to get him talking about animal rights without someone interrupting and changing the subject. She thought that if he invited her to his flat she would not decline any offers of drink. Perhaps she could get him to the 'loquacious' stage of inebriation without risking too much sexual aggressiveness on his part.

A day later Liz accepted Barry Goff's invitation to enjoy another pub meal. However, she made it a stipulation that she would pay, telling him that he was no more than a poor student like she was, so he couldn't always be paying for the both of them. He agreed to her proposal without further argument. He said that his new flat was costing more than he had anticipated, because he had had to buy kitchenware and other housekeeping items. He would welcome her financial help. That evening neither George nor Richard were in the pub, so after eating their meal, they did not linger. To Barry Goff's obvious delight Liz agreed to round off the evening with a couple of drinks at his flat.

Liz was quite taken with the small flat. It was one of two in a semi-detached house that had been converted. Whoever had done the conversion was very good at design. Within the space occupied by Barry Goff's flat the converter had managed to fit a room containing a double bed and a large wardrobe which had a build-in set of drawers. Part of that room had been walled off to enclose a toilet facility including wash basin, toilet and stall shower. The second room of the flat had a kitchenette which occupied the whole of one side of the room, an eating area with a small table and four chairs and a living area with a settee and two overstuffed chairs. Mounted on a bracket on the wall was a small television. Next to that was a bookcase which was filled with books, most of which, Liz noted, were concerned with physics.

Liz was particularly charmed by the kitchenette which consisted of a counter along one wall that contained a full-sized sink and a gas hob. Above the counter on one side was a good-sized cupboard which held dishes and glassware in one half and various foodstuffs in the other half. Under the counter on one side of the sink was a small fridge, and an electric oven with a grill was in a similar position below the gas hob.

Liz expressed genuine delight with the design of the flat, so Barry Goff suggested that she have a good look 'round whilst he got rid of some of the liquid that he had taken on in the pub that evening. It was that instruction that led her to a discovery that quite surprised her and changed her whole view of Barry Goff.

Going around the kitchenette she looked in the fridge, seeing that in the door was a bottle of white wine; presumably the drink that they were to have that evening. She looked at the oven which appeared to be quite modern; it was of a type that was self cleaning. Also, she noted, it looked like it hadn't been used very often. Then she looked under the sink, noticing a small wine rack that held three bottles of wine. However, resting on the floor to one side of the wine rack were three small plastic bottles. The bottles were identical to the one that had contained petrol and had been put through the mail slot in the door of Anita Brinton's flat! She quickly closed the door to the cupboard under the sink and went into the area of the flat that served as the living area.

At that moment Barry Goff came out of the toilet. She covered the shock she had been given by seeing the plastic bottles under the sink by enthusing over the design of the flat. He told her that his landlord was a carpenter and joiner and had bought the building and had converted it for the express purpose of renting it. "Mr Howard is quite a good bloke, really. He's an East Ender who's made good. When he learned that I was from around here he told me he wouldn't charge me the rent he normally charged. He said he was all in favour of East End kids bettering themselves, so he'd do his bit to help. He's really being very kind to me. There's another flat like this one in the building which is still for rent. I've seen what that's going for, and it's nearly double my monthly rental!"

Liz seated herself, whilst Barry Goff went to the fridge to remove the bottle of wine which he then opened, pouring some of its contents into two glasses. Her plan for the evening had altered. Seeing the bomb-making bottles had done that. Whilst Barry Goff was occupied with the wine, Liz was silent, thinking hard about her discovery and how she would have to overcome her shock. He had noticed her change of mood because he said as he brought the two wine glasses into the living area, "you seem to have gone quiet all of a sudden; is something the matter?" Liz said that she was just thinking what a lovely flat it was and how she would love to be able to live in something like it. He agreed that he had been very lucky. "You should see some of the dumps that I've lived in over the past few years. Some people seem to think that just because we're students we don't deserve a decent place to live. Anyway, I'm thinking of doing post-graduate work, so I am very pleased to have found this place; it will make life much more pleasant during the remainder of my time at QMW."

A short time later it became obvious that her companion would have preferred that they got right down to love making activities. However she had blocked that from the first by saying, falsely, that it was a bad time of the month for her. It was obvious that he understood what she meant because he didn't attempt to persuade her. Because of the proximity of the end of the teaching semester at QMW, Barry Goff expressed concern that soon she would be returning to Durham. He said that he really had enjoyed knowing her, and he hoped that they might keep in touch. Liz expressed her gratitude to Goff for helping to steer her through the semester at QMW. "I am sure that I would have found things very much harder if you'd not been there." She went on speaking, but he didn't seem to notice that she was saying nothing about meeting again sometime in the future.

Although Barry Goff offered her a second glass of wine she declined, using the excuse that she had had quite enough to drink that evening, and she had best be getting on her way. As previously, he walked her to the underground station. In order to lessen his disappointment in her she told him that he had such excellent kitchen facilities, if he would like she would cook a meal for them sometime before she had to return to Durham.

Once home in Plaistow Liz wasted no time in attempting to contact DCI Lawrence. She knew that he would not like it, but she felt that what she had to say could not wait for morning. She telephoned through to the night-duty sergeant at the Mile End station and persuaded him to give her the DCI's home number. She had been right. From the sound of his voice quite patently he was irritated by being rung so late at night. However, his mood changed when she explained fully what she had seen at the flat of Barry Goff. He told her to break whatever plan she had for the following morning and to call in at the station. They would work out a plan of how they would use the information.

* * *

Liz had planned out in her mind what she thought would be a workable scheme that would enable the police to search Barry Goff's flat. Ordinarily the police would apply to a magistrate for a search warrant. However, even if that procedure were successful, which Liz doubted it would be, it might prove to be counterproductive. It certainly would alert Goff to a police interest in his activities, and that would complicate Liz's investigation. She had decided that the only way forward would be to search Goff's flat without him being aware. Of course, any evidence discovered by such a method would not be admissible in a court of law, but it could form the basis of further investigation.

Liz met DCI Lawrence as well as the station superintendent in the DCI's office the next morning. To her surprise both of her superiors accepted her ideas about the way to discover if her suspicions were well founded.

Liz very quickly found a telephone number for a Mr Robert Howard, builder. When she rang the number the 'phone was answered by a woman who identified herself as his wife. Liz said that she had seen a really wonderful small flat in a converted house on Mantiss Road close to Queen Mary College. She had been told that there was another such flat for rent and had been given Mr Howard's name and the number to ring. The woman said that, indeed, there was one flat remaining; she told Liz the monthly rental. Liz said that she definitely was interested, but that she would like to have a look at it first. Missus Howard wrote down the telephone number of Liz's flat in Plaistow and a name which Liz gave as Elizabeth Webb. Missus Howard said that she would have her husband ring that evening.

The conversation with Mr Howard was very short, which was fine with Liz; he had a very strong East-End accent and was difficult to understand. As Liz had hoped would be the case he asked her to come by his house the following day and his wife would give her the keys that would let her into the building and the flat that was for rent.

The following morning Liz was driven by PC Ian Winter to the address in Bethnal Green that Mr Howard had given her. Constable Winter had been asked to accompany Liz because he was a member of the specialist staff at Mile End who was knowledgeable about locks. It would be his task to gain entry into Barry Goff's flat. Also, he carried with him equipment that would enable him to photograph any material that Liz thought appropriate. Liz had chosen a time of the day when she knew that Barry Goff would be attending lectures.

Using the key given to her by Mr Howard, Liz entered the building in which the flat was situated. There was no one about, so PC Winter set to work on the door of Goff's flat. Liz was surprised with the speed with which entry was gained, both police officers entering the flat and setting down their equipment.

Liz looked around the two large rooms of the flat, noting that Barry Goff had added a marker board on one wall of the sitting room/kitchenette since her previous visit. It was obvious that he, like she, could be forgetful if he didn't write reminders to himself. On the marker board were listed many such reminders, most of which described things that he had to do over the coming days. Liz thought that that was a good idea; perhaps she would get herself such a marker board.

Her next move was to go to the cupboard under the sink, where, she noted, the plastic bottles she saw on her previous visit were to be found still. She asked the constable to take photos of the bottles and the position that they occupied. Next she went to the book shelf in the living area. However, a careful scrutiny did not reveal any written material that would appear to be connected to animal-rights issues. She did notice that there was a Haynes automobile repair manual there. She thought that it deserved a closer look, so she took it from the shelf. It covered maintenance and repair of Volkswagen Golf models from 1982 to 1987. Suddenly she remembered that the car owned by Dr Brinton in which she had been injured was a 1985 Volkswagen Golf. Liz thought it unlikely that Goff's possession of a Haynes manual for that car was a coincidence. She asked PC Winter to photograph the cover of the book before she replaced it on its shelf.

Liz was aware that in her search she could not displace items, so the search could not be very thorough. However, she looked through all of the kitchen drawers as well as those in the wardrobe of the bedroom. In the bottom of one of the drawers in the wardrobe she found a leatherette pouch containing a small, battery-operated electric tool. Also within the pouch were several drill bits including one that looked to be about the size of the holes that had been discovered in the brake lines of Dr Brinton's car. Probably more revealing was the presence of a roll of electrician's tape in the same drawer. It was the same colour and width as that that had been used to close the holes drilled in the brake line of Dr Brinton's car. Liz had PC Winter photograph the tape and the opened pouch and its contents before restoring them to their former positions. They took with them a short length of tape for analysis.

One object that she had not anticipated finding had been sitting on the table in the eating area of Goff's flat when the two police officers entered. It was the latest model of the BBC computer. Liz had decided to ignore it until the rest of the search of the flat was completed. She had not anticipated finding a computer, and she knew that if it depended upon her, it would take some little time to access it. She hoped that her companion would be able to help.

Constable Winter took only a brief moment to get the computer up and running, noting that its owner appeared not to be concerned about privacy because none of his files were protected by passwords. He said that there were several files in the Acorn word processor, which was called "View." The first such file that the PC opened proved to be a letter sent from a person called "Avenger" to an academic who worked at one of the hospital medical schools in London. The letter threatened the researcher with an action that was unspecified unless cruel behaviour toward animals was ceased. There were other files containing let-ters of a similar nature as well as files containing written descriptions of premises where animals were kept. The two officers discussed the advisability of taking copies of the files because they would have to make use of at least two of Goff's blank 5 1/2" floppy disks. The box containing the blank disks originally had held ten of them, of which eight remained. Liz thought that it would be safe to use two.

On their way back to the Mile End station, Liz had PC Winter drive by the Howard house so that she could return the keys to the property they had 'viewed' that morning. She told Mrs Howard that she and her partner had thought that the flat was "lovely," but that they had decided, reluc-tantly, that it was just too small for their requirements.

* * *

Chapter Six

Liz was happy that in a meeting between herself and DCI Lawrence it had been decided to delay arresting Barry Goff. Once all of the files were assessed that had been gotten off of Goff's computer, the evidence against him was even more damning. Particularly damning was a letter written to Dr Anita Brinton threatening her with "punishment" if she did not give up her experiments. Obviously it was the original of the letter that Dr Brinton had discarded, thinking that it was some kind of practical joke.

Liz still had not got over the shock of discovering that it was very likely that Barry Goff had been the person responsible for attempting to murder Anita Brinton. Even after the discovery of the plastic bottles in the cupboard under the kitchen sink in his flat she did not believe that he had been directly involved in the attack on the victim. She realised that her belief had been based on the fact that she thought that Barry Goff was such a nice, mild-mannered young man.

During her discussion with DCI Lawrence, he had agreed that she should return to QMW until the Christmas vacation. It was hoped that in that time she would be able to get more evidence against Goff. In particular, she was under instructions to attempt to get Goff to reveal to her more evidence that he was the "Avenger" who signed the threatening letters kept on his computer. She was given a portable recording device which she was to utilise whenever she was in Goff's company. Also, DCI Lawrence had told her to be more aggressive in questioning the man about his animal-rights activities. It no longer mattered that that approach might make him suspicious. The risk was worth taking.

Barry Goff seemed very concerned for her when Liz explained her two-day absence from QMW as being due to a very bad cold. He said that he had attempted to get a telephone number for her from their advisor, Dr Sangstrom, but the man had said that he didn't have one on file. Liz thanked Barry Goff for being concerned but she said that she had managed OK.

He said that he would like them to do something special together before the Christmas vac and they both went off to their homes; would she like to come to his flat for a meal? Liz said that she would like that, but that she would insist that he would allow her to cook the meal. He faked a twisting of his arm, saying that he would look forward to a meal cooked by her. He asked her to give him a list of ingredients, and he would buy them in.

Three days after returning to QMW, Liz had what she thought might be a breakthrough in her attempt to infiltrate the animal rights movement. Barry Goff asked if she would like to attend a meeting with him. He said that the animal-rights group to which he belonged were having a get-together at which they were going to lay plans for their activities over the Christmas vacation. He told her, "undoubtedly you will disagree with some of the things that you will hear, especially from the rabble-rousers, but I think that you will find the meeting interesting. I think that you will find yourself broadly in agreement with most of the people there. I am pretty sure that both George and Richard will attend, so I won't be the only person you'll know."

Liz found the meeting to be interesting, but very little of what was said made interesting reading in the report of it that she had compiled for DCI Lawrence. Liz had got the names and descriptions of three persons there who seemed to be the ones in charge. It was likely that the information would be redundant; probably some branch of government intelligence was way ahead of her.

Whilst at the meeting, Liz had attempted to take in as much as she could of what was said that evening and who had said it. She found that most of the talking had been done by a few individuals in the group; the majority seemed only to nod or otherwise indicate approval for what was said by those individuals. They were discussing a large demonstration that the group was to organise in Trafalgar Square, probably in the week prior to Christmas. One of the more outspoken of the group had suggested that red colouring should be dumped into the water fountains to remind people of the blood that was spilled on a daily basis by the vivisectionists. That idea was adopted as a good one.

Another man said that he thought that an action that someone did in the America that he'd read about would be a good one: "they kidnapped an animal experimenter and paraded him around the town in a cage. I would like to see one of the swine put in a cage and set in the middle of Trafalgar Square." That idea was rejected because it would give the police an excuse to break up the demonstration.

Probably the most valuable aspect of the evening as far as her investigation was concerned came during a discussion that Liz had had immediately after the meeting when she and Barry Goff were having a drink in a nearby pub. For the first time he had said something that had implicated him in the attacks on Anita Brinton. During their conversation she had attempted to goad him a little by suggesting that the attack on Dr Brinton had been rather cowardly. He had said that he agreed, but he supposed that any attack by a man upon a woman would be deemed to be cowardly. When she asked how he knew that the attacker was a man he said, "oh, I just assume that a woman wouldn't know enough about how a car works to think to drill a hole in the brake lines" Liz was very pleased at Barry Goff's statement, but she pretended not to notice, saying, "yeah, I suppose you're right."

Although she allowed the recording device to continue to run she felt confident that Barry Goff had revealed the information that she was hoping to obtain. The details of the method used to tamper with Dr Brinton's car had not been released to the media. Therefore, there were only two ways that he could have known about it: either he had done the tampering himself or he knew who did. Since he was in possession of the implement that very likely had been used to drill holes in the brake line, she was sure that he had been the perpetrator.

That evening she took extra care to properly label the tape that had been used to record her conversation with Barry Goff that day. She decided that she would wait until after her visit to Goff's flat before she told DCI Lawrence about her discovery. Maybe during the visit she could induce Goff to reveal more.

Prior to departing for her last visit to the flat of Barry Goff, Liz had removed the recording device that she wore routinely when meeting him. She anticipated that they might engage in intimate behaviour, although she was determined that it would go no further than kissing and fondling. However the tape recorder that she used was attached to her skirt at the small of her back, whilst the microphone was within her brassiere. She thought that it was unlikely that they could remain undetected during the evening she was to spend with Goff.

It was obvious to Liz when she arrived at Barry Goff's flat that he would take pains to tidy up whenever he was expecting a visitor. When she had been there with PC Winter the place had been very untidy including the bed which looked like it hadn't been made in several days. Also, she noted, the BBC computer was nowhere to be seen. Obviously, he kept it put away whenever she came; probably it rested in the bottom of the wardrobe which was a space large enough to conceal the computer's monitor.

Barry Goff had insisted that they needed to be sipping a glass of wine whilst they prepared their meal, "like that bloke on the television, the 'galloping gourmet'!" He poured her a glass of wine from a bottle of red that was only half full, pouring most of the remainder into his own glass. From his rather jolly demeanour Liz thought it likely that he had had been imbibing prior to her arrival.

She set about preparing a vegetable lasagne, which was one of her favourite dishes both to cook and to eat. Normally she served it with a tossed green salad. When they had discussed what they would have for their meal together, Barry Goff had said that he was not much of a cook, but he was sure that preparing a green salad was something that he could handle. The two of them got busy on opposite sides of the kitchenette. Liz thought it was the wine, but Barry Goff was being very loquacious. As they worked, the thought kept occurring to Liz: "he seems to be such a normal person; how could he have performed such a cold-blooded act as attempting to kill or badly injure Dr Brinton." She knew that she should not allow her emotions to influence the way in which she performed her job, but in this instance, maintaining that position would be difficult.

Later in the evening Liz was aware that both she and Barry Goff had had too much to drink. Once again one of his hands was exploring the area between her legs and she was not objecting. His mouth rested upon one of her breasts which he also was fondling. She knew that her judgement was being influenced by the wine. She decided that she would have to make him stop. However, when she said, "no; please Barry, we mustn't do this..."she found herself ignored. He began kissing his way down toward her navel and then lower as he successfully pulled down her underpants.

When his mouth and tongue began to manipulate the area where his fingers had been previously her objections quickly vanished. She lay back enjoying what he was doing to her. In her mind she was justifying her action with the knowledge that Barry Goff had condemned himself already by the evidence she had on recording tape. He would not be able to complain that she had used sex to trap him. As she did usually, Liz expressed her pleasure with quite a lot of noise emanating from her mouth.

When he had finished he began kissing her, allowing her to taste herself on his mouth. She knew from his actions that now he was intent on intercourse. He was attempting to unbuckle the belt of his trousers with the hand of one arm whilst he held her in his other arm. She knew of only one way of stopping him from going further other than getting up and leaving his flat. She unzipped his flies and took his erect penis in her hand manipulating it. Then she took its head into her mouth. It had been some time since she had done such a thing, but her efforts had the desired effect. He relaxed fully until a few minutes later when she felt the familiar surge of liquid come into her mouth. At such a time never had she been able to ignore the taste of the fluid. It wasn't unpleasant, but, also, it wasn't particularly good tasting either. Of course she had an ulterior motive in her action. She had learned by experience that fellation was a sure-fire method of diminishing a man's desire for intercourse; at least for a time.

Once they were finished and she was resting semi-naked in his arms she gave in to a thought that had entered her mind many times during the talks that they had had since meeting each other. "Do you know, Barry, what you did to me this evening was very nice. It has shown me a side to you that I find very admirable. You seem to have taken the trouble to learn how to give pleasure." He didn't say anything for a time, then he said, "probably I shouldn't tell you, but I was taught to do that by a female cousin. She was three years older than me and used to make me keep at it until I got it right. She never reacted like you, though. She would just lie there; the only sound that came out of her was to tell me when I was getting it right! You sounded like you really enjoyed it. I'm glad." Liz smiled. She knew that she was a noisy lover; she had never been successful in keeping her mouth shut.

Although Liz was reluctant to re-commence pursuit of the goal that had led her to befriend Barry Goff, she felt that she had to do it. She began, "do you know, Barry, ever since I went to that meeting of the animal-rights people with you, I've been thinking about what the people said there and some of the talks that you and I have had. One thing really puzzles me. Most of the people there seem so compassion-ate toward animals. Indeed, I have found you to be a very kind and gentle person. How can they or you support peo-ple who would do what was done to Dr Brinton. I watched her when they interviewed her on Newsnight immediately after she got out of hospital. She's not wicked and horrid. She is genuinely trying to help her fellow man."

Barry Goff sat upright, indicating by his action that he was no longer interested in making love. He remained silent for what seemed like a long time during which period Liz dressed herself. Finally he said, "I don't really know what to say, Liz. Until Dr Brinton was almost killed I had thought that people like her deserved everything that happened to them. I don't know what happened, but when I read about what had happened to her, and, especially, when I saw her on the telly, all of a sudden I changed my mind."

"A few days later I saw Dr Brinton and even spoke to her. That reinforced my view that she had been the victim of a wrong. She was sitting in the JCR with a girl I know who works as an assistant in one of the labs in the biology school. I went to see them on the pretext of saying hello to my friend. I was appalled when I saw Dr Brinton close up. Her face was covered with horrible-looking yellowish bruises and one of her eyes was bandaged still. She said at some point after she crashed into the other car the windscreen had shattered and some pieces of glass had embedded themselves in one of her eyes. She was going to have to have an operation to remove the glass."

"Doctor Brinton then got up and left us, so I stayed to talk to the lab assistant for awhile. The girl said that Dr Brinton hadn't said anything about the worst aspect of her crash. She had been blinded in the one eye, and there was a strong possibility that the operation she was to have would not help. I knew that the girl was sympathetic to some of the ideas of the animal rights movement because we had talked about them previously. However, like you, she supports the sort of research using animals that many of the people in biology are doing. She told me that she was very, very angry with whoever it was that caused Dr Brinton's injuries. She told me that she had never met a more caring and compassionate person than Dr Brinton."

Now it was time for Liz to remain silent. Earlier that day she had spoken with DCI Lawrence who had indicated once again that he thought that she was wasting her time at QMW. He spoke of either detaining Barry Goff for questioning or dropping the enquiry. Liz knew that she had evidence that would force the DCI to adopt the former option. However the mood of contrition that Barry Goff was adopting that evening was intriguing her. She wanted to remain with him for awhile longer to see where it might lead.

Whether or not it was her silence that prompted him, Barry Goff said, "I have a confession to make, Liz. I hope that you won't hate me for it, but it was I who almost killed Dr Brinton. It's odd; only after I caused her car to crash and she was badly injured did I realise the seriousness of what I had done. I must have been in some kind of a juvenile dream before that."

"After I met her and spoke to her in the JCR I went to see her. I decided that I had to do that. I told her what I had done and asked her to forgive me. I told her that I was going to go to the police and give myself up. Do you know, Liz, she didn't get angry or anything. The first thing she said was that I must not go to the police. She told me what I knew already: a conviction for attempted murder would end any chance that I might have for an academic career. She said that she realised that it took a lot of courage for me to tell her, and she insisted that we must forget the whole episode. When we talked about it she told me that she had some sympathy with some of the aims of the animal rights movement, but she didn't think that violence was the way to get the law changed." Liz now knew why Dr Brinton had stopped co-operating with the police a few weeks after the car crash that could have killed her.

The way in which Barry Goff had spoken evoked considerable sympathy in Liz's mind, but at that point she had no doubt what had to happen. She would relate to DCI Lawrence what Barry Goff had said that evening which, she thought, would result in his arrest. She thought it likely that the recording Liz had made in which Goff demonstrated a knowledge of the method used to tamper with the brakes of Dr Brinton's car could not be used against him. However, it was likely that it would be sufficient to obtain a warrant to search his flat. Then, the evidence known to be in that place could be entered officially in the police files.

Despite her thoughts about Barry Goff's guilt Liz told him her true opinion: she said that she was very surprised that such a person as he had done such a thing, but, of course, she didn't hate him. She said that as far as she was concerned it would have to be a matter of his own conscience whether or not he told the police.

As Barry Goff walked her to the tube station at the end of their evening together, she tried not to reveal the confusion in her mind. She found that the certainty evoked initially by his confession now had been altered. She would have to think about what she must do. For his part, Barry Goff was concerned that his confession would alter their relationship. She had tried to assure him that that would not be the case, but it was obvious that he did not believe her.

During the tube ride home her thoughts about what must be her response to Goff's confession so occupied her mind that she almost missed getting off the train at the correct stop.

As usual, when she got back to her flat, she checked the messages on her telephone-answering machine. There was one from DCI Lawrence telling her to come into the station in the morning. They were to have a meeting with the superintendent. During the very disturbed night that substituted for her normal sound sleep, Liz found herself struggling with her conscience. She knew that she had to be a police officer first and a human being second. However, it would be a difficult decision to give DCI Lawrence the evidence that very possibly would convict Barry Goff of a crime. Nevertheless, she would have to do it.

* * *

Chapter Seven

The sleepless night that she had endured turned out to have been spent needlessly. The purpose of the meeting that Liz had with the superintendent of the Mile End station and her immediate boss, DCI Simon Lawrence was for the super to indicate that the enquiry that she was conducting was to be ended. "We simply cannot afford to expend any more time on it, constable, we need you for other duties; I have looked over reports of your activities so far, and even though you obviously have kept your ears and eyes open, we've got nothing definitive. I admit that the materials found in the flat of this Barry Goff suggested that he was involved with tampering with Dr Brinton's car and petrol bombing her flat. However, as evidence, it wouldn't stand up in court. Not only was it obtained illegally, it is all circumstantial. No, constable, unless you can give me a cogent reason not to do it, I'm going to end your enquiry. Another case that is more urgent has just come to our attention, so, Simon, I will expect you to do the necessary to see that DC Andresen is brought up to speed on that."

As she and DCI Lawrence left the super's office, Liz ignored the 'pricks' that her conscience was dealing out. Had the super been just a little more doubtful about the need to close the enquiry into the attacks on Dr Brinton, probably she would have said something. Now, however, all that she had to do was to keep her mouth shut and destroy a recording tape and Barry Goff would be freed from the threat of arrest and, possibly, conviction for attempted murder.

By the end of the day Liz had concluded that she had done the right thing by remaining silent in the meeting with the super and DCI Lawrence. However, she had been charged with the responsibility of returning to QMW to explain to the various people involved in the enquiry the reasons why it was being ended. Also, her private mission would be to see Barry Goff and make a confession of her own.

* * *

Liz had made an appointment with the principal and Professor Edwards at Queen Mary and Westfield College to inform them that the police enquiry into the animal-rights activities at the college had ended; at least for the time being. When she told Professor Edwards that Barry Goff no longer was part of those enquiries he expressed relief. "He is a very talented young man; we are hoping that he will stay on here for a PhD. I couldn't believe that he could have been involved in those dreadful incidents involving Dr Brinton."

When Liz spoke to Dr Sangstrom she thought that his wishes of good luck for her future were a bit too vigorous. She was aware that in some of the tutorial sessions with him she had not displayed an overly-brilliant grasp of some aspects of astrophysics. Obviously, he thought that her stay at QMW very likely had been a waste of both his time and her's.

Next she went to speak to Barry Goff. She was dreading the moment and still had not decided finally what she was going to say. She knew that at that time of day he would be in a lecture; she had been there many times herself. She went to the lecture theatre to wait outside until he emerged.

He saw her immediately when he came out of the lecture theatre and came over to her. "It's a relief seeing you, Liz. I was wondering where you'd got to. I was afraid that you'd gone back to Durham." Liz replied that she had had a few things to do which had kept her away from QMW. She continued, "I want to talk to you about them, Barry. Do you suppose we could go to the JCR and have a cup of coffee?" Barry looked at his watch, saying, "yeah, that'll be OK. I was going to go back to the flat to get some materials for this afternoon's practical, but that can wait."

As they walked toward the JCR, Liz attempted to prevent Barry Goff from asking questions by asking him about his plans for the upcoming Christmas holiday. He said that his parents had invited him to go with them on a skiing holiday in south-eastern France. He was tempted, but he knew that he should stay in London and begin his revision for the final examinations in the summer. He began to ask her about her plans for the Christmas vacation just as they reached the JCR. Their arrival gave her the excuse not to reply except to say that she would tell him about it once they had got their coffee. As usual, there was a queue, so he told her to find them a couple of seats whilst he got the coffee.

As Barry Goff joined her with the coffee he said, "now, Liz, what's this thing you were going to tell me about. Have you had second thoughts about what I told you the other night? I suppose it came as a shock, but I did mean it when I said that I am truly sorry for what I did." She knew that she could not delay any longer, so she said, "I have a confession to make, Barry; I want you to hear me out before you say anything. First off, I am not a physics undergraduate from Durham University. I'm a police officer. My specific job over the past several weeks has been to stay close to you and hope that you would lead the police to the person or persons involved in the attacks on Dr Brinton." She tried to stop him from interrupting but he ignored her, asking, "d'you mean that all of time we have spent together you've only been doing a job?" Then the full implication of Liz's statement hit him and he said, "oh god, what have I done? I've landed myself in the shit. I told you that I was responsible for what happened to Dr Brinton..." She said, "that's why I wanted you to hear me out, Barry. As far as the police are concerned, you're in the clear. My superiors have decided to end the enquiry involving you."

After a pause during which she did not look at Barry, Liz said, "I'm afraid that their decision has left me struggling with my conscience. My superiors don't know about your confession. Had they known about that they may have come to a different conclusion. However, I am taking you on your word that never in the past have you been involved in attacks on other people like those you made on Dr Brinton?" He said, "no; never! I can't believe that I actually did what I did this time. I really am very ashamed of myself, especially since Dr Brinton has been so forgiving." Liz said, "that's another thing that influenced my decision to remain quiet: Dr Brinton was willing to forgive you."

Barry Goff said, "I talked to her again yesterday. She said that she had suspected that I might be involved somehow. She said that that suspicion had arisen immediately after she had appeared on television. She said that she had showed the man who interviewed her a tissue-culture flask like that that had been used to make the petrol bomb that had been pushed through the door of her flat. One of her lab assistants, the girl I told you about, saw the programme. She remembered that she had given me a few of the same sort of flask some weeks earlier."

Liz said, "not to change the subject, Barry, but why did you use the rather peculiar type of bottle to hold the petrol." He replied, "I only meant it to be a warning. I didn't want to burn the building down, possibly hurting innocent people. Therefore I wanted a container that would hold a small amount of petrol but that could be closed fairly tightly with some flammable material. Also, I wanted it to be unbreakable. I read somewhere that petrol bombs made from plastic tissue-culture flasks had been used in America for just the purpose that I intended."

As Liz walked from QMW back to the Mile End station she could not help but entertain guilty thoughts. She and Barry Goff had sat in the JCR talking until well past the time when he was supposed to have been in his afternoon practical. As they spoke he had confessed that he had fallen in love with her and he did not want their relationship to end. She knew that she could not reciprocate his feelings. Although his place in her thoughts had evolved from being merely a suspect in a police investigation to being a friend, she was certain that she never could love him. No. She was certain that the relationship had to end. As a consequence of that conclusion, much of Liz's contribution to the conversation they had had that afternoon was an effort, gently, to make him accept that their relationship was over. She wasn't entirely satisfied that she had succeeded in convincing Barry Goff of that fact, but only time would tell.

* * *

Chapter Eight

Liz was on her way to work, walking along the Mile End Road, having got out of the tube at the Mile End underground station. The Queen Mary and Westfield College campus, past which her route took her, looked to be deserted; that reminded her that it was soon to be Christmas, so the students had all gone down for the holiday.

She, also, was looking forward to a short break over Christmas. A few evenings earlier she had got a telephone call from Pat, who had insisted that she must spend some time with her during the holiday period. Already Pat had laid plans for the two of them to get together during that time. Liz's friend had said that she now was certain that she was pregnant. She had insisted that Liz and she should have a "last fling before I get tied down to being a middle-class wife!" Pat's call had reminded Liz that of late she had been neglecting her mum.

Liz realised that, inevitably, she would have to go to Cambridge to spend part of the holiday. However, she couldn't make any plans until she saw the Christmas duty roster at the station. She was the only female officer stationed there; she hoped that that wouldn't mean that she would be on duty the whole of the holiday period. That had happened the previous Christmas. Although spending time with her mum wasn't usually a pleasant experience, it was better than having to stay in touch with the Mile End station twenty-four hours of the day.

Finally, as if her Christmas obligations weren't already enough, she had to attend a choir performance at the Royal Albert Hall on the Friday before Christmas. She had been practising for that over the previous several weeks.

As Liz passed by one of the tall buildings on the QMW campus she nodded at a vagrant who sat upon a grid that was part of the ventilation system for the building. Because the air coming out of the vent was warm, it made a perfect place for the man to bed down.

Each time she saw the man huddled there in his sleeping bag and blankets she thought of her colleague, Detective Sergeant Bill Rawlings. The last time she had seen Bill, he had been lying in the same place, dead. He had been acting 'undercover' in an effort to apprehend someone who had killed several vagrants in the Mile End area. The killer had not yet been caught, but the killings had ceased.

The vagrant she now saw was there most mornings when she passed by. The two of them seldom spoke but occasionally he would take off the disgustingly-filthy cap that he wore and hold it out to her. That prompted her to dig into her coin purse and pull out a pound coin, putting it into the cap, eliciting a 'thumbs up' signal from him. This time, when he doffed his cap, she gave him two one-pound coins. In response to that gesture he raised his eyebrows in surprise. She said, "it's Christmas." That prompted speech from him: "thank ya kindly, ma'am, and a happy Christmas to ya." Liz smiled and went on her way. She knew that the money she gave him would be used primarily to support his drinking habit. However, she thought that were she in his position very likely she would do little else but drink also.

Once she was at her desk in the detectives' room she checked her IN tray to see if there had been any new developments in the investigation to which she had been assigned after her 'stint' at QMW. There was a note there addressed to her and her colleague, DC Ken Ribak. The two of them were just starting the investigation of the murder of a man whose body had been found lying at the front step of a private house situated on a road in the Mile End district. The body, that of a man in his early forties, had been discovered by the owner of the house as he was leaving for his work. The man was unknown to any of the house occupants. The dead man had been stabbed with a narrow-bladed, double-edged knife. It was assumed that robbery had been the motive, since the man's wallet was missing.

In the IN tray was a notification that a possible identification for the man had been established. On the day of the discovery of the body a Mrs Lazarus had reported that her husband had not returned home the previous evening. She had given the police a description of him and a general description of his car although she did not remember its make or the registration number. A check by the police with the Driver and Vehicle Licensing Centre yielded those details.

Liz and DC Ribak were asked to contact Mrs Lazarus and take her to the morgue of the nearby London Hospital to see if the stabbing victim was her husband. Missus Lazarus hardly reacted when she saw the body; she turned and spoke to Liz and DC Ribak, saying, "that's him. Who on earth would want to kill my Norm; he wouldn't have hurt a fly." Liz suggested to the woman that it would be best were they to return her to her home where they could talk in greater comfort.

Both officers accepted the offer by Mrs Lazarus to serve them tea, thinking that it would help to settle the woman's nerves, although both had remarked afterwards that the woman exhibited remarkably-little emotion. During the conversation that followed, Mrs Lazarus was able to tell them little that was helpful to their enquiries. Her husband had worked as a service engineer for a company that installed and maintained underground fibre-optic cables for the transmission of television programmes and other forms of data transference. Fairly often, he would be called away from his home in the evening to attend to a problem in a system his company had installed. That had been the case on the night that he had died.

In response to a question by Liz, Mrs Lazarus was adamant that her husband never had much money on him. She did know that in the boot of his car he carried some expensive test instruments; possibly the theft of those had been the motive for the robbery. After speaking with Mrs Lazarus, Liz checked with Mr Lazarus' employers who gave her a list of the test instruments that their engineers carried routinely in the boots of their cars.

A week after the finding of the body of Mr Lazarus his car was found. It was parked at the roadside not far from the Bethnal Green underground station. It had been there for several days as indicated by the presence of two parking citations under one of the windscreen wipers. In addition, stuck onto the windscreen was a notice that the car soon was to be removed from the road and impounded. Liz looked hurriedly through her notes on the forensic inspection of the Lazarus automobile, seeing that several such instruments were included in the inventory of the car boot. Obviously, Lazarus had not been killed for the value of the test instruments. She noticed that the fingerprints of three people other than Lazarus and his wife had been found in the car. None of the prints were those of persons known to the police.

Some days later, it was becoming obvious to both DC Ribak and Liz that the investigation of the Lazarus death was leading nowhere. Constable Ribak had interviewed Lazarus' work supervisor and two work colleagues who the supervisor suggested were 'mates' of the dead man. They could tell the constable little that was helpful to the enquiry. One of them did say that he didn't think that Lazarus and his wife "got on too well together."

Liz was hardly surprised when DC Ribak announced to her upon her arrival at work one morning that he was being reassigned. He said that he had been told to help Dai Morgan with some theft enquiries, and she was to go see DCI Lawrence who would tell her about her new job.

The inspector showed her a communication that he had had from the Metropolitan Police at the Euston Road station. It seems that about a week earlier the body of a man had been found in the front entrance of a private house not far from the King's Cross train station. The cause of death was virtually identical to that of the victim whose death she and Ken Ribak had been investigating. Someone who knew what he or she was doing had stabbed the victim through the heart with a thin, double-sided knife. The fact that there was no identification on the body suggested that the man's wallet had been stolen. Consequently, it was likely that robbery was the motive behind the killing.

The police at King's Cross had been able to trace the man quickly only because they got lucky. What appeared to be an abandoned vehicle was reported to them by a traffic warden. They traced the road licence number to an address in Birmingham where it was discovered that the owner of the vehicle, Mr Henry Fruhling, had not arrived home, as scheduled, on the previous day. The dead man was a sales representative and, often, was away from home for several days at a time. The man's wife had not yet notified the police because it was not unusual for him to fail to arrive home on the day that he had told her he would.

Forensic examination of Fruhling's car turned up an intriguing piece of evidence. Some of the fingerprints found in the car matched those that had been found in the Lazarus car.

Chief Inspector Lawrence wanted Liz to liaise with her counterpart at the King's Cross station, a DC James Carron. She telephoned the King's Cross station, speaking to DC Carron and setting up a time to see him that afternoon.

Liz was sure that she and DC Carron were not going to get on well. Although friendship wasn't necessary for the work that they had to do together, she thought that it would make their co-operation easier. First off, he had insisted that she call him "DC Carron," rather than James or just constable. Also, by his attitude he indicated that she would be expected to supply information to him, but he was under no obligation to reciprocate. Consequently, she had told him all that she knew about the background of Norman Lazarus. However, she was given very little background information about the victim who was DC Carron's responsibility.

Mister Fruhling was a representative of a company that sold supplies to small grocery shops. He was a frequent visitor to London. That was all that Liz had learned from her colleague about the man found stabbed to death near King's Cross.

Fortunately, official police records were open to her, so she was able to learn more about Fruhling from them. She was interested particularly by a passage in the statement made by the wife of the victim. The woman had implied that her husband had a "roving eye." When asked to elaborate, she had said only that she had reason to believe that he spent part of his time away from home in the company of other women. She had added that she thought it unlikely that that behaviour had had anything to do with his death, however.

A constable with the Birmingham police had interviewed persons who worked with Mr Fruhling at his place of employment in that city. As far as everyone there was willing to say, Fruhling was one of their best sales representatives. Since payments for all sales were handled by cheque or inter-bank transfers, Fruhling would have no reason to be in possession of large sums of money.

The woman who was in charge of Fruhling's affairs whilst he was out of the office had suggested a possible reason for the robbery. A few months prior to his death Fruhling had acquired a mobile phone. She had thought it possible that he had been killed resisting an attempt by someone to steal that. Liz looked in the forensic reports covering Fruhling's killing, noting that a mobile 'phone had not been listed amongst the articles found either in the dead man's car or on his body.

A month after the death of Fruhling, a third victim was added to the list of possible murders committed by the knife wielder. The body of a man was found at the entrance to a terraced house in a small road in the Pimlico area of London. The house had been converted into three flats, and it was one of the flat owners, a medic, who had discovered the body as he left for work early in the morning. He told the police that it was likely that the man had died only a few hours before the discovery; the body still was fairly warm.

Forensic examination of the victim's body had revealed that the entry wound made by the knife that penetrated the victim's heart and caused death was identical to those seen in the murders of Lazarus and Fruhling. The police force involved in the investigation of the latest killing was that located at the nearby New Scotland Yard.

Liz and DC Carron went to Scotland Yard to meet with their counterpart there, Detective Sergeant Tony Brown. As was the case with the first two killings, the dead man's wallet had been taken, so there was no immediate identification. In fact, it had been some considerable time before the man's identity could be established. That happened only because a neighbour of the dead man grew worried about him. The neighbour, an older gentleman, had not seen him for several days and decided, finally, to notify the police. Although the description of his missing neighbour given by the elderly man was unhelpful, he was able to supply the police with the man's name, Peter Clemings, and details of the car that Clemings drove. A few days later the motor was discovered in an impound lot where it had been taken after being collected from a street in Maida Vale, west London. That the car belonged to Clemings could be confirmed by reference to the Driver and Vehicle Licensing Centre in Swansea.

Forensic examination of Clemings' car made it a near certainty that all three killings that were being investigated by Liz and her colleagues were the work of a single person. That person had left fingerprints in all three of the vehicles belonging to the dead men.

About a fortnight after the body of Peter Clemings had been discovered in Pimlico, and well before the time he had been identified, a fourth victim was found. The latest body was found very near to the place where the first body had been found. It, too, was at the front entrance to a private house. Liz was the first officer to go to the scene when the finding of the body had been reported to the Mile End police station.

She accompanied the body in the ambulance that took it to the morgue of the nearby London Hospital. She hoped that she would be able to persuade one of the pathologists associated with the morgue to have a quick look at the body and make a preliminary assessment of how the man had died. She assumed that the death was due to a knife wound; there was very little blood to be seen on or about the body except for a small patch on the clothing that lay just over the left side of the chest wall.

A preliminary assessment in the London Hospital confirmed Liz's assumption. The only mark found on the body was a single small slit on the left side of chest, just at the level of the heart. Liz returned to the Mile End station to write a report of her findings and to enquire of DCI Lawrence whether or not it would be necessary to ask DC Carron to help her with the enquiries into the death.

She was in the middle of writing her report when the telephone on her desk sounded. It was the DCI. He said that the station duty sergeant had just informed him of a fact that might provide rapid identification of the man found dead most recently. "This morning, a Mrs Thomas rang us to report that her husband, Geraint, did not come home last night. I'll give you her details, Liz; when you're ready you might go have a word with her." Liz decided that she would not need help from DC Carron. She would visit Mrs Thomas and, as soon as possible, establish whether or not the dead man in the London Hospital morgue was her husband. After that process was complete she would contact DC Carron.

Liz grabbed for her and supported the woman who had started to collapse after viewing the body as it lay on a gurney in the London Hospital morgue. That told her what she had to know. The murder victim was her husband, Geraint Thomas. She was glad for the help of one of the morgue attendants to guide the woman to a chair that another of the attendants had hurriedly got from somewhere.

After sitting for a moment Mrs Thomas said, "please let me see him again. Just to be sure." Liz walked with her back to the gurney where the woman spoke quietly, "yes, that's him. That's Geraint. Oh you fool; I told you your womanising would do you. Why couldn't you listen to me? Why didn't you ever listen to me?" The woman then burst into tears.

Liz drove Mrs Thomas home after she had recovered from the shock of seeing her husband's body. There were several points of information that the police required, as well as an explanation of the outburst by the woman about her husband's "womanising."

When Liz began speaking with Mrs Thomas she discovered that no one had informed the woman about the way her husband had died. Liz told her that the police believed that Mr Thomas might have been the victim of a mugger; and asked her if there was any reason why she would dispute that. Missus Thomas said that she would be surprised if the motive underlying her husband's murder was robbery. She said, "let me tell you about my husband, Miss, er, Constable Andresen. He couldn't keep his hands off women. I thank god that we never had daughters; I'm sure they wouldn't have escaped his attentions."

"I blame it on his first real job when we were living in south Wales. He worked as a foreman in a factory that made children's clothing. It was that job got him started. Many of the girls who worked in the factory were just uneducated young school leavers, some of them no more than fourteen.

He was a handsome young man and he certainly had a way with him. He soon found that he was able to charm some of the girls straight into bed."

"As he grew older he found that he no longer could charm the young girls. It was then that he began picking up tarts. Shortly after that he got the offer of a good-paying job in London, so we moved here. This job, he is...was...still working in a factory that makes clothing, offered no opportunity to seduce women. Although most of the employees are female they are all Asian women and they wouldn't give him the time of day. However, that didn't stop him. He relied upon his old habit of picking up tarts. I don't know how he managed to escape getting some horrible disease; he told me he always wore a condom. Nevertheless, I wouldn't allow him near me. I suppose I should have left him long ago, but, you know? Despite his womanising he was a good man. He and I got on well together. I shall miss him."

Liz spent considerable time with Mrs Thomas learning of her husband's movements. She was interested particularly in where Mr Thomas might have been on the night that he had died. The woman said that on that night her husband had telephoned to say that he was working late at the clothing factory. However, she knew his habits well enough to know that when he used that excuse usually he was planning an evening with one of his tarts. In fact, she had got so used to his ways that she didn't any longer bother to ring his office to check up on him. In an ironic voice she said, "about the only reason he was at the factory late at night these days was to make use of the shower there to wash the smell of sex off his body."

Liz decided that it would be best to follow the lead provided by Mrs Thomas and concentrate on finding the prostitute with whom her husband may have been on the night he died. To her question as to how her husband contacted prostitutes, Mrs Thomas said that she had no idea except that she was pretty sure that he did not use so-called 'call girls'. They were too expensive for him. She thought it likely that he would find his young ladies on the streets.

After leaving Mrs Thomas, Liz returned to the station and, as usual, wrote up a report of the woman's statement. As she wrote it the idea formed in her mind that perhaps Mrs Thomas had provided her with a clue as to who the killer was. She read once again the statements made by persons who knew the four people who had been murdered. At least one of the persons interviewed about each of the victims except Peter Clemings had either stated or hinted that either the victim fancied women other than his wife or that he was not 'close' to his wife.

She thought that it would be useful to re-question the elderly neighbour of Clemings to see if he could provide any information about the dead man's relationships with women. Liz realised that very likely she should go through 'channels' and get approval from Scotland Yard to speak to Clemings' neighbour, but that would take time. She decided to 'use her own initiative' as she was told during her police-college training that she should strive always to do. She telephoned the neighbour, making an appointment to go to his flat to speak to him directly.

Liz was gratified that the neighbour confirmed that Peter Clemings did "sometimes arrive home in the company of a young lady," as he put it. He said that he had not thought it relevant to say anything about it to the young policeman who had questioned him previously.

* * *

Chapter Nine

Liz was surprised at the speed with which DCI Lawrence rejected her idea that the killers of Lazarus, Fruhling, Clemings and Thomas might be a prostitute who, probably, they had picked up on the street. He dismissed as "nonsense" that a woman could be capable of such acts. He raised his voice to say, "whoever has been killing these men knows what he is doing. That suggests to me, at least, that it's very likely that he is ex-military; maybe ex-SAS or someone like that. I would be very surprised if a woman would know exactly where to put a knife so that it would penetrate the heart."

Liz had surprised even herself by getting angry with the man, telling him that he wasn't giving her time to explain her idea in detail. That had provoked him into an outburst in which he accused her of being "a typical, scatter-brained female!" It was then she came to her senses, realising that she was engaged in a discussion which, if continued, would do her career no good. She said nothing more not even when the DCI told her that he thought that she had been working too hard.

After a few minutes of an awkward silence he dismissed her. As she left the room he said, in a quieter voice, "perhaps it would be best, constable, for you to go back to the detectives' room and think about things for awhile."

That evening, at home in her flat, after a microwave-heated 'instant' meal and two glasses of wine, Liz was feeling very depressed. Once again she found herself wondering if, perhaps, she shouldn't pack in her career in the police. With a good degree in mathematics she knew that there were other jobs that she could do; she was sure that all jobs would not entail being put down constantly by male chauvinists. She remembered with fondness the time when she had spent several weeks working undercover as a supply teacher in a local secondary school. She had much enjoyed working with youngsters, and all of her colleagues in the school, both male and female, had treated her with respect.

Probably the only person who had stopped Liz from quitting the police before was Lydia Mussett. She thought, "I'll be seeing Lydia tomorrow evening at choir practice; I'll talk about it with her then."

As Liz had hoped would be the case, Lydia invited her to spend the night at her flat. saying that they could discuss DCI Lawrence's actions more fully. "Besides, Liz, I have been missing you terribly since you've been at Mile End. We never seem to manage to get together like we used to before you joined the police."

She and Lydia had spent the night in bed together. At first they had made love, which had forced them both to re-member just how much they once had meant to each other. They swore to each other that they would not allow such a long period as previously until their next intimate get to-gether. The rest of their talk had been occupied with advice by Lydia as to how to 'handle' DCI Lawrence.

Lydia urged Liz not to be discouraged by the actions of the DCI. "As I'm sure you have discovered, members of the police service tend to be rather conservative in their outlook on life. In one way, that is a good thing, but also it prevents some of us from readily accepting new ideas. Obviously, DCI Lawrence thinks that women are not suitable to be police officers. He would never come right out and say it, of course, that would be like putting his neck in a noose."

Lydia continued, "by no means is old Lawrence alone in thinking the way he does. Guess who gets to 'see to' tea

when a bunch of us get together at the 'Yard'?" Lydia concluded by telling Liz to 'hang on' at Mile End as best she
could. "In the not too distant future I hope to be promoted.
When that happens I hope to be able to find a place for you
at Scotland Yard. Of course I can't promise anything, but I
would urge you not to 'step on too many toes' at Mile End.
You don't want old Lawrence going around saying that you
are an 'awkward customer'."

* * *

Liz arrived back at her desk at the Mile End station after
what had been a rather hectic weekend. She had wanted to
do as Lydia had asked and stay at her friend's flat over the
weekend, but she had promised her mum that she would go
to Cambridge. That had involved her in an evening in the
pub during which, she noticed that once again her mum had
had more to drink than was good for her. She had enjoyed
the company of the neighbours, Fred and Rose Paltry. She
liked Fred, especially. He was a very friendly man whose
only apparent real interest was his garden. Liz had no interest in gardening, but Fred spoke about his favourite pastime
in such an amusing way that she enjoyed listening to him.

Fred and Rose were getting on in age, now; they had
known Liz since her birth. Every time she and the Paltrys
got together, Fred would reminisce about what a lovely child
Liz had been. He was always reminding her that, at times,
she had been a rather stubborn youngster. "You kept col-
lecting those woodlice, earwigs and slugs from your gran's
garden and keeping them like they were pets, feeding them
lettuce leaves and all that expensive food. You never would
listen to me when I told you to get rid of them 'cause they
were pests. Finally, you got sensible; remember that? You
rescued that little hedgehog and kept it for a pet for quite

some time. Then, in order to keep it going, you had to feed it slugs and things, which it gobbled up!"

Liz regretted that during her visit to Cambridge she had been unable to do more than speak to Pat over the telephone. Their conversation had got Liz to worrying about her friend. Pat said that she had agreed to marry Roger Moffatt, the father of the child that she was carrying. Liz was worried that her friend's attitude was wrong for a young woman contemplating marriage. She seemed to look upon the upcoming event as a punishment for allowing herself to become pregnant. Liz knew that Pat often displayed a lack of enthusiasm for activities which, once she tried them, she had enjoyed. She hoped that her friend's marriage would end up as something she would enjoy.

Liz had tried to joke with Pat, telling her to look on the bright side, "after all, Pat, you're always complaining that your mum has insisted that you live with her. When you get married you'll have a good excuse to move out." Pat agreed, saying, "that was one of the things I told Roger that he must agree to: he was never to invite my mum to come live with us. The bastard! He was only joking but his response to that was to say, 'oh, damn, and here was I making plans to have your mum come live with us to baby sit the sprog when it arrives'."

* * *

Upon her return to Mile End, Liz found a note in her IN basket telling her that a PC Pringle from the Camden Town police had rung her and wanted her to ring back as soon as possible. A few minutes later she was being told by the PC that the Camden Town police were investigating the death of a man whose body had been found on the front walk of a private house in Hampstead village. The man had died from a single strike of a knife which had penetrated his heart. As in the previous killings, the knife blade had been double sided. Since the most recent killing appeared to have been done in a manner that was identical to two murders that Liz was investigating, the PC had been asked to contact her.

Liz spoke to PC Pringle for several minutes, discovering that the Camden police had been unable to identify the man, as yet, although the death had occurred three days earlier. The dead man's description did not match any of those of men who had gone missing about the same time the body was found. The police had asked local newspapers that served northwest London to publish an article containing a photograph of the dead man. The subjects of the article were a description in general terms of the manner of death and a request to the newspapers' readers for help to identify the murder victim. So far, an article containing the photograph had appeared in only one paper and there had been no response to that.

Liz told the PC that it was likely that the killer would have followed his or her previous procedure and would have taken the dead man's car. "Therefore, it might be useful to send a note round to all the stations of the Metropolitan Police alerting them to pay special attention to reports of vehicles that appear to have been abandoned. That's probably a rather tedious procedure, but I expect that somewhere out there is the victim's car; once you find that, the DVLC will do the rest for you."

Liz was at her desk reading a report that had just come about a young man who had been attacked and beaten along the Mile End Road near Queen Mary and Westfield College. Her interest was aroused because she had recognised the man in the photograph that accompanied the report; it was

Barry Goff, one of the men who had been involved in her investigation of the animal-rights movement a few months earlier.

The report reminded her that ten days earlier a similar photograph and report had come across her desk, describing an assault on a young man outside a pub in the Bethnal Green area. Liz had not recognised the surname of that young man, but she thought that the face in the photograph had seemed familiar. Suddenly it occurred to her; the assault described in the earlier report had been one upon a man called "Richard" who had been a friend of Barry Goff. She knew that both men were active in the animal-rights movement. She wondered if their involvement in that organisation had anything to do with the assault upon them.

Her reading was interrupted when the extension phone on her desk rang. It was PC Pringle from the Camden Town police: "hello, DC Andresen? I thought you'd like to know that we've managed to identify our dead man. We haven't found his car, yet, but we've got all of its details from the DVLC, I expect it will only be a matter of time."

"As it turned out the identification came from an unexpected source. Remember I told you that we asked the local papers to publish the dead man's photograph. Well, a few days ago a woman telephoned the local nick saying that she was pretty sure that she knew the identity of the dead man whose picture she had seen in a local newspaper, the Hampstead and Highgate Express. The call was passed over to me."

"The woman told me that she would talk to the police but she wanted a guarantee that we wouldn't hassle her about what her relationship had been with the dead man. I told her that unless she was doing something illegal there was no reason for the police to 'hassle' her. She told me, 'that's the trouble; what the two of us did together isn't exactly approved of by the law'. I told her that I was fairly certain that if she could supply information that led to the apprehension of the man's killer it was unlikely we would go after her. At that point she said, 'well, I'd better not take a chance. I'll tell you his name, but that's all. The man in the photograph looks like a man I know whose name is Kelvin Donald. He's a professor of some kind at that American college in Regent's Park'. Then the lady rang off."

"I tried to trace the call, thinking that probably I was wasting my time; I'd find that it came from a public call box. However, surprise, surprise; the lady used her own telephone. I guess she didn't realise that the call could be traced. Anyway, I got her name and address from directory enquiries. She's a Mrs Zoë Bletchley who lives at an address in the posher end of Camden Town. Just on a hunch I looked up the name in the police files. She was arrested a couple of times a few years ago for soliciting, but nothing was ever proven. However, I think that tells us how she knew Kelvin Donald. I'm going to try to meet with her in the next few days, getting more details about her relationship with the dead man. Either I'll keep you posted, Liz, or if you'd like I could have you go with me. It's possible that she might be more willing to talk to you than to me." Liz said that she would like very much speaking with Mrs Bletchley.

When next PC Pringle telephoned Liz he said that he now had all of the details about Kelvin Donald. "He was an American academic who worked at the overseas campus of an American university which is situated in Regent's Park. I telephoned them and they gave me his details. The man I spoke to at the college will be coming in to the station in a few days time to make a statement; he told me that he could provide us with a formal identification of Donald then. Also, I've set up an appointment to meet with Zoë Bletchley at her home. I gave her the choice of coming into the station, but she said that police stations made her nervous."

Missus Bletchley proved to be a charming woman who looked to be in her mid-thirties. It was obvious that she was not poor because the house in which she lived was detached and, although technically in Camden Town, it was close to Hampstead Village. Liz found it difficult to understand why she had chosen to make her living in the way that she did. To all intents and purposes she gave the appearance of being a middle-class housewife. She was well spoken and her house was well looked after, suggesting that she had neither a drug nor a drink problem.

Once PC Pringle had assured Mrs Bletchley that she would not risk prosecution by admitting that she was a prostitute, she told of her relationship with the dead man. She said, "he was a regular; we got together at my 'digs' about once every three or four weeks. He never talked much about himself; in fact he never told me any more than his first name. I suppose he didn't want me to know much about him in case I tried to make trouble for him at his work."

"I found out who he was by accident. I was walking through Regent's Park when I saw him come out of one of the buildings of that college there. Just then a young man, a student, I guess, passed me. I asked him if he knew who the man I'd just seen was. He told me that the man was called Professor Donald."

Liz asked her how she got in contact with Kelvin Donald, "did you give him your telephone number?" She replied that she hadn't done that in the past several years; she didn't wish to be bothered with 'nuisance' calls. She said that she had two ways of picking up customers. She preferred going into pubs, but she had to be careful doing that because pub landlords would get 'stroppy' if a girl used their pub too often. Therefore, some nights she would stand at the kerb. She continued, "I found out the hard way that I was less likely to get into trouble if I let the men pick me up in pubs or at the kerbside. The only time I've been caught by you lot is early on when I put cards in telephone booths. Also, I've learned by experience that I want to have a good look at potential customers before I go anywhere with them. I could do that whilst chatting to them in pubs or talking to them through the open doors of their cars. Anyway, once I got to know him, I would meet the professor regularly at one of the pubs in Camden Town."

Liz asked the woman to try to remember details of her activities around the time that Kelvin Donald had died. Could she recall having seen him anytime during those few days? Zoë said that she was sure that he had not come to her then, but once she began thinking about it she was sure that she had seen him around that time. "Yes, the more I think about it, the surer I am that I saw him; except that it was not him but his car. I saw another woman talking to someone who was driving a car that looked like his." That statement aroused Liz's interest, causing her to say, "please, Mrs Bletchley, it may be important. Tell us exactly what you can recall seeing."

Zoë Bletchley told how on the night she was sure that she had seen Kelvin Donald's car she had been standing next to another car 'talking' to the driver when she saw what she was sure was Donald's car pull up to the kerb. "I saw this other girl go over, so I tried to get rid of the man I was talking to. However, I couldn't seem to get rid of him.

He said that he didn't want to do as I suggested and find another girl. I was hoping that Kelvin wouldn't go off with the other woman, but after a short time he did. I was really disappointed. He was one of my best customers and I didn't want him to dump me."

Before Liz could say anything, PC Pringle asked if Mrs Bletchley had known or recognised the woman who got into the car she thought was that of Donald. She said that she did not know the woman, but she had seen her a few times before. "She was kind of an odd one. She never spoke to me or any of the other girls, as far as I remember. Also, either she was very choosy or her prices were high. She'd get into a car, sit there for awhile and then, more often than not, she'd get out again."

Liz asked Zoë Bletchley to describe the woman as best she could. "Well, I don't recall much except that she was about my height, but she was slimmer than me...oh, and she had dark hair. She had a good figure and she always wore clothes that showed it off, most of which were pretty skimpy. I said to her once that she must be cold in the outfit she was wearing, but she just ignored me."

Later, back at the Camden Town police station, Liz helped PC Pringle, who, by then, she was calling, "Jim," make out the report he was writing up outlining the statement made by Zoë Bletchley. The PC agreed with her that it was quite possible that the woman whom Mrs Bletchley had seen go off with Kelvin Donald was a likely suspect for killing him and all of the other victims. She said nothing to him about her difficulty in convincing DCI Lawrence that the men might have been murdered by a woman. She was hoping that the latest evidence finally would convince the man.

* * *

Chapter Ten

Liz's was disappointed in her hope that her report of the conversation with Zoë Bletchley would influence DCI Lawrence to change his mind about the killer of the five men whose deaths she was investigating. She was beginning to think that the man stuck doggedly to his belief that a woman could not have done the crime simply because she had suggested it originally.

When Liz left the DCI's office that day she went directly to the ladies' room of the police station where she knew that she could not be disturbed. Once there she seated herself in a cubicle and allowed the tears to stream from her eyes. After a good cry she wiped her face and blew her nose into a piece of toilet paper. She looked in the mirror to see that it was obvious that she had been crying. She waited for a brief spell and then went back to her desk in the detectives' room. Her colleagues looked at her but none of them said anything.

By that evening, Liz had made up her mind. She was going to resign from the Metropolitan Police. She knew t hat if she telephoned Lydia, her friend would try to talk her out of it, but she knew also, that she had to talk to someone.

Finally, late in the evening, she telephoned Lydia, talking to her for over an hour. Lydia said that in the morning she would have a word with her colleague, Detective Sergeant Brown, telling him of Liz's thoughts about the possible killer. "Poor, old Tony; he's been trying to keep up with the case in which you're both involved as well as two others. I imagine he could use some help. I'll see if we can't get you over here for a time. If that stupid DCI of yours won't listen to you, maybe someone here will." Despite Lydia's optimism, it was several days before Liz heard from Scotland Yard.

* * *

The hiatus in the murder investigation gave Liz an opportunity to speak to Barry Goff. Although she was not yet thinking in terms of an official enquiry, she was intrigued by several passages in the statement he had made after he had be beaten by unknown assailants. First off, she was certain that he had not told the truth to the policeman who had taken the statement. In particular, she thought it likely that the view expressed by Goff in his statement, that he had no idea why he was attacked, was not true.

Secondly, the doctor who had treated him upon his arrival at their A&E Department at London Hospital said that Goff had sustained severe superficial injuries, leaving him badly bruised. However, despite the apparent severity of the attack there had been no bones broken. "We kept him in overnight for observation, but he was able to get himself home the next day when he was discharged. I see here that I actually wrote in my notes that I had got the impression whilst examining him that someone had wanted to make him very uncomfortable, but little else." Liz decided that it would be best to telephone Professor Edwards at QMW; undoubtedly he would know how to contact the young man.

As agreed between the two of them, Liz met Barry in the junior common room at QMW. When first she had contacted him she had been worried that he would not wish to see her. However, he allayed Liz's fears when he called to her as she approached the entrance to the JCR where he was waiting. He told her how pleased he was to see her. It was obvious to her that he had been badly beaten, yellowing bruises being visible still on much of his face. She attempted to delay discussing the main purpose of her visit until they had seated themselves with their coffee.

In response to her question, he said that his graduate studies were getting along pretty well, and that he was looking forward to spending some time in America, in the state of Arizona. His statement that he would be glad to get away from London for awhile led to the subject that Liz was hoping to explore with him: "I will tell you, Liz, but I hope that I can trust you that it will go no further. I was telling the truth when I told the police that I did not know the men who attacked me. However, I was not telling the truth when I said that I did not know why I was attacked. One of the two men told me to give up my messing about with the animal-rights movement or next time they would really work me over. Those were his exact words. Also, the man warned me not to tell the police. He said that he would know if I did because he had some connections there. Again, Liz, those were his exact words. I don't know who those men are, but they're trying to 'put the frighteners' on the whole animal-rights movement; at least in London. Remember Richard Cowling? They got to him a little while ago, and I know of another member of the group who has been beaten up. I don't know if you can do anything about it, Liz, but these men shouldn't be allowed to go around beating people up."

As Liz walked back toward the police station after speaking with Barry Goff her mind was taken up with two thoughts: perhaps it was no bad thing that people who are quite happy to break the law should be forced to contemplate the fact that they, themselves, may become victims of lawbreakers. That thought was supplanted by a second thought. As a police officer, it was her duty to uphold the law. She would have to discuss with DCI Lawrence the implications of what Barry Goff had revealed.

Liz arrived back at the police station after speaking to Barry Goff to discover that DCI Lawrence had been looking for her. She went immediately to see him; it was obvious that he was very pleased about something. He greeted her at his office door with the words, "you should be very pleased, Liz. I've just been on the phone to Detective Chief Superintendent Denham of New Scotland Yard. The 'Yard' has decided to mount an operation to see if they can't catch this person who has been killing men all over London. They're going to explore your idea that a prostitute is doing the killing. They are arranging a meeting tomorrow morning at the 'Yard' which all of the officers who have been on the investigation so far have been asked to attend. I guess they are thinking in terms of a London-wide operation, since the killer seems to have spread himself, sorry, herself around."

Liz had tried to detect signs of irony in the DCI's voice but she could not. To her surprise he was actually indicating his approval of the idea and the fact that it had been her suggestion that had prompted it. She left the man's office feeling quite 'chuffed', thinking, "perhaps I've judged him too harshly." All thoughts of Barry Goff and the attacks on animal-rights activists had been driven from her mind. Now she was pleased that she would be taking part in an operation in which, perhaps, she and Lydia would be co-operating.

The meeting at Scotland Yard proved to be very interesting, even though Lydia was not to be involved in the investigation. It was obvious that the 'Yard' had every intention of taking charge. The meeting was begun by a very senior officer, Chief Superintendent Denham, who provided a résumé of the five murders that had occurred up until then.

He told the assembled officers to bear in mind that only one fact was known that positively connected the murderer to the crimes: the fingerprints that were found in the cars of all five victims. "That consistency is unlikely to have arisen by accident. However, all of the other 'facts' that we have, such as the nature of the knife used to kill the victims, could be due to coincidence. Also, we have no definite proof that the killer is either a woman or a prostitute. That supposition derives from the testimony of one person, herself a prostitute. Of course, we have good evidence that three of the victims consorted with prostitutes, so Mrs Bletchley's testimony should not be ignored. Finally, officers, I urge you to attempt to keep an open mind whilst you discuss the way you think this enquiry should go."

Liz was surprised when Chief Superintendent Denham left the room after his introduction. She had resigned herself to sitting in the room with her fellow junior officers being told how the investigation was going to be conducted.

Because of the prior thinking that she had done about the murders Liz found herself unable to keep herself from speaking out. One of her colleagues remarked afterwards that Liz had virtually led the discussion. At the time she had thought that that comment was code for the fact that the officer thought that Liz talked too much.

Everyone had agreed that it would be counterproductive for the police to patrol known red-light areas. That was done already to some extent just to discourage both soliciting on the part of prostitutes and kerb crawling by their potential clients.

Liz put forward the idea that the police should take advice from Mrs Zoë Bletchley. It was possible that Mrs Bletchley had seen the killer. Undoubtedly she would recognise the woman if she saw her again. Liz continued, "perhaps it would be useful to have a police officer accompany Mrs Bletchley in the evening. It might be a slow process but possibly in due course the murderer would show up at the same place where Mrs Bletchley was 'working'. It might take some persuasion, but I am pretty sure that the lady will do it."

That idea was accepted by the group, following which there was quite a lot of laughter when Liz said, "since I'm the only woman in the group it seems pretty obvious who will have to accompany Mrs Bletchley." Everyone agreed that as a safety measure there would have to be radio backup.

Sergeant Brown had said nothing whilst Liz was speaking, but once she was finished he said, "I wonder if perhaps another approach might be made either as an alternative or in addition to that suggested by Liz. First off, we are by no means certain that Mrs Bletchley will co-operate with us. Also, it seems to me we're giving an awful lot of weight to the lady's testimony. She could have been mistaken that it was Donald's car that she had seen that night, or it may have been Donald's car she saw, but it hadn't been on the night he was killed. In other words, our 'killer prostitute' might not be the woman whose description Mrs Bletchley has given us."

"On the other hand, it seems a reasonable assumption that we have the killer's fingerprints. So far we've found no evidence that any of the five dead men knew each other, yet all of them appear to have been in contact with the same person; the person who left fingerprints in the car of each of them."

"I suggest that it would be a good idea for all of us involved in the investigation, except DC Andresen, of course, to act as kerb crawlers and collect the fingerprints of all the women we encounter. We shall have to think up some kind of ruse both to obtain the woman's fingerprints and to keep from having to follow through with the pick-up. However, I have one or two ideas on that score."

Constable Pringle spoke up to say that Tony Brown's idea appealed to him because it would give him a chance to take an active part in the investigation. "However," he added, "I think that we should hedge our bets by doing what Liz suggested also."

It was agreed quickly that Liz should approach Mrs Bletchley to see if she would be willing to take part in the police operation. The rest of the meeting was devoted to a discussion of ways to obtain fingerprints from the prostitutes without them becoming aware.

There was embarrassment on the part of Liz as well as her male colleagues during the ensuing discussion, especially when the ruse that was adopted finally was discussed. Sergeant Brown had proposed: "after she gets into the car, each prostitute should be handed a photograph depicting something really nasty; we'll have to work on that one when Liz isn't here. Then the woman should be asked how much she'd charge. Probably at that point the prostitute would get out of the car. However, if, in fact, she names a price, the officer will have to say that the price she offered was far too high, and he would ask her to leave the car." One of the PCs on the team asked, "what happens if she lowers her price?" Sergeant Brown smiled and said, "well, you'll just have to use your own initiative!"

* * *

Zoë Bletchley became quite willing to help the police once Liz had assured her of two things: first, that they would not arrest her once they found the woman they were looking for and, second, they would help her out financially. She argued with Liz that "if we are to make this thing work I can't be going off for long periods all of the time while you're standing there. I shall have to refuse customers." Liz had passed on Mrs Bletchley's stipulations to Sergeant Brown, after ascertaining what level of payment the woman needed. She was surprised at how little Mrs Bletchley made in an evening. Sergeant Brown told her that Chief Superintendent Denham had anticipated the question about possible arrest; that would not happen. However, he had to get the chief superintendent's agreement for any payment to the woman.

The day before she was to begin her stint as a prostitute Liz visited Mrs Bletchley who had promised to help her with her appearance. Zoë had told her that her normal dress would not be adequate for appearances sake. She said, "I hope you will pardon me for saying so, constable, but you'll have to wear clothing that makes you look like a tart! Also, you'll find that you should dress fairly warmly; it can get bloody cold just standing."

After a few nights with Mrs Bletchley, Liz had decided for herself that it wasn't only what they did for their clients that earned prostitutes their money, it was having to stand out in the open for long periods. She could see why so many of them had problems with drugs and alcohol. Fortunately, Zoë Bletchley was easy to talk to and the two women found soon that they were becoming good friends.

During the nights that she was with Mrs Bletchley, Liz carried a personal radio in her jacket pocket which she was to use as a radio only in an emergency. However, the instrument had been modified so that it could be used for silent signalling. On her right wrist she wore a small device that vibrated when it was activated, and that only happened when her radio received a signal of a certain wavelength. That signal was emitted by radios located in the unmarked police cars being used by other members of the team hunting the killer prostitute. It indicated that one of the cars was approaching the place where Liz and Mrs Bletchley were standing. Her response to feeling the vibration was to press the face of the device causing a signal to be sent from her radio to the radio of the car driven by her colleague. The signal travelled only a few feet and served as a warning for the officer not to waste time stopping at the place where Liz and Mrs Bletchley were standing. Liz thought that the vibrator had been quite useful because it had been activated three times so far.

Each morning the police officers who were involved with the attempt to apprehend the woman who, by then, had come to be known as the 'killer prostitute' met in one of the detectives' rooms at New Scotland Yard. The primary purpose of the meeting was the collection of evidence from the investigating team. Each of the bogus kerb crawlers brought with him a few plastic evidence bags, each containing a photograph on which a prostitute had deposited her fingerprints. Attached to each bag was a note written by the police officer. That note detailed the date and time of encountering the prostitute and her description. It was the writing of detailed notes that took the time during the evening, thereby limiting the number of women that the police officer could encounter. After the evidence was taken away by the fingerprint experts, there was a general discussion of the events of the previous night.

During the third such meeting at New Scotland Yard, DC James Carron admitted that he had become so upset with one prostitute that he had failed to get the required evidence. He said that the event had raised a serious issue as far as he was concerned: "I know that we've been told to concentrate on the investigation at hand, but are we supposed to do that and at the same time ignore serious breaches of the law?"

Sergeant Brown asked him to explain further. "Well, last night I picked up a young woman. Before I had a chance to begin my routine about showing her the photograph and all that, she told me the most disgusting thing. She told me that it was my lucky night and that she could really do something for me. She showed me a photograph of a little girl who was lying on a bed, naked. Someone who was out of the picture had a hand placed between the child's legs. The kid was holding the adult's hand with both of hers and she had a smile on her face. It didn't take any imagination to know what was happening. Then the woman told me that the kid was her six-year-old daughter. She said that if I was willing to pay the price I could have her."

"To be honest I didn't know what she meant at first. I didn't think it likely that she was offering to sell me her daughter to keep, but it seemed unlikely also that she had some other thing in mind. So I asked her, 'how do you mean, have?' It was then she said, 'you know what I mean; it'll cost you 50 quid for an hour with her.'"

"I told her to get out of the car, that I had never heard anything so disgusting in my life. However, as I drove away I realised that I had neglected to get her fingerprints. I wrote down a few notes about what she looked like and the time I picked her up, but I was really upset. To be honest, my first thought was to radio in and ask whether or not I should go back and arrest her. I knew that it might jeopardise the operation; that's why I hesitated. Nonetheless, I still can't forget that poor little kid in the photograph. To think what she must go through with a depraved mother like that."

Sergeant Brown said that DC Carron had brought up a point for which he had no answer. He said that he'd have a word with Chief Superintendent Denham and then let the team know what future policy would be.

* * *

Chapter Eleven

For the first time since they had begun working together, DC Carron spoke more than a few words in general conversation with Liz. He was disgusted by the fact that Chief Superintendent Denham had made it clear to Sergeant Brown that all members of the 'killer-prostitute' team were to keep their efforts focused on apprehending the woman that they were looking for. The Chief Superintendent had indicated that the only exception to that 'rule' would be an instance where a serious breach of the law had occurred and an arrest could be made without compromising the operation.

Constable Carron told Liz, "it's obvious that it has been a long while since Chief Superintendent Denham was on the firing line. I think that he's being unreasonable. I don't know how I could have arrested that woman without letting her know that I was a copper. What worries me is what is happening to that little kiddie, whilst we're trying to find some other woman. So help me, DC Andresen, if I run across that woman again, I'm going to make certain she can't go on doing what she's doing. You and me both know that there are plenty of men walking the streets these days who would happily take her up on her offer. That poor little kid."

* * *

As DC Carron was sitting on the tube train on his way back to Euston Road, his thoughts were on his encounter of the evening before. Ever since it had happened he had been unable to get out of his mind the image of the pretty little girl smiling at him from the photograph that that woman had showed him. He had to admit that some of the pictures of children that he had seen in magazines that the police had confiscated had got him excited. The little girl he saw in the photograph that the woman had showed him was so pretty. He wondered if she had been smiling because she enjoyed what the hand between her legs was doing.

It was those thoughts that had disturbed him the most. Never would he have thought of himself as a paedophile; he had never touched a child. He was certain in his own mind that he could not do such a thing. Therefore, even if he had been excited, it must have been the pornographic image that was at fault. He saw it as his duty to remove from society those people who promulgate pornography. In his mind they were far guiltier than were the people who purchased their wares. Despite what Chief Superintendent Denham had said, he reasoned that he should have arrested the woman who showed him the pornographic image of her child. In the future he would not hesitate to take such a woman off the streets.

Although she knew that it was a violation of procedure, Liz found herself discussing with Mrs Bletchley DC Carron's encounter with the prostitute who had offered him her child. The subject seemed just to have come up naturally whilst the two of them were standing at the roadside during one of their evenings together. Zoë's response, when Liz mentioned DC Carron's comments, was a complete lack of surprise. She said, "I tell you, Liz, there are some strange people about." She paused for a moment and then said, "yes, I know, that sounds funny coming from me, but I mean really strange."

"A couple of times I've had men ask me if I had any little kids that I'd be willing to hire out. That may be what made that woman your 'copper' friend talked to say what she did. She's probably learned that some men get turned on by dirty talk involving young kids."

"Some of the prostitutes that I've known will do almost anything, even let themselves be cut badly with knives; all to get the dosh to buy their drugs. I remember one time I found a young girl; she couldn't have been more than sixteen or seventeen. She was lying next to some dustbins where she had crawled after being dumped from a car. She was bleeding all over her front. She told me that a man had offered her 50 quid if she would let him cut her on her breasts. The terrible thing was that once he'd cut the hell out of her he didn't pay her the money. All I could do for her was to ring for an ambulance. I've no idea what happened to her after that."

"It's a crazy ol' world, Liz; to tell you the truth, every now and then I seriously consider packing it in. I used to think that there was no job worse than teaching school, but I'm growing rather tired of this one, even if it pays better than school teaching. It'd be great if all my customers were like poor, old Professor Donald. He was even better than my ex-husband. He didn't demand too much of me in bed and he wasn't bad in the love-making department. Also, bless him, he was never tight with his money. Usually, he would take me out for a meal before we got down to it, and he didn't even deduct it from my bill!"

* * *

It was quite obvious that Chief Superintendent Denham was agitated by something because he rarely turned up at the morning meetings of the 'killer-prostitute' team unless something had made him angry. Liz was in the middle of a résumé of the activities of her and Mrs Bletchley the previous evening. The Chief Superintendent waited until she was finished, then he spoke: "I'm afraid there's been another killing, and, very likely, it is our killer at it again. This time the incident occurred in Pimlico. The cause of death hasn't yet been established, but the known details will sound familiar to you. It was a male in his late thirties or early forties who was found lying in the doorway of an apartment building early this morning. The body was found by a milkman, who, I gather, stumbled over it, dropping the several pints he was carrying. It was the sound of the breaking glass that caused the householder to turn on the porch light, thereby revealing what caused the milkman to fall. According to the preliminary report I got from the head of the forensics' team, the only external evidence of injury on the body was a small amount of blood on the clothing immediately over the left-hand side of the chest. As usual, there was no identification on the body."

Following his opening statement the Chief Superintendent launched into a monologue about how he was coming under increasing pressure because the investigation under his direction seemed not to be going anywhere. He asked the question: "are we any closer to solving this thing than we were at the beginning?" The silence that followed the question gave him his answer. As he left the room he said, "I know that you're all doing your best; let's hope that we get a break soon."

After the Chief Superintendent had left, Sergeant Brown got up from where he had been sitting on the top of his desk, saying, "Chief Superintendent Denham must be getting more flack than usual. He doesn't usually apply pressure quite so openly. Anyway, has anybody got any new ideas?"

A thought had occurred to Liz when Chief Superintendent Denham had said that the latest death was in Pimlico. She waved at Sergeant Brown, who said, "Liz?" She said, "It seems to me we have been spreading ourselves out rather thinly over the ground we've got to cover. Missus Bletchley and I can cover only one road during the evening, and the lads in the cars can only do perhaps two or three times that number. We have a whole mound of fingerprints, but none of them match those of the woman we think is the killer prostitute. I wonder if it wouldn't be better to concentrate our efforts more?"

"The murders that have occurred so far have been confined to the vicinity of only four of the several roads in London frequented by prostitutes and their clients. Perhaps it would be useful to confine the search for the killer to those four roads. We could try that for a short time and if it produces no results, go back to the way we have been doing things."

Sergeant Brown said, "it sounds like an idea worth trying, at least. It's obvious we've not got very far the way we've been doing it. Any objections, anyone?"

* * *

James Carron approached the road where he knew that he would have to pick up yet another woman who would smell like a perfume shop. Although he wondered what they would smell like once all of their clothes were removed, he had no intention ever of finding out. He retrieved the handset to his car transceiver from it place of concealment in the car glove box and pressed the button that sent a signal to DC Andresen's personal transceiver. There was no answering noise, so he re-concealed the receiver and drove alongside a woman who was standing at the kerb. Only when the woman opened the door of his car and spoke to him did he realise that she was the one whom he had encountered several nights earlier; the one who had offered up her little girl as a sexual partner for him. He had long since resolved that if he ever again encountered the woman he would not allow her to continue her nefarious ways.

At first, when the constable began speaking to the woman he attempted to obscure his face, fearing that she would recognise him. However, after speaking to her for a short time, it became obvious that she had not recognised him as someone to whom she'd spoken previously. He listened carefully to what she had to say, telling her that he would like very much to visit her daughter. She insisted that before she went off with him in his car he would have to pay her the fifty pounds. That request made him suspicious, but he complied, removing a fifty-pound note from his wallet. She got into the car and he drove off, following the directions that she gave him.

As he drove, DC Carron was in two minds as to what he would do. He knew that he would have no proof of an illegal act unless he allowed the woman to at least attempt to permit him to sexually assault her daughter. With that thought in mind he followed her instructions. She directed him to a quiet residential street of a part of London he knew well: a road that was not far from the police station where he worked.

At the place she designated, he parked the car. He followed as she opened the gate that led through the front garden of a house. He was puzzled by the fact that he thought it most unlikely that the woman ever could afford to own or even rent a house in the area to which she had taken him. However, rather than speak, he followed her until she got to the front door of the house. At that point she turned and whispered to him, "you seem such a nice man, I know that my daughter will like you. In fact, I would like to 'have a go' with you also. I won't charge you any extra." After she said that she surprised him by putting her arms around him and kissing him. He tried to remove himself from her embrace, but she proved to be very strong. In the darkness he did not see the rapid movement of her right arm as it plunged the knife into the side of his chest. Momentarily he was conscious of a feeling of pain followed by an inability to breathe. He expended almost the last amount of air he could force from his lungs to utter a strangled cry; then he fell to the ground.

He spent his last moments gasping for breath. He was aware that the pockets of his jacket were being searched. He tried to speak but no words would leave his mouth. Moments later he was no longer conscious and, minutes later, he was dead.

$$* * *$$

As she did routinely the woman searched the newspapers, hoping to discover who it was that she had killed that evening two days previously.

When she had begun her campaign she had expected that eventually she would be able to count a vicar as one of her victims. She had told herself that she would stop the campaign at that time unless she had been apprehended beforehand. She knew that she was doing what she was doing in memory of her father, who had molested her from an early age. He had been a Church of England vicar.

Until she had left her father's house at the age of eighteen she had endured the words of her father's parishioners, mostly women, telling her how lucky she was to have such a kind, compassionate and loving father. She knew that it was her father who by his treatment of her had taught her the hypocrisy of the adult world. A world that condemned, openly, the behaviour that it practised covertly. However, she now had set the record straight, so to speak, with seven victims. She had no doubt that she would be caught, but that did not bother her. Even if she spent the rest of her life in prison that could be no worse than the prison in which she had been living from the age of four.

* * *

The day following the discovery of the body of DC Carron there was a general mood of quietude in one of the detectives' rooms of New Scotland Yard. The body of the police officer had been found very quickly by the owner of the house in front of which the DC had died. The house owner explained to the police that he had become a very light sleeper since he had been burgled some weeks earlier. Since then every little noise that occurred during the night had caused him to awaken.

On the night that the policeman had died he had been awakened by a sound which the house owner knew was that made when his front gate was opened. He had purposefully neglected to lubricate the hinges just so that he would be warned when someone entered his front garden late at night. A short time after he had heard the noise made by the gate, he had been certain that he had heard someone cry out. That had caused him to turn on the light that illuminated the front porch. "When I looked through the 'spy' hole I had had installed in the front door I could see nothing. However, just to be sure, I opened the door. It was then that I saw the body. It scared the hell out of me, so I closed the door and rang emergency services."

It was assumed by everyone on the team of which he'd been a part, that DC Carron was the seventh victim of the 'killer prostitute'. That assumption was confirmed within the two days that followed the death. The police car that he had driven was found quickly, parked in a residential road in West Hampstead. Fingerprints matching those that had been found in the cars of the previous six victims of the killer were found in it.

Meanwhile, Chief Superintendent Denham had suspended the police operation to find the killer and the members of the investigative team where sent back to their home stations until further notice. The Chief Superintendent had made it clear that the suspension was ordered because it was thought possible that DC Carron's death had compromised the operation. A search of his body had revealed that his warrant card was not there. It was assumed that the killer had found it and had discovered that her victim was a policeman.

Liz had only just resigned herself to returning to Mile End and serving under "the male chauvinist" when she got a call from the 'Yard'. It was Detective Sergeant Brown who told her that the "killer prostitute" operation was going again. He said that Chief Superintendent Denham had been worrying for nothing, thinking that the killer would have discovered that DC Carron was a copper. "Denham got this call from one of the lads in the evidence room, asking him what should be done with DC Carron's warrant card. The DC said that that was the first he'd heard that the warrant card had turned up; he said that he'd thought that the killer had taken it and, therefore, knew that Carron was a copper. The bloke in the evidence room said, 'no, forensics has just turned it over, saying that they found it locked in the glove box of the car that DC Carron was driving that night.' Anyway, Liz, Chief Superintendent Denham has decided that we can go ahead, so I'm calling a meeting for ten o'clock tomorrow morning, I hope that everyone will be able to make it."

* * *

Chapter Twelve

Liz had developed quite a fondness for Zoë Bletchley, and the two women had extended their relationship to getting together occasionally during the day when they were not otherwise engaged. Not long after they had begun working together she and Zoë had gone for lunch at a restaurant in Soho which had a reputation for serving good food at prices that weren't outrageous. They had acted like French women, taking almost three hours over the meal thereby attracting 'looks' from the serving staff. During the meal Zoë had confessed that she had made up her mind to abandon her life as a prostitute. She had flattered Liz by telling her that the conversations that the two of them had had whilst 'working' on the streets had made her realise that being a prostitute was no life.

She told Liz, "here I thought that I had been so clever: earning more than twice as much as I did when I taught school. However, I was ignoring the fact that then, at least, I could look at myself in a mirror and see a woman, not an object. I look at you and see that you are happy just being a woman, and that doesn't stop you from doing a job that you like. Oh, I know, Liz, you complain about the male chauvinism of some of your colleagues, but I can tell that you love what you're doing. Your happiness is in the work you do, not in spending the money you make doing the work you do. I've decided that I'm going to explore the possibility of getting back into teaching. I haven't done it for ten years and I've no idea how easy it would be to take it up again. Fortunately, I've got enough put by so that I don't have to rush right out and take the first thing on offer."

Liz was very pleased to hear of her friend's decision, but she had to choose her words of approval carefully. She wanted to avoid giving Zoë the impression that she had disapproved of her occupation as a prostitute, which, indeed she had. However, Liz had encountered sufficient numbers of prostitutes in her police work to know that Zoë was rather unusual. She had not become trapped within the occupation either by drug abuse or alcohol dependence or, what seemed to be occurring more and more in recent years, physical imprisonment. Liz had offered to help Zoë in any way that it would be possible.

It had been four months to the day since Liz had begun her stint as part of the 'killer-prostitute' team at Scotland Yard. Although she had been relieved of most of her official duties at the Mile End station, she visited there every few days for at least a few hours in order to keep in touch with investigations being undertaken by her colleagues.

To those men, Detective Sergeant Morgan and DC Chris Houghton, to whom she was closest, Liz had expressed her frustration with the 'killer prostitute' enquiry. She was beginning to wonder if perhaps the contribution she was making was just a waste of time. She wondered how long it would be before the whole police operation would have to be called off due to lack of progress.

Privately, Liz and most other members of the team had begun to believe that something must have happened to the woman whom they were seeking. Her first seven victims had died at about fortnightly intervals. However, now it had been just over a month since DC Carron, her last victim, had died. Chief Superintendent Denham was insistent that the operation should continue. He was of the opinion that the woman was a 'thrill' killer; doing it because of the challenge. He was convinced that the woman would continue to do it until she was caught.

* * *

When the break came in the hunt for the 'killer prostitute' it came from a source that was completely unexpected: Zoë Bletchley found the woman.

Liz was visiting with her friend, Lydia Mussett at New Scotland Yard where she had spent most of the day, since the meeting of the 'killer prostitute' team in the morning. She had not bothered to return to Mile End after the meeting because that evening she and Zoë would be spending their time on a street in nearby Pimlico.

Lydia had answered her extension phone and, after a pause, she had said, "she's here; just a second." She then handed the 'phone over to Liz. A voice said, "Liz, its Chris Houghton here. Sorry to bother you, but there's a woman by the name of Mrs Zoë Bletchley who's anxious to speak to you. I told her that you were spending the day at Scotland Yard, but she didn't know how to get hold of you there. Anyway, I said that I would try to get you and then pass on a message to you that she wants you to call her. She thought that you had her number, but just in case she gave it to me anyway."

Liz tried the telephone number that DC Houghton had given her. Zoë answered rather tentatively but when she heard who it was her voice became excited: "Liz? I'm almost certain that I have found our mystery woman. The woman I've seen certainly looks like her. However, the only thing that makes me wonder is the fact that she's a school teacher, and has been one for over six years. I thought I'd better ring you to see whether or not we should go to Pimlico this evening. However, once I thought about it I figured that you would say we should. I can't be positive that the woman I've seen is the killer." Liz suggested that they meet that evening and that Zoë could tell her all about her encounter at that time.

When Liz met her, Zoë had lost her enthusiasm. "I'm sorry, Liz; the more I've thought about it the more I think that the woman I saw this morning isn't our killer." Liz asked Zoë to tell her the complete story.

"Well, as I told you I have decided to return to teaching if they will have me. When I taught previously, I taught modern languages, specialising in French and German. I know that language teachers are in short supply, so I thought that from that angle I shouldn't have any difficulty. However, I haven't been in a classroom in the past ten years, so I didn't know whether or not I would have to do something to update my experience. I thought that the best way to find out would be to go directly to the source. Much to my surprise I still had the number of the school where I last taught in my address book, so I rang that."

"The woman who answered was rather short with me at first, wanting to know how I had got the number. All I could think to do was to tell her who I was and that I had taught at the school several years ago. The woman then became all friendly, saying that she remembered my name and all of that sort of thing. Anyway, the next surprise came when she told me who the headmistress of the school was. It was a former colleague with whom I'd been good friends. She passed me over to my ex-friend, Imogene Coggins, and we had a good old 'natter'. When Imogene heard why I was calling she insisted that I come right to the school; she said that she wished to grab me before anyone else did!"

"Well, I arrived at the school just at their dinner break, so Imogene suggested that we go into the school's cafeteria and get some sandwiches and a drink. She kept telling me how things had changed since I had taught; the quality of the food in the cafeteria being one!"

"I tell you, Liz, I almost dropped my tray when Imogene and I joined the queue at the serving counter. Immediately in front of us was a woman who either is the killer you're looking for or she is the killer's spitting image. Imogene introduced the woman to me as Clarissa Stafford, telling me that she was one of the PE teachers. I tell you, Liz, it was really odd standing close to that woman and trying hard not to let on what I was feeling. I asked her how long she had been at the school; it turns out that she had been there six years. In fact, almost everything she told me made it seem impossible that she could be the killer. However, she looks just like the woman I saw that night with Professor Donald."

* * *

The morning following her talk with Zoë Bletchley, Liz got to Scotland Yard early so that she could speak to Sergeant Brown before the regular meeting of the 'killer-prostitute' team commenced. She wanted to ask his advice about how to proceed with the lead that Zoë had given her. Tony Brown got very excited and insisted that the two of them inform Chief Superintendent Denham immediately.

Liz felt like she was a bit of a fraud because the Chief Superintendent insisted on giving her credit for the discovery that Zoë had made. However, the important thing was the plan of procedure that he suggested that she was to follow: "now as you've told me, DC Andresen, your informant isn't absolutely certain that the woman that she has seen is the killer. Therefore, we shall have to use some caution.

Give me the details of the school and the name of the head-mistress and I'll attempt to get hold of her and set up an appointment for you to see her today. What we need to do first is elicit her co-operation in helping us to get the sus-pect's fingerprints. That will get us a lot closer to knowing whether or not she's our killer. If we can establish whether or not the woman's fingerprints are the same as those found in the cars of the seven victims we will be on much firmer ground for further proceedings. You and Tony go off to your meeting now, but come back and see me when it's over. Also, probably, it would be as well not to say anything about this during your meeting. Better to err on the side of cau-tion and assume that your friend was mistaken."

It was obvious to Liz that Chief Superintendent Denham had been careful in setting up an appointment for her with Mrs Coggins. The headmistress greeted her without giving any indication to persons in the school's main office that she was a police officer. Only when they were in her private of-fice did Mrs Coggins allow her bemusement to show. "I can-not think what the police would be wanting with Clarissa Stafford. She is one of our best teachers; very popular with the students, especially the girls of the upper forms. I am sure that there must be some mistake."

Liz allowed the headmistress to continue with her mon-ologue on the qualities of Miss Stafford, listening carefully for clues that might be useful to the police in the future. Finally, Liz was able to introduce the subject of the reason for her visit to the school into the conversation:"we believe that Miss Stafford may have been involved in a crime. The easiest way of proving or disproving that would be to com-pare her fingerprints with those that were left at the crime scene. We would like your co-operation in obtaining the young woman's fingerprints. Let me assure you that should her fingerprints not match those we have in police records we will destroy them."

* * *

The tube journey from Camden Town to St James Park seemed to take no time at all, probably because Liz was engaged most of the time writing up notes of her interview with Mrs Coggins. The headmistress had been full of praise for Miss Stafford, assuring Liz that the police would be wasting their time investigating the teacher.

In a plastic evidence bag in her handbag Liz carried four sheets of paper: forms on which teachers reported the names of pupils absent from their classes on any one day. Absence Report forms related to Miss Stafford's PE classes. Usually the forms would have been taken to the school's main office by a different student each day. Consequently the fingerprints of that student would be on the forms. However, fingerprints from only one person, Miss Stafford, would be found on all four of the forms.

Liz had been most interested in much that Mrs Coggins had had to say, except that she ignored her protestations on behalf of Miss Stafford: "this is the sixth year that she has been with us; she did her university at Loughborough and then did a postgraduate certificate of education there. She came straight to us after leaving Loughborough. She is a very shy young woman and tends to keep herself to herself; a trait which, I fear, doesn't endear her to some of her colleagues. However, she is very popular with the students, the upper-form girls, especially. Each year she runs courses teaching the girls how to handle themselves should they be attacked on the street. That doesn't find favour with some of the male teachers; they think that she is a man hater and a bad influence on 'impressionable female minds', as they tend to call the girls who attend Miss Stafford's courses. Also, I think it irritates some of the more macho men that Miss Stafford is really quite strong, probably because she's a body builder."

* * *

Chief Superintendent Denham had seen to it that everything would be in readiness to act when Liz arrived back at Scotland Yard. The Absence Reports that she carried were taken directly to the forensics lab and a short time later it had been confirmed: on each of the report sheets were the fingerprints of the same person who had been in the automobile of each of the murder victims.

Liz knew that Chief Superintendent Denham held strong views about the utility of fingerprint evidence. He had made it obvious from the start of the investigation that he did not consider that sort of evidence to be conclusive in proving that a particular suspect was the 'killer prostitute'. He had said several times that it was the kind of circumstantial evidence that was easily refuted by a good barrister. He would be satisfied only if the murder weapon could be recovered. He felt that she would have to be very skilful to remove all traces of her victims from that.

Bearing in mind the Chief Superintendent's views, Liz was surprised when he asked her to brief her colleagues on her views as to how the detention of Miss Stafford should be attempted. Obviously, he had listened when she résuméed her conversation with Mrs Coggins. Also, he had been unimpressed with her argument that several police officers should be involved in the detention of the young woman. He told her to ask just three of her 'killer-prostitute' team colleagues to accompany her.

* * *

Missus Coggins was speaking to one of the secretaries in the main office of her school when she looked up to see DC Andresen and three men enter. She told the secretary to excuse her and then went to speak with her visitors. Before she could say anything, Liz told her, "Mrs Coggins, I am very sorry to disturb you, but I would like you to take me and my colleagues to the place where Miss Stafford is at the moment. We have a warrant for her arrest. We will try to create as little upset as possible." The head teacher left Liz briefly to consult a file that obviously was the teaching timetable. Then she spoke to the secretary, "I'm just off to the hall, Dorothy. See if you can get hold of Mr French who's on his free period and have him go there to meet me."

Earlier, as they had driven to the school, Liz had discussed with her colleagues the procedure that they should use in detaining Clarissa Stafford. She had warned them that the young woman was reputed to be very strong. If she attempted to resist arrest she might be difficult to overcome. Also, they should bear in mind that there was a possibility that she would be armed, so she should be approached with caution.

On the way to the place where they were to find the suspect, Liz asked the headmistress to describe the physical layout of the hall in which the PE teacher worked. As she had feared, a person wishing to escape from the hall would have several choices. The hall, itself, had three exits, one of which led out onto the school playing field. To make matters worse there were two changing rooms at one end of the hall. Should the suspect wish she could escape into one or the other of those. Each of the changing rooms had an exit. Liz wondered whether or not she and her colleagues should delay until they had more backup. However, by the time she decided that that would be a wise move, the headmistress was entering the hall where a number of teenage girls were playing basketball, whilst others watched. Standing at the far side of the hall was a woman whom Liz was sure was Miss Stafford.

When the woman saw the headmistress and four strangers enter the hall, she spoke to one of the girls standing next to her and then came over to where the headmistress was standing. Before the headmistress could say anything she spoke: "I know why you're here. Please don't make a fuss, I don't want you to disturb my girls."

Once back at Scotland Yard, Chief Superintendent Denham began the interrogation of Clarissa Stafford. However, he stopped the interview when the suspect refused to speak to him. She said, "I will speak only to that female officer who helped to arrest me. I'll never get any of you men to understand why I've done what I've done." When asked to explain those words she refused to say anything further.

* * *

Chapter Thirteen

When Liz began interrogating Clarissa Stafford she was able to satisfy her curiosity about something that had bothered her since the arrest of the woman; Clarissa's comment that she had been expecting them when the four police officers had entered the hall where she was teaching.

Miss Stafford told Liz that she had recognised Mrs Bletchley when the woman was introduced to her by the headmistress. "Her face was familiar, but I couldn't remember where I'd seen her before. However, finally it came to me. I had seen her a couple of times standing at the kerbside when I was there. Since Mrs Coggins told me that Mrs Bletchley was at the school talking about a teaching post, I realised that she couldn't have been a prostitute. The few prostitutes I've spoken to don't talk like her. Also, she seemed rather nosy, asking questions about my personal life. Finally, it came to me; she must be from the police. I couldn't think of any other reason that she was at the school and was interested in talking to me. I figured that somehow or other, the police had found out where I worked. So, when you and those three men came into the hall yesterday, I had a pretty-good idea who you were and why you were there."

Clarissa Stafford did not hesitate to admit her guilt in the killings for which she was arrested. In fact, Liz got the impression that the young woman not only lacked remorse, but that she was actually proud of what she had done, saying, "do you want me to tell you about it or don't you really care? You've got me and I have confessed." Liz told her that she, for one, was always interested in the motives that drove people to commit crimes, adding, "I don't find it difficult understanding why someone kills in a fit of anger or unintentionally, as in a car accident. However, I do find the killing of innocent people for no apparent reason inexplicable."

A plainly agitated Clarissa broke into Liz's narrative raising her voice to say, "but you don't understand; they weren't innocent. They were all child molesters. That..." Liz interrupted saying, "how do you know that? The last man you killed, James Carron, was an unmarried police officer; I doubt very much that he was a child molester."

Clarissa was patently surprised by what Liz had to say, "that man was a police officer? He acted like all of the rest. He took me up on my offer to allow him to have sex with my daughter. An innocent man wouldn't do that; he wasn't to know that I had no daughter."

Liz said, "I think that it is most likely that his agreement to your offer was done in the line of duty. He talked about you to me. He realised that the only way a criminal charge could be brought against you successfully would be to apprehend you in the commission of a criminal act. You may not remember, but the night you killed him was the second time he had encountered you. The first time he had ordered you out of his car for making what he described as a 'disgusting proposal'. Since then he had been looking out for you, intending to gather sufficient evidence so that he could arrest you. He was not to know that you were a killer." At that point the interview was interrupted. It was obvious that Miss Stafford was distressed; she would not respond to questions put to her.

Liz suggested to the PC who was in the interview room with her that it might be time for a tea break. It pleased her when he didn't demure, but got up from where he was seated to go get the tea. She wasn't a militant feminist, but she saw no reason why it was always a female who had to perform such tasks.

Once the PC was out of the room, Clarissa Stafford looked at Liz and asked, "what's going to happen to me?" The tone of the young woman's voice caused Liz to feel pity for her. However, she had to answer truthfully: "I really don't know, Miss Stafford. My knowledge of criminal law is sufficient for me to know what is an illegal act and what is not. However, when it comes to the application of the law, I'm afraid that's something with which I've had little experience. Although you have admitted to us that you have killed seven men, you may find that a lawyer will insist that you reconsider your position when it comes to answering charges in the criminal court. I really don't know."

In order to break the awkward silence that followed her answer to Miss Stafford's question, Liz said: "you know, Miss Stafford, something that you said early in the interview has puzzled me. Off the record, what did you mean when you said that none of your victims were innocent; how did you know that?"

For what seemed like a long time to Liz, the young woman looked at her steadily without speaking. Finally she spoke: "for you to even begin to understand how I knew that those men weren't innocent, you must understand about my father. He began molesting me when I was a little girl; I think maybe I must have been about four because that was my age when my mother died, and I know that it started about then. I learned when I was older that at different times women of the village where we lived had offered to help my father by keeping house for him. Had he not refused perhaps life would have been very different for me."

"After my mother died my father took over the tasks of managing our house although he insisted that I help him where I could. However, from about the age of nine I became my father's wife in every sense of the word. I slept in his bed and, many nights, he fucked me. Outside of school hours I kept house for him and even acted as his secretary."

"What I haven't told you yet was that my father was a Church of England vicar. He was pastor of the church in the small village where we lived. I suppose it was that that most distorted my view of life. Here he was, molesting his own daughter on a regular basis, meanwhile everyone in the village thought that he was a saint. I had to stand there smiling when everyone in the village told me what a wonderful man my father was. They would tell me how lucky I was. Also, they would say to each other that the vicar was lucky because his 'lovely young daughter obviously adored him'. If only they had known. As I grew older I decided that I would repay him for his hypocrisy when I was able to do so. I would kill him. However, I never got the chance. He was killed when I was seventeen."

"He didn't arrive home after evensong one night. I was just as glad because when he was very late he wouldn't wake me up to make me fuck him. When he was still not home in the morning, I went by the church on my way to catch a bus to go to my school. I found the door standing open. Because of that I assumed that my father was still there, so I didn't bother to go into the church. Normally, the door was kept locked when there were no services or my father or the verger weren't there. Several pieces of valuable ceremonial silver were kept in a locked cabinet in the vestry, and my father was always worried that they would be stolen. Do you know, detective, I was actually disappointed when

I was told later that day that my father was dead. However, my disappointment arose only from the fact that his death robbed me of the pleasure of killing him. In my mind I had worked out exactly how I was going to do it. I wanted to see the look on his face when the full realisation of what he had done to me was brought home to him. However, whoever killed him robbed me of that pleasure."

"Our village constable came to my school and got me. He wouldn't tell me what the problem was, but I figured that it must be something serious to warrant all of the attention I was getting. Well, it turned out that had I looked just inside the church door that morning I would have seen my father's body. Since the ceremonial silver was missing, the police believed that my father had caught burglars in the act of stealing it and had made the mistake of attempting to stop them. He had been killed with a ceremonial dagger that was kept in the cabinet where the silver was kept. It was one of a pair owned personally by my father. I think that you will recognise the dagger that killed him when I say that it had a narrow, ten-inch blade and was sharp on both edges of the blade. I have its twin. If the police haven't found it already, I will tell you where it is located. It's in the inner pocket of the jacket I wore when I acted as a prostitute"

"After my father was dead I experienced a feeling of not being a prisoner for the first time that I could ever remember. I could hardly contain my anger when my father's parishioners came to the house, fawning all over me. They interpreted my inability to experience even the slightest feelings of sorrow as 'oh, aren't you a brave girl'."

"Of course, my father's house was owned by the church, so after a brief period allowing me to 'mourn' I was informed, in very polite terms, of course, that I would have to vacate the premises. Several people in the village offered to put me up at least until I finished school. However, I was saved by the new vicar, a woman; she offered me accommodation for as long as I required it, saying that the house was much too large for only a single person. I offered to pay her using some of the money that I had got when my father died. The C of E paid something like six months salary, I think it was. I was glad that she took up the offer because I did not want to be indebted to her."

"I used most of the money I got after my father's death to go to university. I had decided that I was going to make myself as strong as possible so that never again would I be forced to give in sexually to a man. I had grown to hate the act of fucking. I never was able to derive any pleasure from it. In one sense, I suppose, I am still a virgin. My father is the only man I have ever fucked. Please don't get me wrong, DC Andresen, I am not using what happened to me as an excuse for my actions. I have no intention of making excuses. In fact, I am proud of what I did, except, maybe, killing the policeman. If what you said about him was true."

Just at that point the PC re-entered the room with a tray, setting it down on the table between Liz and the prisoner. Liz noticed that it had only two cups of tea on it, so she asked the PC if he wasn't having any. He said that he'd taken his in the tea room; that was why it had taken him so long.

After she and Miss Stafford had finished their tea Liz glanced at the clock, which confirmed what she had thought; it was growing late, and still she had not managed to persuade the prisoner to finish a critical part of her statement: her motive or motives for killing seven men. Miss Stafford had alluded to a motive early on in her statement, but then the two women had got to talking on other subjects.

Liz decided that the best approach to the subject would be one that was direct: "you mentioned early on, Miss Stafford, that the men you killed were child molesters. Why did you think that; you didn't know any of them did you?" Clarissa Stafford said, "no, I didn't know any of them, but let me tell you what I did know. As I was growing up I lived under the illusion that my father was a one-off. Other men didn't behave like him toward children and that what was happening to me wasn't happening to any other children. Then, I found out different."

"Ever since I was a teenager I have tried to keep myself fit by running. I didn't have any friends, so I had to run by myself. During the first few years that I was running I was approached three times by men who tried to get me to run with them. I had no interest and I told them so. However, just after my father was killed I was running when a man approached me who was really frightening because he wouldn't go away when I told him to. When I got back to the vicarage that day I took my father's keys and went to the church. I was hoping that the twin to the dagger that killed my father would still be there. It was. For a long time after that I carried it every time I went out by myself. However, when I went to university I took up bodybuilding. I wanted to make myself as strong as a man, so that if one of them tried to rape me I could defend myself."

"It wasn't until a few months ago that I got the idea to try to do my bit to rid the world of child molesters. It all started when I was running one morning at Primrose Hill. I noticed this man who was walking along in front of me holding onto the hand of a young girl. I noticed them because it looked like the man was almost dragging her. When I got close to them the man turned and saw me. At that moment he put his hand over the child's mouth. I couldn't help noticing that she was only five or six. I thought of stopping, but much to my regret I didn't."

"A couple of days later the local paper carried a picture of the young girl and a story about her having been kidnapped from a local primary school. It said that she had been taken to parkland at Primrose Hill, raped, and left for dead in some bushes. Kids playing with a football found her. One of them kicked the ball into the bushes where the little girl lay. The one who went searching for the ball found her. It was a miracle that she was found, otherwise she probably would have died from exposure."

"I telephoned the police and they sent someone to my school to talk to me. I gave them a description of the man, but the policeman who spoke to me said that they would be lucky to find him. He told me that that sort of thing was happening these days and there wasn't too much the police were able to do about it unless they caught someone in the act. I remembered the look on that little girl's face and I decided that even if the police couldn't do anything to prevent such things happening, I could."

"The idea of acting like a prostitute came because I figured that it was one way to find men who were sexually abnormal. I think that any man who pays women to let him fuck them is sick. How they could do such a thing, I don't know. Anyway, I read an article in one of the London tabloids where the police were attempting to stamp out kerb crawlers. It named some districts in London where activities by prostitutes and their clients were creating a nuisance. I think you know the rest. All I did was ask each man who stopped his car near me if he wanted to have sex with my six-year-old daughter, telling him it would cost him

£50 for an hour. If he said yes I got in his car and directed him to a house or apartment block that I had sussed out beforehand."

Clarissa Stafford stopped talking, so Liz waited for a time and then began to conclude the interview. At that point, the young woman began speaking again, "All along when I was killing those men I expected to get caught. In fact, I still am surprised that I lasted as long as I did. I know that when I asked you earlier what was going to happen to me you thought that I was worried. It wasn't that at all. I asked only to learn what will happen now that I have been caught. All that I know for sure is that murderers no longer are hanged, so that that won't happen to me. Also, I know that I will go to prison and, probably, spend the rest of my life there. However, that holds no fear for me. As I said before, I have been in a kind of prison since I was four years of age."

Liz concluded the interview at that point. She knew that she would have to report to Chief Superintendent Denham before going home and give him a brief résumé of Miss Stafford's statement. Also, she wanted time to reflect on the story that Clarissa Stafford had related during the time the interview was not being recorded. She wondered whether or not to include that in her résumé to the chief superintendent. She decided not to. She was sure that it would be considered irrelevant to the police case against the young women, if entirely relevant to her defence.

* * *

Chapter Fourteen

Liz was not overly pleased to be back at her desk at the Mile End station. Even though she had felt somewhat homeless during the almost two months that she was working with the 'killer prostitute' team out of New Scotland Yard. Usually, she saw her colleagues at Mile End on a regular basis, but only rarely was she able to attend their morning briefings which would keep her up-to-date with their activities. It was her colleagues, excluding DCI Lawrence, that she had missed.

By way of contrast to her treatment by Chief Inspector Lawrence, Chief Superintendent Denham had treated her as though she might have a brain cell or two. He had sought her advice concerning aspects of her part of the 'killer prostitute' investigation and, frequently, had acted upon what she had told him. She had not agreed with the hard line that he had taken concerning the guilt of Clarissa Stafford. She was well aware of the trap that often ensnared upholders of the law: focusing on crimes, rather than the victims of crimes. Liz had not thought that she was ignoring the plight of the 'killer prostitute's' victims. However, she had to admit that it was difficult to have much sympathy for the men who had gone with Clarissa Stafford only because they wanted sex with a child.

During her tenure at the 'Yard', Liz had renewed her friendship with Lydia Mussett, although her night-time work pretending to be a prostitute had prevented them from seeing each other much during that time. However, being able to spend even brief periods of time with someone with whom she could be intimate made Liz realise how much she missed that kind of company. She resolved that she would do something about that when she returned to Mile End.

Her 'stint' at New Scotland Yard had involved her in quite long duty periods. In compensation for that, she was entitled to take several days off. In the past she had not bothered because, for the most part, she had no place that she particularly wished to go. However, now, she decided that she would spend a few days in Cambridge. It had been some time since she'd visited her mum, and, also, she wanted to see her friend, Pat, who then had reached the last month of her pregnancy.

Of late, whenever Liz talked to Pat on the 'phone, her friend, who usually made light of her troubles, had sounded rather down. Pat was only half joking when she made the usual complaint that her husband, Roger, had "spent only five minutes of his life, whilst I've had to put up with eight months so far of puking every five minutes, a bad back and looking as large as London bus." When Liz asked whether or not Roger was helping her at all, Pat retreated a little in her argument, saying, "well, he has been pretty good. Of late he's been doing quite a lot of the household tasks so that I don't have to be on my feet for too long at one time. I just wish the whole damn thing would get itself over with. I'm getting fed up!" Liz hoped that if she spent a few days visiting in Cambridge she might be able to cheer her friend.

* * *

Liz had been in Cambridge for only a day when she had begun to regret her decision to spend some time with her mother. Ever since she had been a teenager Liz had felt that her mum had seemed incapable of acknowledging the fact that her daughter was growing up. As she had done when Liz was a youngster, Audrey had insisted upon lecturing her daughter on how she should live her life. Now that Liz was away from home the situation had changed little except, perhaps, to get worse. The few constraints that her mother might have had in voicing opinions of Liz's way of life tended to disappear when the woman had been drinking, which was often. Liz had been largely successful in ignoring the theme of her mother's main complaint; that she was living 'far' away from the one person who loved her. However, fortunately, so far Audrey had not taken up the theme which had been a favourite of Liz's grandmother when she was alive: being in the police was not a proper occupation for a woman.

Liz's Nan had wanted her to marry, settle down and have children; "the way women should do," which was the way the Nan usually had phrased it. Liz had found that argument impossible to combat, so she had ignored it.

Liz had expected to spend some time with Pat and her husband, but that plan had to be abandoned because Pat was in hospital. During the latest of her ante-natal health checks the midwife had found that Pat's blood pressure was quite high. The midwife insisted that Pat should go into hospital for a check-up, frightening her by telling her that she was showing signs of pre-eclampsia, an often fatal condition brought on by pregnancy. However, more extensive tests done during the two days Pat was in hospital showed that her condition was the more common 'pregnancy hypertension'. She was sent home and cautioned to get plenty of rest during the last month of her pregnancy. However, by the time Pat was out of the hospital, Liz was back in London. She had made excuses with her mum and had gone back a day early.

* * *

Liz arrived back at Mile End to find that DCI Lawrence had been asking for her. Liz had gone to see him, not knowing what to expect since she had not had a chance to speak to him since returning to duty. He surprised her by being full of praise for her work at New Scotland Yard. "Bill Denham told me that I could be proud of you; you were sort of the leading light in that investigation; he thinks that you'll go far. There; I'll bet that will make you feel good." The DCI's remarks had made her feel good, but that feeling was generated more by the hope that the remarks indicated a change in the view that Chief Inspector Lawrence had of women in the police.

Liz made a few modest comments before asking, "will that be all, sir?" The DCI said, "no, I almost forgot what it was I wanted to talk to you about." He picked up a file folder from his desk and held it out to her. "I want you to have a look through this. In the past four months or so there have been several incidents; five, as I recall, in which four men and a woman have been badly beaten up. The beatings are unusual in that none of them appear to be racially motivated and drunkenness does not appear to be involved. I am asking you to take over the investigation because you know one of the assault victims: a young man called Barry Goff. I thought that you might have a word with him to see if he can give you any insight into why he was beaten up."

The mention by the chief inspector of Barry Goff's name made Liz recall her conversation with Goff immediately before joining the 'killer prostitute' investigation: he had said that the victims of the beatings had been chosen because they were part of the animal liberation movement. Liz decided not to say anything about that to the DCI. She realised that she should have spoken up quite a lot earlier and that to do so now might diminish the man's present amicability. She took the file and went back to her desk in the detectives' room. A careful reading of the file indicated that only one characteristic seemed to be held in common by the five victims of the beatings: all of them had been beaten by just two men. However, the descriptions of the men doing the beatings varied considerably. In their statements, none of the victims had been able to offer a reason for why they had been set upon. Liz knew that those statements were lies, at least with respect to that of Barry Goff, and, possibly, Richard Cowling. The file did indicate that most of the victims had been arrested at previous times for relatively-minor offences, such as creating a public nuisance, unruly behaviour or common assault.

Liz was sure that Barry Goff could provide her with information that would be valuable in her investigation, but there was one line of enquiry she had to make before speaking to him. At the time Barry Goff had been attacked, Liz had spoken to the medic who had examined him in the A&E Department of the London Hospital where he had been taken. The man had expressed his opinion that Goff had been beaten very professionally. By that he meant that there appeared to have been no intent to inflict serious injury, merely to make the victim feel and look poorly. Liz set out to interview the doctors in the A&E departments of the hospitals where the other beating victims had been taken.

That exercise had proved to be rather futile. It was too long after the fact. Of the four medics she attempted to contact only two were still working at the same hospitals. The others had moved to other jobs outside of London. One of the two doctors that she interviewed had forgotten all about the incident, and he had not kept notes. Even though Liz made no comment he defended himself by saying, "have you ever spent any time in an inner-city A&E department, constable, especially on Friday and Saturday nights?

It's a bloody madhouse. It's almost impossible to look after the people who keep coming in, let alone sit down long enough to write up case notes!"

Although the other doctor to whom Liz had spoken had kept brief notes, they were of no help to Liz in indicating what she wished to know. She concluded that there was nothing for it; she would have to interview the victims themselves. In order that she may do that she would have to contact Barry Goff once again. Undoubtedly he would know all of them.

Barry was very pleased to hear from Liz, telling her that he would help in any way he could to apprehend the two men who had been beating up members of the animal-rights movement. That statement told Liz part of what she wished to learn, namely, very likely it was the same two men who had administered the beatings. She made a date with him to meet in the Junior Common Room bar at Queen Mary and Westfield College.

* * *

Liz's meeting with Barry Goff had been quite pleasant. He had only just got back to London from a short stay at an astronomical observatory near Tucson in Arizona. He had enjoyed every minute of it, especially the astronomy and the Mexican cooking. He had encountered the latter for the first time. He had been unable to 'get over' the fact that during his time there the nights were almost continuously cloudless, permitting extended periods of optical observations. He contrasted that to Britain, which, he thought, had had to develop radio astronomy because of the almost continuous cloud cover. Liz listened patiently to Barry extolling the virtues of Arizona, biding her time until she could get him talking on subjects closer to her interest.

Finally she was able to ask him if he was continuing still with his participation in the animal-rights movement or had he been dissuaded by the two men who had beat him up. He said that he had done very little with "the movement," but that was merely because of the lack of time. "I'm still in complete sympathy with what they're trying to do. However, Liz, there is something funny going on. All of us who have been beat up have been given the same message: 'drop your activity in the animal-rights movement and don't tell the police. Consequently, I don't know if I should be telling you; you probably know about it already."

That remark puzzled Liz, so she asked Barry to explain it. He told her "there's a suspicion amongst us that it's the police who are behind the beatings. First of all, we're certain that it's the same two men who have attacked all five of us."

That remark puzzled Liz because she had deduced from her reading of the file given her by DCI Lawrence that several different men had committed the assaults. However, that had been based on the descriptions of the victims, which, at the best of times, were subject to error.

Barry Goff continued, "also, you remember George Baird, don't you. He was one of the men we used to meet up with occasionally when we went to that pub near where I used to live. Anyway, George swears that one of the men who beat him up is or at least was a copper. He is sure that he had seen him a couple of times policing animal-rights demonstrations."

Liz hoped that she had been successful in convincing Barry Goff that the police were not involved in the beatings. "I would hardly be here asking you questions if I knew the answers already, Barry; I don't like wasting my time."

He agreed that the idea had seemed rather far-fetched to him, but that George had been so positive.

Liz used Barry's expression of doubt in an attempt to engage him in a scheme that she had planned prior to meeting with him: to arrange for her to meet as many of the beating victims as was possible. She knew that he would have to keep the fact that she was with the police a secret. However, she did have one advantage: previously she had been seen with him by members of the group to which Barry belonged. Liz returned to the station having made a date with him to have a meal in the pub where they used to meet Richard and George. Barry said that usually the two men could be found there on a Saturday night.

Liz knew that she was under obligation to report to DCI Lawrence the results of her interview with Barry Goff; however, she decided to leave out the bit about the suspicion that the police had been involved in the beatings. Although she had dismissed the allegation when Barry Goff had expressed it, upon reflection, she wondered if there could be an element of truth in it. She knew that the job of a part of the security services of the country, MI 5, was to keep an eye on groups like the animal-rights movements. She wondered if, perhaps, they were involved in the beatings. Were that the case, she had heard enough about their operations to know that the civil police very well could be kept in ignorance about their activities. Liz concluded that were MI 5 involved in the beatings of Barry Goff and his associates she would find out soon enough. Someone would attempt to discourage further investigation on her part.

* * *

Chapter Fifteen

When Liz and Barry met in the pub with George Baird and Richard Cowling, it was obvious immediately that her scheme had failed. George Baird greeted her by saying, "ah, yes, you're Barry's copper friend. I'm afraid coppers aren't in good odour around her just at the moment." Liz spent the entire evening in rather lively conversation attempting to convince Barry's friends that the police had not been involved in beating them up. Although they were not convinced by any of her arguments, she did manage to get all three men to agree on a description of the two men who had assaulted them. She hoped that the descriptions would be adequate for a police artist to make relatively-accurate drawings of the men's faces.

At first, none of the men was willing to go with her to Scotland Yard to assist a police artist. Finally, however, Barry Goff agreed to go, but only after Liz had agreed to come to his flat and cook a meal for the two of them.

The next day Liz met Barry at the Mile End station and then the two of them went to New Scotland Yard. Barry told her that he had seen the famous revolving sign many times on TV, but he never imagined that he would actually be visiting the place one day.

Liz was surprised how quickly the artist was able to complete his work, producing drawings of the two men which Barry Goff said were as accurate as he could remember. She asked him to find his own way back to Mile End, since she had arranged to have lunch with Lydia Mussett.

* * *

Upon her return to the Mile End station, Liz was told that DCI Lawrence wanted to see her. He came straight to the point. "Liz, whilst you were away this morning I got a telephone call. It has been suggested that we should drop our enquiry into the beatings of those animal-rights activists. Although it was put in the form of a 'suggestion', it was made pretty clear to me that it was more like an order. To be honest with you, I am not too sure what to do. I want to get your views on the matter because, of course, you are the one doing the investigating."

Liz put into words the first thought to come into her mind: "I don't see how we can drop the enquiry, sir. After all, five crimes have been committed. We have what I think are fairly accurate descriptions of the two men who have committed those crimes. I don't understand; has whoever spoke to you said or implied that the beatings weren't crimes?" The DCI said, "no; it's not so straightforward. The person that spoke to me said that by our investigation we were interfering with another investigation that was more important because it was more in the national interest. In other words, Liz, one of the security services is involved, probably MI 5. I think that we shall have to follow the advice I have been given and drop the enquiry. I'm sorry, but I am putting that in the form of an order. You'd best return the file on the case to the documents room."

"Maybe now would be a good time for you to take off those days you didn't take when you got back after your stint at Scotland Yard. There's not much going on at the moment, so I'm sure that we can get along without you for awhile."

Liz left the chief inspector's office feeling very frustrated. She did not want to drop her enquiry just when she felt that she was getting some results. She was sure that if she went through the Met's database she would be able to find likenesses of the two men who had been going around beating up on animal activists. However, the DCI had made it quite clear that he had been frightened off, even if he didn't say so in so many words.

She put the file that she carried under her arm in a drawer of her desk, rather than return it to the documents room. Despite Chief Inspector Lawrence's orders, she would continue her interest in its contents. In spare moments she would search through the Met's database to see what turned up.

* * *

Liz was pleased to return to her flat having to contemplate nothing more pressing than a quick microwave meal, a glass of wine and the prospect of a few days away from rather routine police duties. She would go to Cambridge, and, of course, stay with her mum. However, she hoped that that would not preclude a long visit with her friend, Patricia Moffatt.

After her meal Liz telephoned Pat's number. The 'phone was answered by Roger, Pat's husband. He told her, "oh, you're a couple of days too late, Liz; Pat's still in hospital. I only just got back from visiting her."

"You'll be pleased to hear that yesterday she gave birth to an eight-pound, three ounce boy. We're calling him Andrew. Despite his size they thought that he was a week early, but I doubt it; Pat must have miscalculated. Anyway, he's going to be a big lad; he was 21 inches long. She will be coming home tomorrow or the next day; I'm not sure which."

Liz congratulated Roger on his new son and told him to give Pat her love when he visited her next. "Tell her I'll ring in a few days time."

A disappointed Liz put down the receiver. Here she had been almost ordered to take a few days off and she could think of no place to go. She was sure that she did not wish to visit Cambridge whilst Pat was unavailable. Maybe she would just stay around her flat and relax. Then she said to herself, "no, that's no good; c'mon woman use some imagination. Think of some place to go." Other than Pat the only other person that she could think of with whom she'd wish to spend a few days was Lydia. However, during their lunch together the previous day, Lydia had enthused to Liz about the investigation with which she was involved at present. She reckoned that the team of which she was part were just about to round up one of the largest rings of drug dealers in London.

Liz resigned herself to spending a few days wandering around some of her favourite London places. It was at times like these that she wished that she had a companion. Most other times, she enjoyed her solitary life.

She had just finished writing a long note to herself, résuméing her thoughts about the investigation she'd just been asked to drop, when her extension 'phone sounded. It was Zoë Bletchley who was profuse in her apologies for not having called Liz earlier, "but," she said, "it's taken me longer to re-organise my life than I thought it would when I started. Now, however, I think I have just about done it. I got that teaching job that I went after, but I don't start full-time work until the start of the school year in the autumn. Meanwhile, to get used to 'wearing the harness' again, I'm doing some supply. I could do that full-time if I was up to it, but that's a mug's game. The kids are really quite relentless when it comes to giving temporary teachers a bad time. I suppose it's always been like that, but I never did any supply work before. Anyway, Liz, the reason I called; I'd like you to join me for a meal; the sooner the better. I should have invited you long ago, but you know how it is."

When Zoë learned that Liz was taking a few days off, she volunteered that she would do the same. "Why don't the two of us take a couple of days to explore London? That would be really exciting. I haven't done anything like that since I was a teenager, and then I couldn't do much 'cause I didn't have the money! Why don't you come stay with me; that way we can plan out what we're going to do each day and not waste time having to meet someplace in town!"

That evening, Liz arrived at the door of Zoë's house with a small bag containing all that she would need to last her the three days that she and her friend would be staying together. Once again, she was charmed by the house.

In response to Liz's remarks about how lovely it was, Zoë told her how she had 'earned' the house. "I owe my former husband for a lot of things, including this. I didn't find out until after I married him, but he was completely under his mother's thumb."

"I don't know how he managed to persuade her that I was suitable for him to marry because once we'd made our vows his mother could find nothing I did as being right. After a few months of marriage to him I began to wonder what I had ever seen in him. In addition to being a complete mother's boy, he was addicted to prostitutes. He worked in the City as a stockbroker; his mother had bought him a seat on the stock exchange. However, he was never very good at it. I used to tell him that if he spent more time at the exchange and less time with his tarts he would do better."

"Anyway, when we'd both finally had had enough he agreed that we should be divorced. However, he told me that he would give me anything I wanted, within reason, if I would take the blame for the break-up of the marriage. He said that if his mother thought that it was his fault she would be heartbroken. I knew better than that. If she discovered how he carried on, what with prostitutes and all, she wouldn't have been heartbroken, she would've disowned him. He'd have been in a real pickle then. He was really very dependent upon her financially."

"I was really only joking when I offered to take the blame for the break-up of our marriage, if he would give me the deeds to this house. To my surprise he agreed. I suppose it didn't really bother him, his mum had given it to him as a wedding present when we got married. Also, I'm pretty sure that she would be happy to see the back of me. So, Liz, that's how I got this lovely house, free and clear. I tell you it makes a difference to the housekeeping not to have to worry about mortgage payments."

"Also, it was my former husband who gave me the idea about becoming a prostitute. He was always very secretive about his finances; he had a personal bank account as well as our joint account. One time I inadvertently opened up the envelope in which his monthly statement came. I was staggered because almost all of the cheques he had written during the previous month were to four women, each for the sum of £50. It made me wonder when he ever found the time to be a stockbroker. Also, I saw that he had paid each of the women in a single month as much as I earned teaching school. I was certain that my former husband was not their only client."

During their first night together, Liz and Zoë planned out the itinerary for the following day, in a convivial atmosphere created by the consumption by the two of them of a bottle of white wine. Zoë said that normally she drank very little, but that she was really looking forward to the next three days. It had been a long time since she had been with someone she really liked as a companion.

As her friend was saying that, Liz was thinking similar thoughts. She was feeling quite affectionate toward Zoë, so she hugged her. That provoked a reaction that Liz had not expected: her friend hugged her and kissed her passionately. Before Liz realised what she was doing, she responded with equal passion. A short time later the two women were in bed together, neither of them caring or thinking about where their behaviour was going to lead them.

The plans that Liz and Zoë had made for their three days together were implemented only partially. They managed to visit one major tourist site on each day, starting with the Tower of London, Liz's favourite of all of the capital city's tourist attractions. As a schoolgirl she had become fascinated with the history of medieval Britain. In consequence there was little about the Tower that she did not know. She delighted in showing Zoë around the place and detailing its history. The second day was Zoë's choice, and she took them to the Museum of Childhood in Bethnal Green. Despite working not very far from the museum, Liz had never been there. She found the exhibits fascinating.

On the third day, it was a toss-up between the Greenwich Maritime Museum, which was Zoë's choice and the National Gallery, which was Liz's choice. The coin came down tails, so Zoë got her choice. That had the advantage of a boat ride down the Thames, which both women enjoyed.

From the first night when she and Zoë made love, Liz had determined that she would not think about what was happening between the two of them. She would just enjoy their time together and hope that everything turned out for the best. She realised that a relationship between herself and Zoë could not go anyplace. Fortunately, during the time that they had spent together, Zoë had not said anything that would indicate that she expected the relationship to last.

After their first time of making love, Zoë had seemed anxious to talk with Liz about what they had done and how each of them felt about that. She had expressed surprise that Liz had responded to her, saying, "I was half expecting you to slap my face, but I just couldn't help myself. I knew that I was interested in other women, but I didn't think that you were." Liz hadn't known what to say. She didn't think of herself as being interested in other women. In fact, she wasn't really interested in men, either, except as friends and colleagues. She knew that her love for Pat and Lydia was of a sexual nature, but they were the only persons she thought of in that way.

Liz's silence encouraged Zoë to continue. "Until I divorced my husband and started being a prostitute I always thought that my rôle in life was to be a wife and mother. Then one night I met a woman in a pub who asked me to go home with her. I don't know what made me do it. I guess it was just an impulse. I remember thinking as we drove along in her car what in the world she expected me to do. I hadn't the foggiest idea what to do with a woman. However, when we got there she had me undress and take a shower with her. Then she told me to relax and just do to her what I did to myself to give me pleasure. After that it was very easy. I even found myself willing to have oral sex with her; something I had done for my male clients, but had never thought that I would do with a woman."

By the time their three days together were nearly complete, Liz had made up her mind what it was that she wanted from her relationship with Zoë; she hoped that a situation would arise that would allow them to discuss it. She thought that she had detected 'hints' in some of the things that Zoë had said that indicated that her friend desired a permanent relationship. That was not possible. Even if she loved Zoë, which she didn't, it would not be possible for them to live together.

As it turned out, Liz need not have worried. On their last night together, Zoë seemed less enthusiastic in her love-making than she had during the previous two nights. Finally, after they had finished their activity in bed, Zoë told Liz that she wished to speak to her about the future. Liz waited apprehensively, until her friend stated, "I think that you know, Liz, that this relationship can go nowhere. After all, I am at least ten years older than you. Also, I have decided that I want to get on with my life. I feel that I wasted the six years that I was married and the four years since when I was a prostitute. Now I am going to do the selfish thing and throw myself into my teaching career. Also, I'm going to sell this house, which is far too large for me, and buy a flat. Any money I have left over from the sale, and there should be plenty, I shall invest. Then, when I am ready to retire from teaching, I shall have enough money to travel. Maybe then I will tie myself down with someone to act as a travelling companion. Am I being too selfish, Liz? Are you disappointed in me?"

Liz hoped that the relief that Zoë's words gave her was not too obvious. She said only that she agreed with her friend's sentiments because she felt somewhat the same way herself.

* * *

Chapter Sixteen

Upon her return from the brief holiday spent with Zoë Bletchley, Liz discovered that the case involving the beatings of the animal-rights protesters had been re-activated. However, now, it involved a death. Detective Chief Inspector Lawrence briefed Liz, telling her that a sixth protester had been set upon by two men, as before, only this time there had been a witness. The DCI told Liz, "we're not too certain of the details, but clearly the man was attacked not long after leaving a pub where he had spent part of the evening. He was found in an alleyway about half way between the pub and his home. The man who discovered the victim was out walking his dog. He said that normally he would never go into an unlit alleyway at night, but his curiosity was aroused when two men almost bumped into him as they exited that place. It was the fact that they were running that made him suspicious. After he had advanced a few feet into the darkness he heard a noise that sounded like someone calling for help. A moment later he virtually stumbled over the victim, who let out a yell."

"The dog walker talked to the victim long enough to discover that the man had been set upon by two men and badly beaten. The victim complained that he was suffering terrible chest pains; he asked the dog walker to get an ambulance. Fortunately, the dog walker had a mobile phone on him which he used to dial 999, alerting both the ambulance service and the police. The informant said that whilst he and the victim were waiting for the ambulance the victim fell silent. Unfortunately, the victim was dead by the time the ambulance got there."

"Our first thought was that this beating was not the usual one because the victim had been killed. However, then it turned out that the cause of death was a heart attack. Apparently, the victim wore a pacemaker which became dislodged during the beating."

"In my view, the death of a victim puts the beatings back onto our agenda, and I think that we should go ahead with our investigations. I had a word with Scotland Yard and they told me that they knew nothing about any security-service involvement in the investigation. Therefore, Liz, unless I get another telephone call telling us to butt out, you'd better get that file back out of the documents room."

As she left the DCI's office Liz breathed a sigh of relief that she had decided at the last moment before going on holiday to put the file back in its proper place.

The man who had seen the faces of two men who were running away from the place where the latest victim had been beaten agreed to come into the police station to look at the sketches Liz would show him. Without hesitation, he picked out the two that depicted the men whom Barry Goff had described to the police artist. It had taken some time, but Liz had gone to a lot of trouble to procure four sketches of other criminal suspects made by the same police artist. She reasoned that if the man could pick out the two drawings of the suspects from amongst six sketches shown to him, very likely the sketches accurately portrayed the suspects.

* * *

That evening, from home, Liz rang Lydia and asked her advice. Lydia suggested that Liz should go to the 'Yard' and have a look through the police database that was held there. She said, "we're not quite to the point of a computerised national data base, but that's coming in the near future.

Unfortunately, your search will have to be by manual means which will be tedious but I can't think of any other way to do it. You can have one consolation, though. Whilst you're here, you and I can have lunch together!"

After two days of sifting through the Met's database of persons convicted of crimes, Liz had not found faces that closely resembled the drawings of the faces of either of the two men suspected of assaulting animal-rights activists. Liz had got excited when, on the second day of searching, she had found a photograph that had features that were similar to those of one of the suspects. However, further checking revealed that the man depicted in the photo was in prison and had been there for the previous five years.

Liz returned to Mile End disappointed and wondering where she could turn next. It was then that she opened a drawer in her desk to discover a sheet of A4 paper that had been folded in half. On it was printed in bold letters with a felt tip pen, "Liz, read this!" She recognised the note as something she had written to herself prior to the time a few days earlier when she had taken some time off. It was an analysis of something that Barry Goff and his friends had told her about their belief that at least one of the two men involved in the beatings of the animal-rights activists was a policeman.

At first she had explored the idea that one or both of the two men assaulting the animal-rights activists had infiltrated their movement. However, then she remembered that Barry Goff had told her very early on in their discussions that there was no such thing as "the movement." Animal-rights activists generally belonged to small, local groups and really only got together in large groups when there were plans for a public demonstration. The six activists, the assaults on whom had come to the attention of the police, had belonged to three separate groups. It seemed unlikely that the men responsible for the assaults had infiltrated all three groups. In Liz's estimation, that strengthened the idea that one or both of the suspects would have to be someone who would have access to information on the membership of several, perhaps all groups of animal-rights activists.

In her notes Liz had concluded that very possibly the friend of Barry Goff had been right. At least one of the men administering the beatings to animal-rights activists was either a policeman or a member of the security services. That might explain the telephone call that DCI Lawrence had received in which he had been told to drop the investigation into the beatings.

Although she had said nothing at the time, Liz had disagreed with his previous decision to terminate the investigation of the beatings. As far as she was concerned, they were crimes and the people who perpetrated the crimes should be brought to justice. Furthermore, she had not been persuaded by the DCI's argument that another branch of law enforcement would bring the criminals to justice. Liz knew that the Metropolitan Police kept records of the personal details of all officers serving in the force; those details included an up-to-date photograph of each. However, the DCI refused to take seriously her request that she be permitted to go through the Met personnel records. He had irritated her by asking, "do you realise just how much time that could take?" She attempted to add weight to her argument by emphasising the fact that the beatings had resulted in the death of one of the victims. Nevertheless, the DCI was adamant: Liz was to explore other aspects of the investigation.

* * *

As she did normally, Liz stood aside as the tube-train door opened, allowing the passengers who were getting off at Mile

End to get out of the compartment. As usual, she was aware of people standing behind her and on either side; all hoping to gain some advantage over neighbours in entering the carriage. She was one of the last persons to enter, never quite having the 'brass' to push others out of her way to do so. Once in the carriage she made her way to its interior. She had learned by experience that that manoeuvre was the most likely to allow her to avoid the crowding that always occurred on the underground during the rush hours. Most people preferred to bunch up near the doors so that they could get out of the carriage as quickly as possible. However, Liz had only a few stops to go and then she would be home. She got a firm grip on one of the floor to ceiling supports provided for standing passengers and settled herself for the short ride to Plaistow.

Her usual way of passing the time was to read the advertisements that formed panels just above the height of her head on either side of the carriage. As she read her attention was diverted for a moment to the face of a man who was standing a few feet away from her. She looked away quickly. She was absolutely certain that she knew that face. It was that of one of the two men she was seeking. She glanced again at the man, but he appeared not to have noticed her.

The rest of her time on the train until she reached her stop, Liz spent trying desperately to think of what she should do. She was certain that her sighting of the man was not coincidence. She thought it likely that he was following her. Then a thought entered her mind that had made her smile because it was hardly appropriate for the occasion. For some time she had debated with herself whether or not to buy a mobile 'phone. To that point, the arguments against that act had prevailed, namely the 'phones were expensive and probably she would not make a lot of use of one. Whilst she was on duty, at least, she could make use of her police transceiver. However, now she could use some means to summon help and there was none. She knew that a mobile 'phone would be useless whilst the train was in an underground tunnel, however, toward the end of her journey she would have been able to use it. She thought briefly of making her way into the last carriage of the train where the guard was positioned, but because of the crowding that would take more time than she had. Also, very likely, it would alert the suspect and he might disappear. She concluded that it would be best were she to behave normally until the suspect gave some indication of what he had in mind.

As she got off the tube train Liz reminded herself that she had some shopping to do for her tea. Normally she did that in a small market that was not too far from the Plaistow underground station.

As Liz made her way to the ticket barrier she held back several times, allowing her fellow passengers to crowd ahead of her. She noticed that the suspect made that manoeuvre also. Finally, she went through the barrier, the man being just behind her. Before leaving the station she searched in her handbag for her notepad. As she was writing on it she noticed that the suspect passed her and went out of the station. She was just as happy that he had done that; she would prefer to have him in front of her where she could keep an eye on him.

Once out of the station, Liz saw that the man was nowhere about. That seemed onerous to her, so she was glad that the route to the market was well lighted. Once there she would give the market owner, a very pleasant Bangladeshi, the note that she had written which asked him to contact the Mile End police to have them get someone to her flat as quickly as possible. She was sure that she had not seen the last of the suspect.

Within the market, as usual, Liz engaged the proprietor, Mr Ashri, in conversation. He knew that she was a police officer, but he rarely asked her questions about her job. She, however, always could find a ready topic of conversation by asking him about his twin daughters. She was pleased to hear from him that both had just got acceptance notices from the London Hospital Medical School which, now, was part of Queen Mary and Westfield College. It was obvious that he was very pleased and proud of his girls.

There was an awkward moment when Liz went to pay for the groceries that she had bought. The total came to £13.95, so Liz handed Mr Ashri a twenty-pound note, hidden beneath which was the piece of paper on which she'd written her message to be passed on to the police. Mister Ashri separated the two items, handing back to Liz the small piece of paper, telling her she'd given it to him in error. That forced her to hand the message back to him, saying, "please, Mr Ashri, read what's on the paper and do as it says after I leave your shop." The tone of her voice caused him to hesitate, but only for a few moments. He opened the till and placed her message in one of the compartments. Then he counted out her change and bade her a pleasant "good evening."

After walking a short distance, Liz got the strong impression that she was being followed. That impression was worrying because she was approaching the road on which the building containing her flat was situated; it was not well lighted because the lamps in two of the light stanchions had burned out. She turned, stepping off the kerb and into the road, looking both to the right and the left affording her the opportunity to see if there was anyone in her near vicinity. When she looked to her right, back toward the food market, she saw a man who was walking towards her. He was too far away for her to discern whether or not he was the one who had been on the tube train. She continued across the road, walking in a direction that would take her away from the flat. She had no idea where she was going, but she was frightened and she believed that she would be unwise to go into a darkened area.

After several minutes of walking Liz crossed the road once again. This time she saw no one. To be absolutely certain that there was no one about, she stopped by the kerbside and carefully studied the road in her vicinity. Still, there was no one. Relieved, Liz turned and went in a direction that would take her to her flat. Now she was beginning to worry that the milk that she had bought at the market would be getting too warm.

As she approached her flat she could see that there was a police car parked at the kerb opposite her front door; it had its parking lights illuminated. She breathed a sigh of relief, going up to the car and knocking on the window to let the driver know that she was there. The driver was PC Ed Norton, whom she knew well. She invited him into her flat to get warm and, also, to explain to him what had prompted her to call for help.

After two cups of coffee, Liz was able to persuade PC Norton that the danger was past and that he could go back to the police station. He had offered to stay with her, but she told him that that was not practical. Anyway, she said that she felt secure. Shortly after moving into the flat she had had a number of security devices installed including an alarm system. Also, the front door had double locks and a security chain, and all of the windows had lockable handles

* * *

Chapter Seventeen

Liz awoke when a hand gripped her face, preventing her from opening her mouth. She could smell the distinctive odour of latex, so that she knew that whoever was holding her was wearing disposable gloves. She could feel the weight of a body that was resting on her, pinning her down. She screamed, but the only sound that she heard was muted by the hand that covered her mouth. Her first thought was "this is it; something terrible is about to happen." It was a fear that she had had since childhood. She had no idea of the origin of the fear but it had been there always. Inches away from her face was that of a masked, hooded figure. The image before her increased her attempts to scream, but still only a muffled sound escaped from her mouth.

Then a not-unpleasant-sounding voice spoke to her, saying, "just listen to me, Miss Clever Cloggs. You have done a good job hunting us down, but from now on you are going to give it a rest. We know perfectly well what we are doing, and believe me, it's in the country's interest. We cannot have a bunch of anarchists dictating to the government what its research policies will be. All we are attempting to do is persuade some of them that they had best think again about what they are doing. We are sorry that that one man died; that was an accident. We were not to know that he had a pacemaker fitted. However, remember, the animal rights people have killed also. They always excuse it by saying that they are only killing murderers of animals or that it was an unfortunate accident even when it's the result of a fire started deliberately or a bomb planted someplace. So take this as a final warning, constable. Next time we won't be so gentle."

Liz pulled at the man's hand, but she was unable to dislodge it. It was obvious that he had finished speaking to her when he turned and spoke to someone else who was in the room with them: "give me a hand, here; let's fix it so she won't be going anywhere for awhile." Liz feared the worst; she closed her eyes expecting the blows to begin. Instead the hand at her mouth was replaced by a length of what she later discovered was duct tape. Her wrists were placed together behind her back and secured with something that had sharp edges which she could feel when she moved her wrists. Then duct tape was used to immobilise her arms and ankles. Finally, she was placed on her back and the bed clothing was pulled up around her body, 'tucking' her in.

The man who had spoken to her before said, "you may like to know that there are some scissors on the dresser. You will undoubtedly need them, those wrist bands are pretty tough. Also, I am putting twenty quid there. That's for the repair of the window we broke getting in here. I'm afraid we had to make a bit of a mess of it because of the double glazing. Just as a hint, constable: you shouldn't leave the keys in the window locks. It makes it too easy for someone to get in once they've broken the window. Don't forget what I told you. If you are really clever and value your career in the police you will close this case and ask DCI Lawrence to put you on to something else."

"Finally, I hope you realise that what has just happened to you never happened, if you get my meaning. We'll leave by the front door, which, I've noticed, has a Yale lock on it so it will lock behind us. However, as soon as you get free you'd best go down and throw the dead bolt, as well as lock the broken window. Also, don't bother handing over the duct tape to forensics; that won't tell you anything."

For several minutes after she heard the front door slam Liz lay in her bed, motionless except for the shaking that accompanied her sobs. Her physical reaction had been due to the feeling of helplessness that she had felt in the hands of the man who spoke to her. Her tears were driven by both fright and anger. After a few moments she began to form in her mind the procedure she would follow to free herself. She realised that the band that held her wrists was too tight because one of her hands had gone numb. She decided that she would concentrate first on that.

After freeing herself, the first thing Liz did was to retrieve her radio transceiver from her handbag and report to the Mile End station what had happened to her. She said only that two men had invaded her bedroom. She was certain that she knew exactly who the two men were, but she kept that information to herself. Once she had made it clear that she had not been harmed, the officer to whom she spoke told her that he would send out a couple of police constables. They would stay with her until morning. At that time she was to remain on the premises at least until a scene-of-crime team arrived.

* * *

As Liz had expected, a forensic examination revealed nothing that would prove to be useful for tracking down the two men who had broken into her flat. As one of her assailants had told her would be the case, the duct tape revealed nothing; it was of a type that could be bought at any do-it-yourself shop or builder's merchants in any city. The plastic straps that had bound her wrists were a little more specialised; they were of the self-locking variety used by gardeners to bind plants to supporting stakes. Again, available not only at DIY shops but at most gardening centres.

And, of course, the assailants wore gloves so that there was no fingerprint evidence.

As the assailants walked around in her bedroom their movements made a rustling noise. That indicated to Liz that they were wearing protective suits of some kind; probably of the type worn by police when moving around a crime scene. As a consequence of that no traces of the men's clothing were found. The men had even taken the trouble to wear shoes that had featureless heels and soles. They left no impressions in the soil of Liz's back garden.

When Liz spoke to the policeman in charge of the Scene of Crime team, he said that he doubted that they would have much chance of getting further evidence. They would have to examine all dust bins and other places where rubbish was dumped in the area around Liz's flat. The assailants would have been quite conspicuous appearing on the street dressed in the way they were when they were in her flat. Therefore, they must have dressed after entering her flat and undressed before leaving it. That meant that they might have disposed of the clothing locally or carried it to and from the flat in a bag of some kind.

* * *

A fortnight after she had been assaulted in her bedroom, Liz was on indefinite leave, having been ordered by an assistant commissioner at New Scotland Yard to go away and think about her future in the Metropolitan Police. The man, Assistant Commissioner Bradstock, had got quite angry with her when she had complained that "everyone" was covering up for one of the security services, and was colluding in illegal acts. He had not denied her allegations but had told her, "stop banging your head against the wall, constable; there is nothing that either you or I can do about it."

Following those words Liz had left his office. Although she had intended to meet with Lydia following her meeting with the AC, instead she left Scotland Yard, taking the tube back to Mile End. She had decided that she had had enough of the police; she would hand in her resignation to Superintendent Cleary that afternoon. She didn't wish to speak to Lydia because she knew that her friend would attempt to talk her out of her decision.

She knew that there was an element of self pity in her thoughts, but she didn't care. She had grown tired of being a woman in an organisation which was still living in the nineteenth century when it was founded as an all-male preserve. She had not even begun to think of alternatives for a career, but those thoughts were not far from her consciousness. Now, she had to get through the next few days when she would have to leave her colleagues, most of whom she liked.

Just as she had feared would happen, London underground was experiencing delays to their services due to what a difficult-to-understand announcement delivered over the public-address system described as "engineering works." The same announcement said that trains going east of Bank station were amongst those affected. Unlike most of her fellow passengers, Liz did not grumble. She was happy to have the time to organise her thoughts and to think about what she was going to say to Superintendent Cleary.

Liz's musing recalled her conversation with the AC. Even he had admitted that she was in the right. She had told him, "the police have sketches that are good likenesses of the two men who are going around beating up people. Like everyone else, I think that it is likely that the men are members of one of the security services, probably MI 5. That should make it an easy matter to put names to the two like-nesses that we have. However, no one wants to do anything about it."

"Sir, it was drilled into me at Hendon that no person, official or otherwise, was above the law." The assistant commissioner's last words to her had been, "however much I might admire your pluck, young lady; I fear you've got to learn the hard way. I am ordering you to take some time off to think things over. I'll square it with your superintendent at Mile End."

By the time she arrived at the Mile End station Liz had plotted out the procedure that she would follow before leaving the place for good. First she would type out her letter of resignation; then she would take it to the superintendent. Finally, she would leave the station for home. She knew that she would not be able to face her colleagues and answer their questions as to why she was doing what she was doing.

Superintendent Cleary expressed surprise after he had read the resignation letter. He responded by saying, "now, constable...Liz. I don't blame you for being angry. I would be too. However, I don't think it's as serious as you think it is. Commissioner Bradstock told me that he thought that perhaps he had been a bit hard on you, so don't let that worry you. Do as he says and take some time off to think about things. I'm sure that when you cool down you will see that the AC is right."

Liz persisted, telling the super that she had resigned and that was all there was to it. Finally, she said "sir, I don't wish to be disrespectful, but I believe that you have no alternative but to accept my resignation. I am leaving now to go back to the detectives' room and clear out my desk."

Superintendent Cleary said nothing more; he just shook his head. After Liz had left his office he took the resignation letter and placed it in the top, right-hand drawer of his desk, saying out loud, "we'll just put that away for safe keeping until you come to your senses, young lady."

Two days later Liz was seated on the train to Cambridge, as usual, staring out of the window and day dreaming. This time she was musing about the events of the immediate past. Although she had left the Mile End station without saying anything about her resignation to her colleagues, they had not allowed the matter to rest there. All of them had telephoned her that first night. Each of them had expressed it in different words, but all had sympathised with her position. In addition, all had told her that they thought that she was "a good copper," and they didn't want to see her leave the police. Even DCI Lawrence had rung her. However his message had been much less friendly. He thought that she was being a "damn fool; risking your career for a bunch of anarchic idiots!"

Probably the words that meant most to Liz were those of her friend, Lydia Mussett. Lydia said that she agreed with Liz's motives for resigning, adding, "I'm sure that I wouldn't have the courage to do what you've done." However, Lydia begged Liz to reconsider her resignation. Both women burst into tears when Liz told her friend that it was too late. She had made up her mind.

* * *

Prior to going to Cambridge to spend some time with her mum, Liz rang Pat. She hoped that she and her friend could get together during the visit, and that Liz would have a chance to meet Pat's son, Andrew, who was just a few weeks old. Liz decided not to hold back speaking to her friend, she would tell her that she had resigned from the police.

Pat expressed surprise that Liz had resigned, saying, "you seemed to be so happy being a copper. It's quite a shock, Lizzie. What are you going to do now?" Liz said that she had not thought that far ahead, but that she was going to spend some time exploring various options. "First, I'm going to come back to Cambridge and spend a few days. Then, probably, I'll go back to London and start looking into things that I can do. I did some supply teaching awhile back and I quite enjoyed that. I want to look into the possibility of getting a teaching qualification, but I'm not too sure what's involved."

It was then that Pat said, "oh, Liz, do you think that your mum would mind if you stayed with me? I could use some moral support just about now. I wasn't going to say anything to anyone, but something has happened to me since Andrew was born. I just seem unable to cope. I didn't realise that I would be such an inadequate mum otherwise I wouldn't have had the poor little mite. He's such a sweet baby; he needs a mum who can really be a mum. I'm sure that you could help there; I've seen you, you're good with babies. Also, I think it would really give me a boost if you could stay with me for a time."

Liz asked about Pat's husband, Roger, and was told: "oh, he's being no help at all. In fact, he's hardly home any more. He keeps telling me that it's my fault because I won't do anything with him. He just won't realise that I can't help it; I don't have any energy. It's all I can do to keep poor, little Andrew fed and his nappies changed. I think that I am going to have to stop breast-feeding him 'cause he's depriving me of my sleep. I tried to get Roger to help, but he got all embarrassed when he saw me using a breast pump. Since you've got the same equipment maybe you won't be embarrassed. It's funny, he doesn't get embarrassed when he sees some young thing on the high street with her tits hanging out all over the place. The only thing Roger's got going for him as far as I'm concerned is the fact that he adores his son. I've never seen a man go so completely 'ga-ga' over a baby."

Liz told Pat that she would be delighted to stay with her; "to be honest with you, Pat, I was dreading spending time with my mum. I dare not tell her that I've resigned. Otherwise she will start planning my future life for me; that will involve me returning to Cambridge and living with her. Your suggestion that I stay with you is just perfect. I'll stay as long as you'll have me. Maybe I can look into the job situation in Cambridge. Also, of course, I can help out with Andrew."

* * *

Chapter Eighteen

Liz knew that she was being cowardly, but she had decided, finally, that she would not inform her mother that she would be in Cambridge. Pat had pleaded with Liz to plan on staying with her for a long time. Liz had no intention of doing such a thing. However, no matter the length of her stay in Cambridge, she knew that her mum would insist that she stay with her. She could just hear Audrey telling her, "Pat is a good friend, but she's not family." In fact, as far as Liz was concerned, she and Pat were family, but never had she dared to even intimate such a possibility to her mother.

Liz took a taxi direct from the train station to Pat's flat, which was in a lovely location in the centre of Cambridge bordering the river. She was surprised when, in response to her knock on the door, Roger, Pat's husband, admitted her. He said that he was there to have a brief session with his new son; that he would not be there long. He said that until his wife was feeling a little better he thought that it would be wise for him to keep out of her way. He said that he was staying with one of his work colleagues.

It was not difficult for Liz to discern that Roger was very unhappy at the turn of events since his son's birth. He was obviously distressed by Pat's moods of depression, which seemed to erode the 'reserve' that usually he exhibited in Liz's presence. He told Liz that he felt helpless to help his wife. He wondered if, perhaps, he had been mistaken to insist that the two of them should marry after Pat got pregnant.

A short time after Liz arrived, Roger announced that he was leaving. She accompanied him to the door of the flat where he turned and gave her one of his business cards, saying, "I would really appreciate it, Liz, if, in the next couple of days, you would give me a ring and tell me what you think is wrong with Pat."

After Roger's departure, Liz thought over her conversation with him. She wondered if, in fact, Pat's behaviour was, indeed, connected to the fact that her friend resented having had to marry Roger. She remembered that Pat had expressed such thoughts when she had discovered that she was pregnant. However, Liz had not heard her friend complain about it recently.

Liz's experience with babies had been confined to their care as a temporary baby sitter when she was a teenager. She had never had complete responsibility for the long-term care of a child. However, she discovered quickly that it was Pat's intention that Liz would be the mum that Pat felt that she could not be. Fortunately, Pat's little boy, Andrew, was a very easy child to manage. He was only a few weeks old but already he seemed to know how to charm everyone who looked at him; he simply smiled and giggled. However, Pat was something else again. She had lost her normal vivacity. Often she would get angry with herself for being unable to accomplish tasks that she was used to doing routinely. Such fits of anger usually would end in tears. At other times she would burst into tears for no reason that was apparent to Liz.

After the first week of staying with her friend, Liz found that she was becoming like a mum to Andrew. As far as she could see, Pat had got worse since Liz's arrival; now she was unable to sleep during the night. Also, her milk production had diminished, so Liz had taken over most of the baby's feeds, relying on powdered formula which had to be sterilised once it was made up.

Liz urged her friend to seek medical advice; she had heard of a condition that was called 'post-natal depression'. She wondered if, in fact, Pat could be suffering from that. However, Pat refused to visit her GP. She said that she felt "down," but she'd get over it soon.

One morning, after a night in which Pat had been particularly restless, Liz had got a call from Roger. Only then did she remember that he had asked her to call him. She apologised to him, telling him that it was her opinion that his wife was not responsible for what was happening to her. "I have tried to get her to make an appointment to see her GP, Roger. I'm afraid that I know nothing about it, but I have heard of a condition called 'post-natal depression'. I've told Pat about it, but she says that it's just all nonsense. However, I wonder if there is anything that you could do to convince her to see someone." Roger said that he would ring Pat's GP and see what the woman suggested. "I'll get back to you, Liz. I hope that there is a simple answer to this thing. It's so unlike Pat; usually she's so lively."

That evening, Liz had just fed and bathed Andrew and had put him down when she answered the telephone to hear the voice of Dr Turner, Pat's GP: "Mr Moffatt has told me about Mrs Moffatt's problem, Miss Andresen. However, he wasn't able to give me much detail. He asked me to speak to Mrs Moffatt, and I shall do that in due course. However, first I should like to hear from you since you have been staying with her for some time, now. I hope that you don't mind."

Liz was impressed with Dr Turner's approach. The woman asked Liz to describe a "typical" twenty-four hours in Pat's life. Liz did that as best she could, emphasising the fact that her friend seemed to be tired all of the time, yet she seemed unable to sleep at night. The doctor concluded that Pat very likely was suffering from a condition known as post-natal depression or PND for short. "However, having said that, I don't want to give you the impression that I know what PND is. I don't, and neither does anyone else. For some reason, some new mothers have to suffer through it for a few months or even up to a year. As far as I know the only medical treatment is anti-depressant drugs. I believe there are some attempts to treat it with psychological counselling, but that's outside my realm of experience."

"I don't like to put my patients on anti-depressants, especially when they are breast feeding. What I am going to suggest may seem unorthodox, Miss Andresen, but I would like to enlist your co-operation. I'll have a word with Mrs Moffatt first, but very likely I shall give her a mild sedative; that will help her sleep, and, I hope, relieve some of her anxiety. If that doesn't help, I'll try something else later. Now, Miss Andresen, I shall tell Mrs Moffatt that I am giving her something that cures post-natal depression. I hope that that will do the trick. If not, I'll have to think again. Now, let me speak to Mrs Moffatt, please. I'll see if I can persuade her to come into the surgery tomorrow."

Whilst Pat spoke to her GP, Liz went into the second bedroom of the flat which she was using as her own. After a very brief time, Pat came to see her, saying, "Dr Turner has talked me into going to her surgery in the morning. I wanted her to make out a prescription for the stuff she wants me to take, but she said she must examine me first. Also, she wants to see Andrew to see how he is getting on. Would you mind very much coming along with me, Liz? I just don't trust myself anymore. I might step off the kerb into the path of a car, and I wouldn't want to do that with Andrew in my arms."

Liz tried to ignore the implication of what Pat had said, but she could not. Never before had she heard her friend state that her own life was of little consequence. Now she was really worried about Pat. She wondered if she should ring the GP and seek further advice.

* * *

Still, Liz was finding it difficult to adjust to the change that had occurred in Pat's behaviour since the visit to Dr Turner's surgery. She had begun at once to take the tablets that the doctor had prescribed and for the first time since Liz had come to stay, Pat had slept through the night. The following day, Pat was almost her old self, once more being able to help in Andrew's care and suggesting that she and Liz take the baby for a stroll on the nearby Midsummer Common. That evening Pat insisted upon cooking the evening meal. Both women had a glass of wine with their meal; Pat had said that she wished no more than a glass of wine because she intended to resume breast feeding Andrew. During the ensuing few days it became clear that Pat's recovery was almost complete, so that Liz was thinking that soon she would be returning to London.

Whilst living with Pat and Andrew, Liz had had precious little time to plan a future life. Now, however, she was dreading having to tell Pat that she would be leaving soon. By many of her actions and statements since her recovery Pat had intimated that she expected Liz to stay with her and Andrew indefinitely.

As Liz had feared would be the case, it was clear that Pat had no plans that did not include her. When Liz spoke to her about returning to London, Pat said that she wanted the two of them to continue as they had been when they were teenagers. "Only now we know what to do when we get into bed together." Liz needed convincing. She knew that she loved Pat, and she very much enjoyed what they did in bed. However, what Pat seemed to be suggesting was a permanent relationship. Although there no longer was a constraint on such a relationship forced by Liz's job, she felt that her friend was ignoring other difficulties.

When Liz asked where Roger fitted into her plans, Pat had been quite blunt: "he doesn't; it's quite simple, Liz. I'll divorce him. I didn't want to marry him in the first place." Liz had questioned the grounds upon which Pat would base such a divorce, but her friend chose simply to joke about it, saying, "how about I plead 'non-consummation'?" Liz was pleased that her friend's sense of humour had returned, but she told her to be serious. "You can't ignore the fact that you will have to show cause in order to obtain a contested divorce." Liz was in no doubt that Roger would contest such a divorce. It was obvious from his behaviour that he loved his son very much and, she thought, he must love Pat also. He had been sufficiently concerned about his wife to consult medical advice on her behalf. As much as she might be tempted, Liz knew that living with Pat would not be a practical proposition. She would have to return to London.

After a full day of discussion and many tears produced by the two of them, Liz and Pat agreed to part. Liz had managed to persuade her friend to be truthful with herself; she had wanted to marry Roger as much as he had wanted to marry her. At one point in the discussion, Liz had said, "remember, Pat, you told me soon after you met Roger that if you were ever to marry, it would have to be a man like Roger. What has happened to make him less desirable?" Pat had not attempted to answer that question. However, after a time she began to be persuaded by Liz's arguments, finally agreeing to telephone Roger at work and ask him to come home. Liz was delighted.

* * *

The one thing that Liz had dreaded whilst living with Pat and Andrew was encountering her mum in the centre of Cambridge where Audrey worked. Had that happened and Liz had not been able to convince her mum that she had just arrived in Cambridge, she knew that she never would have heard the end of it. However, the only question that was asked when Liz showed up at the Audrey's house by taxi early one morning was, "where have you been, Elisabeth; everyone has been looking for you!" Liz was puzzled by the question, but she thought that she would ask about that later. She lied to say that she had just arrived in Cambridge, and she was taking a few days off from her work. Audrey repeated what she had said before about "everyone" looking for her, so Liz asked, "who is everyone?"

"Well, that lady policeman you know in London called you awhile back. She didn't say what she wanted, but she wanted you to call her; she said it was urgent. Then about a week ago, I think it was, a policeman came to the door, telling me that he was from the Cambridge police. He said that you had contacted them because you needed a document that you had left here some time ago, and you wanted them to fetch it. He said that you had said that you thought that you'd left it in the room where you normally sleep when you're here visiting. I took him to your room and told him I'd leave him to it because I was right in the middle of washing clothes. Some time later he came into the kitchen saying that he was finished. He didn't answer me when I asked if he had found what he was looking for. I must say, Elisabeth, despite the fact that he was a copper, I didn't much like the look of him. He was rather brusque and he made a mess of both the front room and your room, taking stuff out of drawers and not putting it back properly."

Liz was pretty sure that the "lady policeman" who had called was Lydia, although she had no intention of returning the call. However, everything that Audrey had said about the policeman who had come to the house was puzzling. She asked, "you didn't, by chance, ring the local police to confirm that the man was a policeman? Did he show you any identification?" Her mum said, "he showed me something that said 'police' and had a picture on it; I didn't look at it too close, but it looked genuine. No, I didn't telephone the police. Should I have done? When he said why he was here I assumed that you knew about it."

Her mother's story got Liz thinking that there was only one possible explanation of why a so-called policeman had searched her room. He must have been one of the men who had visited her that night in her flat. She wondered what he was looking for. It was then that she remembered that she still had copies of the two sketches made of the men who had assaulted the animal-rights protagonists. She had forgotten about them and had not left them behind when she had cleared out her desk on the day she resigned from the Met.

* * *

Chapter Nineteen

Despite her fears, Liz found herself enjoying the time she was spending in Cambridge. Her mum had moderated her drinking and no longer was insisting that every evening be spent in the pub. Also, Audrey seemed to have made a conscious decision not to nag her. Her mum had not questioned her about the time she was spending away from her job in London, thus relieving Liz of the necessity of lying. In reality, Liz had not yet made up her mind where she was going to live. The apparent change of heart by her mother in her treatment of her made Cambridge a distinct possibility.

After thinking about it for a few days, Liz decided that she would explore the possibility of training as a teacher. She would begin her investigation in Cambridge, going to Homerton College, which, she believed, offered a one-year course that led to a postgraduate certificate of education or PGCE. Also, she had no idea how she would support herself. She had managed to save a few thousand pounds from her police salary, but she was sure that that would be inadequate to keep her for very long. If she stayed in Cambridge very possibly she could live with her mum.

The woman at Homerton College to whom Liz spoke, Mrs Holland, was very encouraging, telling Liz that she would have no difficulty finding a secondary-school job as a teacher of mathematics. In fact, the woman had stated that really it would not be necessary for her to acquire a PGCE, although there was little doubt that the qualification would be useful.

Missus Holland told Liz the story of her first experience as a teacher: "I read history at university, and I had no real interest in being a teacher, even though my mother was one.

However, once I had graduated I found that jobs for historians weren't thick on the ground, so to speak, so I decided to give teaching a try. Much to my mother's surprise, my first job application, which was to a girl's public school, was successful."

"I remember still my first day teaching; it was pretty traumatic. The one piece of advice given me by my mother that I followed was, 'before you enter your first classroom make out a detailed lesson plan for each of your classes'. I followed her advice to the letter, entering my classroom full of confidence and with a sheaf of papers under my arm. Much to my horror half way through the hour I had covered everything in the plan for that class. I had to improvise for the remainder of the time. Fortunately, after a few days I adjusted and I didn't have any trouble after that. That's where doing a PGCE would be helpful. It concentrates on methods of teaching; a knowledge of those probably would save you some grief when you first get started."

Liz had come away from Homerton thinking that she was very glad that she had spoken to Mrs Holland. The lady was just full of good ideas. Missus Holland had suggested to Liz that she might do supply work until a good full-time job came along. She said that most school districts were very short of such temporary teachers, especially those who were qualified in specialist subjects, like maths. Liz was going to follow Mrs Holland's advice, but not in Cambridge; she was going back to London. The only factor that had made her consider remaining in Cambridge was her lack of money; living with her mum would have helped there. However, if she could earn a reasonable amount of money doing supply work she could afford to stay in London in her flat. Also, Mrs Holland had told Liz that in her opinion she would find far more opportunities for long-term supply in the East End of London.

* * *

Liz expected that her flat would be cold: before she had left London, she had turned down all of the room radiators to a position that did no more than keep the water pipes from freezing should there have been a prolonged frost in her absence. However, the flat was really quite cold. Furthermore, when she turned on the light in the front room all she observed was disarray. Upon going into the kitchen she discovered the reason why the flat was so cold: the double glazing had been removed from one of the kitchen windows. The kitchen, also, was in complete disarray, a condition that she discovered in all other rooms of the flat, even the bathroom.

Liz was of two minds whether or not to inform her former colleagues. She was pretty sure who it was who had broken in, and, also, she was certain that she knew what they were after. That it was her 'friends' from MI 5 was confirmed in her thoughts by the fact that she could discover nothing that was missing. Consequently, it would be a waste of time to report the break-in to the police.

She set about cleaning up the mess. When that was done she opened the bottle of white wine that had remained, undisturbed, in her fridge. She thought that she could use a couple glasses of that if only to help her through the period until her flat became warm.

In her bed that night she decided that she would carry on her life as she intended it to be at least for the immediate future. In the morning she would search for a job as a supply teacher; also, of course she would have to contact the man who had repaired the kitchen window the last time the MI 5 agents had broken it. She was hopeful that she had saved the man's bill which had his contact details. Also, sooner rather than later, she had to return her police warrant card to the Mile End station.

* * *

It had been only three days since Liz had begun work as a supply teacher in the London borough in which Plaistow was situated. Missus Holland had been right; Liz had had no trouble finding work. Every day since signing on as a supply teacher she had been working. Each morning she had received a telephone call from a local secondary school anxious to find someone to take the place of a teacher who had called in ill that morning or who was away from the school on official duties. Liz had found it awkward not having a car because most of the schools who had called her were at some distance from her flat and she didn't know the local transport system very well.

A new addition to Liz's flat was a telephone answering machine; a device that she had avoided buying previously. She greatly disliked having to leave messages on the machines of other persons. However, a woman at one of the schools where Liz had worked had suggested that she buy one. The woman, who was responsible for obtaining temporary staff for her school, told Liz that the possession of such a device would allow her to obtain more long-term employment. The woman had said that where possible most schools attempted to engage supply teachers well in advance of the day of their need. Therefore they would call the person involved and leave a message on their answering machine.

Despite its intended purpose, the first person to leave a message on Liz's new answering machine was Lydia. Liz had been dreading her first contact with Lydia because she knew that her friend would remonstrate with her for resigning from the Met. She wanted to keep Lydia as a friend, but she would be unable to cope if her friend continued to display disapproval for what Liz had done. However, the message on the answering machine betrayed nothing of Lydia's former anxiety about Liz's resignation. Her calm voice said merely that she was wondering how Liz was getting on and could they get together sometime soon. The message ended with Lydia making a plea for Liz to call her, "either at home or at the 'Yard'."

Once Lydia answered her 'phone Liz was happy that she had rung. Her friend seemed so pleased to hear from her, and they nattered on for over an hour, finally making a date for Lydia to come to Liz's flat for a meal. After she rang off, Liz went into the kitchen to pour herself a glass of wine. She was satisfied that her friend had accepted the fact of her resignation from the police, although the subject had not been raised during their telephone conversation.

* * *

Liz had got home just a few minutes before the knocker on the front door of her flat sounded. She had stopped off on the way to buy the ingredients for the meal that she was cooking for Lydia. She looked through the spy hole that she had had installed in the front door of her flat; a precaution that had been recommended by her colleagues after the visit to her by the 'MI 5' officers. The person standing there was a woman, but she could not make out the facial features. She put on the security chain and opened the door hearing a familiar voice saying, "you took your time, Liz. One would think that I was here to rape you...hm, maybe that's not such a bad idea!"

Liz admitted Lydia, who had brought a small case with her. That meant only one thing, the thought of which delighted Liz. Once the door was closed behind her Lydia put her arms around Liz and gave her a kiss that caused her to become aroused. She responded accordingly and a few minutes later the two women were in bed together.

As Lydia suckled her breasts, Liz could think only that it had been such a long time and she really had missed the friend that she loved dearly. Then Lydia changed her position and began to 'fuck' Liz; that action had its usual effect: Liz opened her mouth, gasping for breath. As her climax drew near Liz's gasps became louder causing Lydia to increase the frequency of the fucking motion. Both women then ceased their active love making, with Liz lying in Lydia's arms whilst cuddling together.

Liz knew that she was not the only woman with whom Lydia made love, but she didn't care. She loved Lydia and, if it were possible, she would move in with her and the two of them would spend the rest of their days together. However, always inserting itself between them was the lack of understanding of their colleagues in the Metropolitan Police; that was an obstacle that was then insurmountable.

After a prolonged shower and a change of clothing, Liz served Lydia and herself a glass of white wine, asking her friend to seat herself in the front room whilst she got on with the evening meal. As Liz busied herself in the kitchen, Lydia insisted on keeping her company, at first talking about generalities having to do with recent activities at the 'Yard'.

Then Lydia startled Liz by saying, "you know, don't you, that you're still a copper?" Liz started to object, but Lydia stopped her, saying, "I know, I know; you think that you resigned six weeks ago, but unfortunately or fortunately, depending upon how you look at it, a resignation has to be accepted before it becomes effective. Your super, Cleary, just stuck your resignation letter in a drawer in his desk and never acted upon it. He was hoping that you would change your mind. Haven't you wondered why a couple of pay checks have gone into your bank account as usual." That caused Liz to remember that she had not checked her bank statements recently, so she wasn't aware that she was richer than she thought.

When Lydia had begun to speak, Liz was in the middle of preparing a dish she had not tried previously, a Chinese-style stir fry, which had looked easy except for the necessity to cut raw pork into small pieces. Lydia's statement had startled her sufficiently that she cut herself on the thumb rather severely. At that point Lydia took over the getting of the meal whilst Liz tended to the wound. She was happy to have the break because in addition to a thumb that was sore she was feeling the effects of the second glass of wine, which, rather unwisely she realised, she had poured for herself.

It was obvious that Lydia was far more adept than was Liz at talking and preparing food at the same time. She said, "irrespective of your status as a serving copper or a civilian, we need your help, Liz. I don't know if you've heard, but there have been two more beatings of animal-rights activists. That has caused someone in the hierarchy of the 'Yard' to realise that whoever is responsible for the beatings has no intention of stopping. Consequently, the official attitude toward the beatings has changed. My boss has been drawn into the enquiry, and he has asked me to see if I can't get you to co-operate."

Liz said, "I don't know, Lydia, I don't think that you will get very far. I think that the security services are involved and you know how secretive they are." Liz said, "well, I'm not sure that that is true. One of the bigwigs at the 'Yard' who has the clout to get answers from politicians told my boss otherwise. He said that he had been assured by a very senior civil servant in the Home Office that no one in either of the security services was involved with the beatings."

Liz interrupted Lydia at that point, "do you really believe that? The two men who broke into my flat that night as much as admitted that they were responsible for the beatings and that I was to 'butt out'. Unless they were connected with the police somehow, how would they even know that I was involved in investigating their activities? They also knew that my boss was DCI Lawrence. Also, Lydia, I haven't told anyone yet, but a man in a police uniform turned up at my mum's house in Cambridge; he was looking for something, I don't know what, because he searched almost the whole house. Then, when I got back from staying in Cambridge I found that my flat had been broken into and the place taken apart. What they're after, I don't know, but they sure made a hell of a mess looking."

By that time, the food was ready to serve so Lydia said, "let's have our meal whilst it's hot. I've got more to say, but it can wait until after we get some food in our stomachs."

After eating and then clearing up the dishes, the two women sat down to talk. Lydia continued on the subject she had opened prior to the meal: "as you surmised, rightly, when you talked to AC Bradstock, the 'Yard' was not very interested in pursuing an investigation that might get them involved with the security services. However, that was before two events occurred. The first I already told you about: the denial by the Home Office that the security services were involved in the assaults on animal-rights activists. However, the second was more serious. The originals and all of the copies of the sketches that you had made of the faces of the two men suspected of doing the beatings disappeared also. That must mean that someone connected to the police, and more specifically, New Scotland Yard, is involved in the beatings. Alternatively, someone at the 'Yard' has done a favour for the men doing the beatings. Neither alternative is acceptable to the Metropolitan Police."

When Lydia mentioned the stolen sketches, Liz said, "yes, I'm pretty sure that MI 5 or whoever made visits to my mum's house and broke into my flat, probably were looking for copies of the sketches. Fortunately, I forgot to leave behind the copies that I had when I left Mile End. I have them in my handbag." Liz went to her handbag, and after searching, found copies of the sketches of the two men in one of the side pockets. She handed them to Lydia, who responded by saying, "oh, Liz, that's brilliant! I've tried to get the victims to help, but all of them refused. A couple of them made it clear that they felt that if they did help they would be putting themselves in further danger. I'm afraid that most of the victims take the view that it is the police who are behind the beatings; none of them trusts us."

At that point Lydia got a grave look on her face, saying, "please, Liz, is there no chance at all that you will agree to help us? This thing has gotten beyond an investigation into the beatings of a few animal-rights activists. The higher ups at the 'Yard' are worried that there may be some major police corruption. They have asked me to try to persuade you to help, even if it doesn't involve permanently returning to the police service. You are the one person, other than the victims, who has first-hand knowledge of the two men involved in the beatings."

* * *

Chapter Twenty

Liz was uncertain what her reception would be when she returned to the Mile End station. She had been away for almost two months and as far as she knew most of her colleagues would not have been aware that her resignation from the Metropolitan Police had not been acted upon. She was pleasantly surprised when she entered the station and the duty sergeant welcomed her back. His welcome contained a clue as to the reason that had been given for her absence. He asked if she was feeling better. She hoped that she had betrayed none of her ignorance of what he was talking about when she replied to his question, "yes; much better, thank you."

In the detectives' room the response of her CID colleagues was equally warm, all of them expressing their relief that she had been able to return to her job. They had invited her to go with them at lunch time to one of the local pubs; they wanted to celebrate.

The explanation of the behaviour of her colleagues came a short time after when she spoke to Superintendent Cleary. He said that he had taken it upon himself right from the start not to accept her letter of resignation: "I thought it very likely, Liz, that you would change your mind. You're a damn good copper, and I think that it is in your blood. I know that you told everyone that you were leaving the police, but I told them that they weren't to take you seriously; you were just overtired and needed some time to think about things. I must confess that when nothing had been heard from you after six weeks or so I was beginning to worry that I'd misjudged you. However, now you're back and ready to go again, and that's all that matters."

The superintendent said that he had been liaising with Detective Superintendent Murphy at Scotland Yard: "his CID group has been put in charge of trying to sort out the persons responsible for beating up those animal-rights activists. I know that you are friends with Detective Sergeant Mussett, who is a member of Murphy's team, so what I've told you will be old news. However, I've had a chat with DCI Lawrence and we've agreed that until it's no longer necessary you can assist the Scotland Yard enquiry. I'm not sure how much of your time will be taken up with that enquiry, but just let the DCI know when you are finished. There are one or two enquiries here that could use some more help."

* * *

Even though Detective Superintendent Murphy was very personable, at times, when he spoke rapidly, Liz found it difficult to follow his Belfast accent. He treated her as some kind of 'guru' which she found flattering. He said that it was her persistence in believing that the two men administering the beatings to the animal activists had to have some official status that was determining the approach with which the enquiry would begin.

Liz knew that what Superintendent Murphy was saying was based on at least two false premises: she knew that she had concluded, probably wrongly, that one or the other of the security services was involved in the beatings, not officers from the Metropolitan Police. Furthermore, as far as Liz knew, the factor that had suggested that the two miscreants were policemen; in fact, officers serving at Scotland Yard, was the fact that the file held there containing their likenesses had gone missing. Liz was certain that it was Lydia who had been responsible for her getting the credit the superintendent gave her when he spoke to her. She thought, "good on you, Lydia; I owe you one!"

Liz had not realised that the Metropolitan Police had so many officers. Lydia had taken her to the records office and introduced her to the clerk who was in charge. It was to be Liz's task to go through all of the files held on male officers of the Met. Each file held a photo of the head and shoulders of the officer whose details were included therein. At first, Liz had compared the two sketches made by the police artist with each photograph, but after a short time she had committed both likenesses to memory. That had speeded up the process of comparison.

Very quickly, Liz found the first possibility. Although the man's features were similar, they were not identical to those of one of the men of whom sketches had been made. Also, this man was not stationed at New Scotland Yard. Liz put the file aside: the first in a pile that was to contain all of the 'possibles'.

After two days of searching, the 'possibles' pile consisted of four folders. However, none of them was a file giving the details of a police officer who was serving at New Scotland Yard. When she discussed the result with Lydia, her friend suggested that they should not let that result determine anything. "Let's just go ahead and assume that two of the four men represented by those files are the culprits. If we are able to establish that fact then we'll try to discover how they got access to records held at Scotland Yard."

The results of Liz's investigation led to a difficult situation. It had been anticipated that the identification of the two men would be far more definitive than it had turned out to be. She agreed with Superintendent Murphy that before any of the men were approached the identification that Liz had made should be confirmed by at least one of the beating victims. That conclusion led to a double dilemma: all of the victims had been contacted by the police and none of them was willing to co-operate in identifying the men who had attacked them. Secondly, even if one or more victims could be persuaded to aid the identification, the manner in which that could be done was in some doubt.

Liz had suggested that in her opinion a feasible approach to the identification would be the simplest one: show the victims actual photographs of the four police officers. However, Superintendent Murphy had frowned at that, saying, "we might hit it lucky, but in my experience that doesn't always work. I've seen men picked out of a line up whose photographs had not been recognised when shown to the same victim. I think it would be best if we dreamt up some excuse to get the four men to the 'Yard' so that the victims can see them 'in the flesh', so to speak. That is, of course, if you can manage to persuade any of the victims to help us."

Liz said that she would contact one of the victims, Barry Goff, who was the most likely to help. "Also, Goff knows at least one of the other victims, Richard Cowling; he might be able to persuade Cowling to help. However, sir, I think that it is unlikely that either of those men will want to come to the 'Yard' or any other police station as far as that is concerned. Both Detective Sergeant Mussett and I have had direct experience of the fact that the beating victims are very mistrustful of the police. At least one of them thinks that this whole business is a conspiracy by the police to intimidate the animal-rights movement. Even if they are willing to co-operate with the investigation I'm pretty sure that we'll have to find some way of doing it that doesn't involve their appearance at a police station." Superintendent Murphy said that whilst Liz was doing her bit he would call the team together and see if anyone had any bright ideas.

* * *

Liz rang the telephone number that she had for the laboratory at Queen Mary and Westfield College in which Barry Goff worked; she left a message for him to ring her when it was convenient. After two days she had not heard from him; that caused her to worry that her best hope for confirming the identification of possible 'rogue' police officers would not be useful.

Finally, however, she heard his familiar voice when she answered her extension 'phone. He apologised for not calling sooner, saying, "I've only just got your message, having got back into the lab after being in hiding in the college library for the past three days. I'm supposed to be second author on a talk that my research supervisor has agreed to give at the upcoming British Association meetings, and he, bless his pointed head, has insisted that I write it. He says that the experience will be good for me. Have you ever noticed, Liz, that when someone wants to dump something on you they tell you it'll be good for you?" In truth, Liz didn't entirely agree with Goff's cynicism, but she indicated her agreement just to be sociable.

Barry Goff did not wait for Liz to suggest that they meet. He said that the meal she had cooked at his flat had been the best he'd had in a long time; he was hoping that she would be willing to repeat the performance. "I'm a little richer now than I used to be; I finally got a studentship. I'll buy in all of the ingredients if you'll tell me what to get and I'll even provide the wine. I've kind of missed our evenings together, Liz. I thought that we used to have fun."

After she had rung off, Liz thought over her conversation with Barry Goff. She found that she was looking forward to their evening together. Usually, she was too busy to realise it, but she was really rather lonely for companionship. She couldn't rely on Lydia and now even her relationship with Pat had cooled noticeably.

Since returning to London from Cambridge Liz had spoken to Pat only once and that was because Liz had telephoned her friend. From the 'gist' of that conversation it was obvious that Pat was trying to distance herself from many of the things that she had said when the two of them were living together. Obviously, Pat had made up her mind that she would try to make the best of her marriage to Roger.

Liz had always known that she was the sort of person who did not make friends easily; consequently, all of her life she had had very few friends, and, so far, only Pat and Lydia could be called close friends. She decided that if her friendship with Barry Goff looked like developing into something that would give her pleasure, she would not attempt to stop that.

After setting her date with Barry Goff, Liz telephoned Lydia Mussett at Scotland Yard to see if any decision had been made about how the rogue-officer suspects and their victims would be got together. She would need that information before she spoke to Barry Goff. Lydia sounded quite enthusiastic: "I had what the super thought was a brilliant idea. Why don't we film the police officers without them knowing it? Lord knows the 'Yard' has plenty of covert surveillance equipment and expertise. Anyway, Liz that's what we're going to do. We'll make videotapes of the four men. The super would like you to help out with that."

Liz had decided that for her get-together with Barry Goff she would try to keep the meal simple; she would make a quiche. She remembered with amusement her first attempt at a quiche; the whole thing had been runny and had fallen apart, giving it the appearance and consistency of cheese-flavoured scrambled eggs. However, with time she had become quite adept, producing quiches that tasted good and looked good; even if she did say so herself. As it turned out, Barry Goff proved very easy to please. He told Liz that he'd never eaten a quiche; he had grown up in a "meat and two veg household. As far as my mum was concerned, adventurous cooking consisted of taking the roast out of the oven before it was well done."

During the meal Liz was aware that Barry Goff was doing his best to keep her wine glass filled. Her first response to his attempts to 'top-up' her glass was to put her hand over it, but he persisted, and she could feel her resistance melting away. By the end of the meal she knew that she had had too much to drink. Goff told her to seat herself on the settee and that he would clear up the dishes since she had cooked the meal. She discovered that to him "clearing up" meant putting the dishes in the sink to be done later.

She watched him as he cleared up, trying to make up her mind what response she would make should he attempt to make love to her. She was fairly certain that he would try.

Some time later, Liz was lying back on Goff's bed as he applied his mouth to the pleasure zone between her legs. She had been surprised at the speed with which Goff had begun his 'campaign' of seduction. She thought that her state of intoxication had aided the process for him, but also she had learned from previous experience that he was an expert at oral masturbation. She felt that she owed a debt of gratitude to Barry's female cousin who's instruction had been responsible for his prowess. However, on this occasion, oral masturbation had been his response when she had refused, gently, to have sexual intercourse with him. She admired his gentlemanly behaviour. When she told him that she wanted the two of them to know each other better before they had sexual intercourse he had stopped at once.

Barry Goff was sufficiently good that Liz was becoming very noisy; suddenly, his mouth was applied to hers and his tongue was occupying her mouth. At the same time she could feel the pressure of his erect penis as it pushed against the opening to her vagina. Her first impulse was tell him to proceed, but then she felt pain. That had happened to her before and she wondered what the matter was. Pat had told her that it was normal to feel pain the first few times but that she would soon get used to it. However, it became obvious to Liz that her relative inexperience at sexual intercourse caused her still to be uncomfortable. Finally she reached down and grabbed his penis, pulling it away from her. Moments later she had finished him off; it was obvious that his arousal had been very high.

Their sexual experience together caused Liz to have a warm feeling toward Barry Goff. A feeling she'd not felt toward a male since she had been a teenager. She accepted his invitation to spend the night with him. She lay in his arms whilst they talked; an occupation that went on until well past midnight, when he signalled to her by kissing her passionately that he was ready to have another session of love-making. That session was even better than the first. He began by orally masturbating her; her reciprocation was even more vigorous the second time than the first, causing him to say, "oh, yes; oh, yes, Liz." She had had very little sexual experience with men; however, until that night she had never heard one give voice to his pleasure.

* * *

Chapter Twenty One

Liz thought that Superintendent Murphy's team at Scotland Yard had done brilliantly. They had managed to obtain videotape footage of the four police officers whose faces most resembled those of the men who had assaulted the animal-rights activists. Not only that but they had obtained recordings of their voices. The whole deed had been accomplished by the simple expedient of asking the men to take part in a film that was being made for recruitment purposes. Video recordings were made of the men whilst they answered short questions about why they chose the police as a career and what had happened to them since doing so.

The advantage of the video recordings was that they could be shown in the homes of the victims, always assuming, of course, that they had the proper equipment to view the recordings. Unfortunately, it rather looked like the whole exercise would prove to be a waste of time. Liz had contacted all of the assault victims by telephone: two had hung up on her when she told them who she was. With the exception of Barry Goff, the others had steadfastly refused to co-operate, two of them becoming rather abusive in their insistence that the police were not their friends.

The next disappointment came when Liz watched the recordings on her television. None of the voices was that of the man who spoke to her after breaking into her flat and immobilising her. In fact one of the questions asked of the four police officers during the interviews had been designed specifically to elicit a response that would use the word, 'interest'. The man who spoke to Liz in her bedroom that night had used a phrase, commonly used by politicians and government officials, "in the country's interest." However, what was not common about the usage by the intruder was the pronunciation of the word, "interest." He had substituted a letter 'n' for the first 't', pronouncing the word, "innerest." None of the four men interviewed had duplicated that pronunciation.

Liz telephoned Barry Goff to set up a date for her to visit him so that he could watch the video recordings. He told her that he would do it, but only under one condition: that she would allow him to take her out for a pub meal and then they would return to his flat to "watch television." She teased him by saying, "blackmail is an ugly word, Barry; you know that I can have you arrested." He teased her in return by saying, in a voice that attempted to mimic the film actor, Humphrey Bogart, "those are my terms, baby; take 'em or leave 'em." She replied, "well, put that way, I guess I shall have to take 'em."

After she rang off she stared off into space for a time, lost in a thought; she wondered if, for the first time in her life, she was falling in love with a man. She knew that she was beginning to have the same feelings toward Barry Goff that she had toward Pat and Lydia.

The evening with Barry Goff proved to be disappointing for both of them. Before she met him at the pub Liz had made up her mind that if the situation arose that evening, she and Barry again would engage in sexual intercourse. If the pain appeared again, she would just have to endure it. Also, unlike their previous encounters, she would insist that Barry wear a condom. She had no intention of becoming pregnant. Before meeting him, she would prepare herself with a trip to the chemists to buy a packet of condoms.

A rather indifferent pub meal started off the disappointing evening. Since, in the past, the same pub had served up excellent food consistently, both Liz and Barry guessed that the place had been taken over by new management.

Back at Barry Goff's flat the second disappointment came. He recognised none of the four police officers who appeared in the videotapes shown on his television. He said that the voices were not those of the men who had attacked him; of that he was certain.

Finally, Liz and Barry had not made love, except for a session of fondling of each other whilst on the settee. Barry had apologised to Liz, telling her that a few hours before meeting her in the pub his mum had called him to say that his dad had been taken to hospital, having collapsed with what had been diagnosed as a suspected heart attack. "My mum told me not to cancel my evening with you because there was nothing that I could do at once. However, early in the morning I have to go to my parents' house, and then we will go off to see my dad. I'm sorry Liz, it's not been a very good evening. I hope we can do it again once my dad gets sorted out. Anyway, you found out what you wanted to know about those four coppers. None of them was responsible for beating me up; I'm certain of that."

As Barry was walking Liz to the tube station he questioned her about where her investigation would go from there. She said that she would have to consult with the head of the investigative team, saying, "obviously we've got to think again about who the culprits might be, since you didn't recognise any of them." He assured her, "really, Liz, I'm not lying to you; since I've got to know you, I wouldn't do that. I'll have another word with Richard Cowling when next I see him. Maybe the two of us together will be able to remember something that neither of us remembers separately."

As a goodbye gesture, Liz kissed Barry passionately. He responded, equally passionately, after which he said, "I'm really sorry about tonight, Liz. As soon as my ol' dad gets on the mend, we'll do it again, only next time I won't be walking you to the tube station, if you know what I mean!"

That night, in her bed, for the first time in several days, she masturbated prior to drifting off to sleep. The fantasy that accompanied her action involved love-making between her and her companion of earlier in the evening. That was how much Barry Goff had come to occupy a place in her thoughts.

* * *

Liz was the first to speak when the team led by Superintendent Murphy next met. She explained the reasoning behind doubts that she had about the value of pursuing the idea that the attackers of the animal-rights activists were policemen. Although Superintendent Murphy thought it likely that Liz was putting too much trust in the word of Barry Goff, that wasn't what he told her. He said that he thought that she might be giving up too easily. "Let's put our heads together and see if we can't come up with some scheme to coerce the victims to identify their attackers. It seems obvious to me that all of the victims have been got at. We'll have to find some way to overcome their fright. Has anyone any ideas about that?"

Sergeant Brown said," I don't know how practical it would be, but I saw a television programme not that long ago where some female psychologist was testing the effectiveness of advertising using what she called 'pupillary response'. She filmed the faces of volunteers as they were shown different adverts. She didn't even have to ask them any questions; she could tell by the dilatation of their pupils whether or not the adverts were effective in getting their attention. I don't know whether or not we could get one of our technical staff to help us."

One of the members of the team who never spoke during their meetings raised his hand. The super said, "ah, DC Lyons, you've joined us." That got a laugh from everyone but DC Lyons who looked embarrassed. "I saw the same TV programme, sir, and as I recall the lady psychologist was at pains to point out that pupillary dilatation merely signified interest. Consequently it would have to be used with caution. Remember, Tony, she used as an example a large photograph showing an attractive girl seated on the wing of a Jaguar convertible? She said that the pupils dilated on most men shown the photograph. However, it proved to be impossible to know whether it was the girl or the car that caused their pupils to dilate."

Liz was expecting some kind of snide remark from the super, but he surprised her by saying, "that's a good point, Jeremy. You've certainly kicked that idea in the head! Now; has anyone else got any ideas, whether or not they're bright?" Again, DC Lyons said, "in that same programme the results of some experiments were shown in which people were hooked up to a polygraph whilst they were shown photographs. It was demonstrated that that method didn't work well in the determination of preferences, but it was very effective in discovering objects the subjects didn't like. Apparently seeing something frightening in a photograph caused both their breathing and pulse rates to alter predictably. Would it be possible to work out some way to persuade the victims of the assaults to take a lie-detector test?"

Superintendent Murphy said that he thought it unlikely that they would such a test voluntarily, given the animosity that they had displayed so far. "However, it may be possible to force them to take part in an enquiry that involved a lie-detector test. Let me think about it for a time. Possibly we could invent an incident that would allow us to bring all of them in. Then we might be able to force them to take a lie-detector test as part of their interrogation. Tony, you and Jeremy put your heads together and work out a scheme to get all of the victims in here. I'll fix it with the technical boys to help us with the lie-detector tests."

Over the next few days all of the animal-rights activists who had been assaulted were brought into Scotland Yard and questioned. Each activist was approached at his or her home and told that they were being detained on suspicion of causing grievous bodily harm to a man who was conducting experiments on animals. The incident about which they were questioned was entirely fictitious, but all but one of the activists were taken in by the subterfuge. The one exception was a lawyer by profession. He had insisted upon having a solicitor present whilst he was questioned. He was not detained.

At the 'Yard' the activists were questioned for a time concerning their whereabouts at the time the animal researcher was attacked. After the preliminary questioning was completed the activists were fitted with the sensors of a polygraph apparatus by one of the forensic staff. All of the activists objected, but they were told that they had no option but to co-operate with the police. It was explained to them that they would be shown photographs of eight men who were known to have taken part in attacks on animal researchers in the past. The current whereabouts of the men was unknown. The activists were told that it was expected that they would lie, rather than reveal the identity of the unknown men; consequently, the police had no choice but to use a lie detector to test their responses to the sight of the eight men. All of the photographs were those of policemen, four of whom where the ones whose facial features resembled those of the two men who had attacked the animal activists.

Liz had felt a sense of relief when none of the animal-rights activists had reacted noticeably when shown the facial features of the eight men. It reinforced her view that the two men who had assaulted the animal-rights activists were not policemen. However, she did not say anything along those lines when Superintendent Murphy called the team together to discuss the results of the interviews.

At the conclusion of the meeting it was decided that the enquiry would be inactivated until such time as new evidence should come to light. Liz was asked by Superintendent Murphy what it was she wished to do: return to duty or take up the option that had been offered some weeks before: terminate her career in the police. Liz didn't hesitate. She said, she hoped not too cheekily, "oh, you can't get rid of me that easily, superintendent." He smiled and said, "good, good; I was hoping that you would say that."

As she sat on the tube returning to Mile End, Liz thought over her decision, which had been made more-or-less on the spur of the moment. She was happy with what she had decided to do, but she felt uncomfortable about the decision to drop the enquiry into the assaults on animal-rights activists. She was unable to chase from her thoughts the idea that the police were overlooking a factor that was important to the solution of the case.

* * *

Chapter Twenty Two

Liz's return to Mile End was welcomed by her colleagues. The resources of the station were being overstretched by a large-scale investigation into drug trafficking that was being conducted co-operatively by several police forces in the south and east of London. Her colleague, Detective Sergeant Dai Morgan, résuméed the results that had been gotten to that point.

The investigation was instigated by the complaint to the police by a Mrs Marjorie Ellington, whose house was located on a road that ran perpendicular to the River Thames in Wapping, south London. Missus Ellington's house was one of two at the very bottom of the road, lying adjacent to the river bank. None of the houses on the road had garages, so all of the car owners parked their vehicles on the road, there being an agreement amongst them that a certain space 'belonged' to each of their houses.

Missus Ellington had become upset because on a few days of each month the same white van would park in her space. She would arrive home from work after it had got dark to find that the van had got there before her. She would then have to park several roads away from her house and walk along dimly-lit streets to get home. She complained that in the part of London in which she lived, the van driver's action put her at considerable risk. She said that she had tried to persuade the driver of the van not to park in 'her' place by putting notes on the windscreen, but he had ignored them.

She said that she figured that the police wouldn't take her seriously when she complained to them that the van driver was parking in 'her' space. However, she hoped that another of the driver's habits would attract their attention.

She had no idea what he did when he was away from his van, but he was responsible for leaving considerable litter when he drove away. Upon leaving her house on the mornings following his visits always she would find several sheets of muddy newspaper scattered about her front garden.

She was certain that the van driver was responsible for depositing the litter in her garden, but she thought that it would be better to be certain before she made a complaint to the police. She had no intention of confronting him directly; there was no telling how he might react.

On an evening when she found the van parked in 'her' space, she kept a vigil from behind the curtains of her front room. Despite the general darkness, the van and the surrounding few feet of the pavement were just visible in the illumination given off by a nearby street lamp.

After a time she saw a movement on the road and then a man approached the rear of the van. To her surprise he appeared to have come from the direction of the riverbank rather than that that she had expected: the top of the road where there were shops and other business premises. Slung over the man's shoulder was a large bag which appeared to be rather heavy because he was well bent over. She watched him as he went to the rear of the van, unlocking and opening the tailgate and setting the bag down inside. Then he seated himself on the floor of the van's load space. Reaching behind him into the van he got out some sheets of newspaper which he used to wipe the Wellington boots that he was wearing. Then he removed the boots and put on a pair of shoes that he removed from the inside of the van. Before lowering the tailgate of the van, the driver did what Mrs Ellington was hoping she would be able to observe. He wadded up the newspapers and threw them over the low wall that separated Mrs Ellington's small front garden from the pavement.

The visit of Mrs Ellington to her local police station came just a few days after a bulletin had gone out to all police stations in the metropolitan area. It asked members of the local forces to be on the lookout for any activity taking place on or near the banks of the Thames that appeared to be suspicious. It said that there were reasons to believe that the river was being used as a means of smuggling drugs into the heart of London.

Had the contents of the bulletin not been fresh in the minds of the local police force, very likely Mrs Ellington would had been told, politely, of course, to go home and stop wasting police time. Instead, she had found herself to have become the centre of police attention; a situation which pleased her enormously. She agreed to co-operate with the police, who asked her to notify them promptly the next time she came home to find the van parked outside her house. That notification then would prompt the activation of a plan that the Metropolitan Police had devised.

First, it would have to be ascertained that the van driver was involved with smuggling drugs. He would be followed to his destination, which, then would be kept under observation by a team of plain-clothed policemen. It was hoped that the surveillance would provide not only evidence of drug activity, but also allow the police to gain some appreciation of the size of the operation.

* * *

Immediately Mrs Ellington had rung the number given her by the police, the plan was put into operation. A police constable was sent to her house where he established himself behind the curtain of her front room. At the same time, two unmarked police cars, containing four plain-clothed police officers were parked on either side of the street at the top of the road on which Mrs Ellington lived. Upon a radio signal from the officer in Mrs Ellington's front room they were alerted to be prepared to follow the van.

The van was followed to an address in Stepney, East London, at which it was observed that the driver removed a large parcel from its rear and carried it into a building which appeared to be a normal house. Subsequently, it was discovered that the building was the distribution depot for quite large amounts of smuggled drugs, which were supplied to drug dealers scattered quite widely over south-eastern England.

Because the drug-distribution house was within the jurisdiction of the Mile End police it was their responsibility to maintain its surveillance. However, once the scale of the drug operation was discovered, several other of the Metropolitan Police forces lent their assistance.

Liz Andresen found herself to be closely involved with that activity. She and her colleagues had set up a point of observation in a house that was on the same road and almost immediately opposite the drug house. The house owner, an elderly widower, had been more than willing to co-operate with the police. He said that he had got "fed up" with all of the activity that seemed to be going on, "cars arriving at all hours of the day and well into the night." He told the police that he suspected that the house was being used as a brothel. They didn't disabuse him of that idea.

* * *

Liz always had found surveillance to be one of the least attractive sides of her job. It involved sitting for long hours doing nothing except keeping her eyes open. The only pleasurable thing about it was the fact that she could indulge her habit of day dreaming, or "musing," as she preferred to call it. Of late she had taken to reviewing in her thoughts the relationship she had with Barry Goff. She wondered what it would be like to have a long-term relationship with a man; a real sexual relationship, that is. Over the previous few years she had had a couple of brief 'flings', but they had come to nothing. She was aware that thoughts of such a relationship did not engender the same fantasies that she had when thinking of her relationships with Pat Moffatt and Lydia Mussett.

The more she thought about it the more she was edging toward the conclusion that she really did not want a sexual relationship with a man. Her experiences had taught her that such a relationship implied marriage or, at least, long-term 'togetherness'. The only aspect of that that appealed was the possibility of having children. Even that source of appeal had not appeared in her thoughts until Pat's son, Andrew, was born. Now she found herself quite attracted to the idea of being a mum. However, realistically, she knew that that was unlikely. Consequently, she would have to hope that she and Pat would retain the close friendship that they had.

Liz's musings were interrupted by a static-ridden message for her on the radio transceiver that she had placed on a table near the window where she maintained her vigil. When she pressed the 'receive' button on the device she heard the voice of the station sergeant at Mile End. He told her that DCI Lawrence had asked him to pass on a message to her: "he would like you to call in on him before going home this evening after you've finished your surveillance duties for the day. He's got something important to ask you about." When she asked what the problem was, he replied that he did not know; he had been asked by DCI Lawrence to deliver the message.

On her way back to the station Liz thought carefully about the events of the past few weeks. She could think of nothing that she had done wrong. However the station sergeant had sounded rather mysterious when she had attempted to discover from him why the DCI wished to see her.

It had surprised her somewhat when DCI Lawrence asked her, in a kindly voice, "perhaps you had best sit down, Liz; I'm afraid I have some rather bad news. This morning a Mrs Rebecca Goff telephoned the station and asked to speak to you. She was told that you were not available, but if she wished to leave a message you would ring her back. It was obvious to the receptionist that she was upset; she was throwing accusations all over the place. Finally, the call was transferred to me. It was then that I learned that she was the mother of Barry Goff, who, she said, you knew well. She told me that yesterday evening she had come home from visiting her husband in hospital to find a police car parked outside her front door. She said that two police officers from Mile End had come to tell her that the police had removed a body from a flat that was being rented by her son, Barry. It appeared that the person had hanged himself. The dead man was identified tentatively as Barry Goff, an identification which was confirmed later by Mrs Goff. She said that when she asked them at the hospital how her son had died they told her that it appeared that he had hanged himself."

Liz interrupted the DCI with a gasp of surprise, "killed himself! Barry Goff wasn't the sort to do such a thing! He had so much to live for!" The DCI said, "I hadn't realised that you and he had become friendly, so it surprised me when Mrs Goff told me that. She told me to ask you; that you would know that her Barry could never commit suicide. That's why I wanted to speak to you, Liz. Not that I expect you to form a judgement about the suicide, but if you knew him well I thought you might be able to weigh the possibilities. Apparently Goff's body was taken to the London Hospital, but as of a short time ago, no formal examination of it had started. However, a pathologist there did say that there was some suspicious bruising on parts of Goff's body that would have been unlikely to have been caused by hanging. Let's give it a few days for them to complete their examination, and if the forensic report indicates suspicion of something other than suicide, I'll put you on it. If it wasn't suicide it may be the work of our mysterious friends who've been going around beating up animal-rights activists. You were the closest person in this nick to that investigation."

After she had left the DCI's office Liz thought about her reaction to Barry Goff's death. She realised that her main emotion had been surprise, but also, there was sadness. He seemed to be such a nice lad and clever with it. She was reasonably certain that he would not have killed himself; he just wasn't the type. He was very interested in his research; he had talked about it when she and he were together. She smiled to herself when she remembered calling him, teasingly, an "astron-o-bore" the few times when he had monopolised their conversation with long explanations about his latest research finding. She decided that she would not wait until the official verdict; however she would telephone his mother that evening and attempt to discover the circumstances of the death.

During their telephone conversation, Mrs Goff résuméed for Liz all that she had been told about her son's death. Apparently, when found, Goff had been dead for three or four days. It was his failure to show up on two consecutive days to physics practicals for which he acted as demonstrator that had caused a Dr Sangstrom, his research supervisor, to make further enquiries. Those led to the discovery of the body by the research supervisor, who subsequently notified the police.

Liz had put it out of her mind, but speaking to Mrs Goff had reminded her: she had gone to Barry's flat four days earlier to have a pre-dinner drink, and then they were going out together to eat in a pub. She remembered that she had knocked on his door and had waited patiently for almost fifteen minutes before deciding that he must have forgotten about their date.

As she thought about that she remembered that when she entered the building in which Goff's flat was situated two men were coming out. In fact, one of them held open the door for her. She hadn't paid much attention to the men at the time, but speaking to Mrs Goff had started her thinking: could those men have had something to do with Barry's death? She decided that she would discuss the possibility with DCI Lawrence, and if he approved, she would investigate. She knew that there were tenants in the second flat of the house in which Barry's flat was located. Possibly the two men had been visiting there.

* * *

Chapter Twenty Three

In speaking with Barry Goff's mother over the telephone Liz had attempted to convey her sympathy to the woman without entangling herself emotionally. It was obvious that Barry had told his mother quite a lot about his relationship with Liz. However, it was obvious, also, that he had considered their friendship to be closer than had she. Now, Mrs Goff was expecting Liz to play the rôle of the grieving girlfriend; a task that Liz had no intention of performing. Liz knew that in the next few days she would have to speak with the woman on an official basis, and she did not wish to complicate that procedure.

The forensic report on the hanging of Barry Goff had suggested that there was a strong possibility that he had been murdered. The body bore all of the classic signs of death by suffocation, so Goff had been alive when he was hanged. However, there was bruising on the upper arms, and the interior of the mouth exhibited signs consistent with the fact that he had been gagged.

The forensic pathologist who had examined the body concluded that Goff must have been attacked by at least two men. Very likely he had been gagged to silence him, since no immobilising drugs were detected in the analyses of the body fluids. Again, it was likely that his body had been lifted up so that his head could be put through a slip-knotted noose that was suspended from a length of iron piping that ran across the ceiling of the kitchenette. In the opinion of the pathologist, it would have taken at least two men to perform that task. Probably the bruising on the upper arms had been caused by the tight grip necessary to keep the victim immobilised whilst his head was put through the noose.

Liz tried not to display her pleasure when DCI Lawrence relieved her, he said temporarily, of her duties with the drug investigation. She much preferred the active processes that would be involved in the investigation of the death of Barry Goff.

Her first move had been to question Barry's mother. As she had anticipated, Mrs Goff knew nothing of her son's activities as an animal-rights activist, so she kept secret that aspect of the investigation.

On questioning Mrs Goff about her son's movements just prior to his death, she said that since her husband had gone into hospital Barry had been a frequent visitor to her house. She said that her son had been "ever so sweet and attentive. Bless his soul, most nights he insisted on driving me when I went to visit my husband in hospital. He was such a good boy!" That statement brought forth a flood of tears from Mrs Goff for which she attempted to apologise, but Liz simply patted the mother's hand in sympathy.

As she had hoped, Liz was able to obtain a key to the door of Barry Goff's flat from the clerk who was in charge of the crime-exhibit storeroom of the Mile End Station. Possessions of the dead man would be given to his parents in due course, but not until the police had completed their investigation of his death. Fortunately, a ring holding several keys had been removed by forensics from a pocket of the trousers worn by the dead man. Liz was certain that one of the keys would be the one to the front door of the building in which the dead man's flat was located. She wasn't certain that the flat would contain anything that would be helpful in her investigation, but it was necessary to have a look.

Liz chose a time to visit Barry Goff's flat when it would be likely that the tenants of the other flat in the building would be at home. She wished to speak to them in case they might have heard or seen something that would be helpful in her enquiry.

Immediately she let herself into Barry Goff's flat, Liz got a feeling that she had not felt in any previous police investigation: that she was invading someone's privacy. The flat was set up in a manner which suggested that its owner had just stepped out for a few moments and would be right back. There were dishes in the sink of the kitchenette and the bed was unmade. She noticed that the BBC computer that sat on the table in the sitting room/kitchenette was still on; animations of a screen-saver programme moved slowly across the monitor.

Then Liz noticed something written on the marker board that Barry Goff used to remind him of things he had to do. Written on the bottom was: "Remember! Tell Liz about my conversation with Richard!" Liz wrote down in her notebook the words that Barry Goff had written. She was sure that the Richard to whom Barry had referred was Richard Cowling, one of the men who had been assaulted by the bogus policemen. Aside from the message on the marker board, Liz found nothing further in the flat that looked like it might be helpful to explain Barry Goff's death.

The couple who rented the flat above that of Barry Goff had expressed shock when Liz told them what had happened to him. They characterised him as a friendly, but very quiet man. The woman told Liz that because of Barry Goff's quiet manner she and her husband had been surprised a few evenings earlier. There had been quite a commotion in the hallway outside of Goff's flat. However, just as her husband had decided to investigate, the ruckus had ended; consequently, he hadn't bothered to go to have a look. The woman couldn't remember exactly the time when the commotion had occurred but she thought it likely that it was during one of the two evenings considered to be the possible time of Goff's death. Also, she stated that she and her husband had not had visitors, male or otherwise. "We've just moved to London because of my husband's job and we don't know anybody here as yet. I hope things improve soon." That statement by the woman made Liz feel certain that the two men she had seen leaving the building had been Goff's murderers.

Liz knew that she would have to interview Richard Cowling about the message that Barry Goff had written on his marker board. She thought it likely that he would not talk to her voluntarily, so she discussed with DCI Lawrence the possibility of bringing him into the station. The DCI demurred, saying, "that's a tricky move, these days, Liz. Of late the Met have been getting some stick on that point. We've been accused of being 'heavy handed' when it comes to questioning suspects. Oh, nothing physical, just not letting them know about their rights; that sort of thing. See if you can't get this Cowling to talk. You say you know a pub he frequents; go there and see if you can't engage him in conversation. If that doesn't work we'll try doing it the hard way."

After two evenings 'nursing' a glass of wine and refusing offers from men to buy her a drink, Liz saw the man to whom she hoped to speak. Richard Cowling entered the pub in the company of George Baird. Liz watched as they seated themselves after George had bought the drinks. They seemed not to have noticed her; she hoped that perhaps they had forgotten that she was a police officer.

As Liz approached their table, it was obvious immediately that neither man had forgotten who she was: "ah, Richard, watch what you say; here comes the snoop. Not content with getting poor, old Barry killed, she wants to get us killed too!" Liz was surprised at the statement because the details of Barry Goff's death had not yet been released to the newspapers. The only comments about the death made in the newspapers had simply stated the name of the deceased and the fact that the police was treating the death as apparent suicide. Either George Baird was guessing or he knew something that she did not. That strengthened her belief that her enquiry would get further if she detained both men for questioning. However, she resolved to try persuasion first.

She said, "I know that you think you have every reason to hate me, but Barry and I were close friends and I am very sad at his loss. I can think of no reason why he would take his own life; I was hoping that you two, who seemed to know him well, might be able to help." George Baird stood up, saying, "you can sit here if you want, Richard, but I'm going elsewhere."

A look of exasperation came over his face as Richard Cowling watched his friend walk to another table and seat himself. He said, "I'm sorry, miss; I really should go over there. He gets all upset when he's in one of his moods. I'd like to help you, but I really don't know anything about Barry's death. I didn't think that he would kill himself, either, but that seems to be the case from what the papers said. I know George is convinced that the same men who are going around beating people up killed Barry. He figures that if he talks to you the same could happen to him. That's one of the main reasons he's so antagonistic against you. He's absolutely convinced that Barry's death wasn't suicide and that the police are just covering up the fact that he was murdered."

In desperation Liz said, "you do know that the police have the power to detain you and George Baird both for questioning whether or not you agree. I didn't wish to do that because it would create a very public fuss, and I'm sure that neither of you want that. Therefore, Mr Cowling, I am giving you a last chance to sit here and talk to me quietly and sensibly; otherwise I shall summon help and take the both of you to the nick." As she finished speaking she reached into her handbag, removing her police radio transceiver.

Richard Cowling glanced at the transceiver, then at George Baird, saying finally, "OK; as I said, I don't know nothing about Barry's death, so I'm not going to be any help there." He started to go on, but Liz interrupted him: "sometime, not too long before Barry Goff's death, you and he talked about something that must have related to the beatings. He left a message on a marker board in his flat which reminded him to tell me about a conversation that you and he had had. I can't think that he would think that I would be interested in any other subject. At least, one that the two of you would talk about."

Richard Cowling shrugged his shoulders, saying, "I don't recall speaking to Barry about the beatings; at least, not recently. I wonder if it could have been anything to do with that video you showed him of policemen who resembled the men who are beating up animal-rights activists? He told me about that, saying that he was pretty sure that none of the coppers were the men who had beat him up."

As Liz was forming her next question, Richard Cowling said, "I do remember one thing we discussed about the men in the videos. We were agreed that the men who attacked us were a helluva-lot older than them. Richard thought that they were in their late forties, at least. I thought that they were even older. Despite their old age they were bloody strong, though." Although she made a note of Richard Cowling's recollection about the men's age, she did not see how that could be relevant. She pressed him to try to re-member more, but he said that he really couldn't: "when me and Barry get together I'm afraid we found lots of other things to talk about, rather than those stupid beatings. I don't know what more I can tell you, miss." Liz decided that she was unlikely to get more useful information from Richard Cowling, so she thanked him and left the pub.

Back at the police station as she wrote up her report of the meeting in the pub that evening, the thought came to her suddenly: "I wonder if I've been looking in the wrong place? Could the two culprits be police officers who worked at Scotland Yard and then retired? That could explain why they might have access still to the records department at the 'Yard'." Liz decided that she would ring Lydia in the morning and discuss the matter with her. Lydia would know whether or not what she suggested would be possible. She didn't wish to discuss it with DCI Lawrence; she was sure that he would consider absurd the idea that the assailants of the animal-rights activists were retired Metropolitan Police officers.

* * *

Chapter Twenty Four

In speaking with Lydia Mussett it became clear very quickly to Liz that her friend considered it most unlikely that retired Met officers could be involved in the beatings. She counselled Liz to look elsewhere for suspects: "for starters, our records department is pretty damn secure. It almost takes an act of parliament to gain access to their files. What you're suggesting is that some copper who isn't even at the 'Yard' any longer could somehow make use of the records. I think that's very unlikely, Liz. I'm sorry that I can't be more supportive of your idea."

Liz decided to try another approach, although she knew Lydia well enough to know that her friend would realise what she was trying to do: "tell me this, Lydia. How long are records kept for Met officers after they retire, and would it be possible to see those records?" Lydia laughed quietly, saying, "you're not going to take 'no' for an answer, are you sweetie? The short answer to your question is: I don't know. However, I will certainly find out for you and ring you back. What do you want to do, go through the files of retirees looking to see if any of them bears a likeness to one or both of your culprits?" Liz told her friend that that was the idea. After agreeing to go to supper and stay overnight with Lydia at her flat, Liz rang off.

Two days later Lydia telephoned Liz to say that she had spoken to Superintendent Murphy: "he thought that your idea was brilliant! That just shows you how much I know! He is going to have a word with a colleague who controls that side of things at the 'Yard', so I'll let you know if and when he gets the OK for you to come here and paw through our retiree records. To be honest with you, Liz, I still think that it is unlikely that the culprits are retired coppers. That would implicate a whole bunch of people not only in conspiracy but, now, murder."

Liz said that she had thought about that and that she had come to the conclusion that perhaps the whole venture had begun innocently enough, but that it had got out of control. "Barry Goff told me that one of the men who beat him up had warned him of dire consequences were he to go to the police afterwards. He told me also that every one of the other assault victims that he knew also had been warned not to co-operate with the police. Maybe once the culprits learned that one of their victims had co-operated with the police, the whole project began to get out of their control. Maybe Goff was murdered because he was seen as a danger to the culprits; he was the only one of their victims who appeared to be co-operating. Therefore, they might have considered him to be the only one of their victims likely to identify them."

"Somehow, the perpetrators have been able to learn secrets known only to the police; that was obvious from some of the things said by one of the men who invaded my bedroom that night. Either they have access to police information or they are doing a good job of keeping an eye on the movements of everyone involved in the investigation of the beatings. No, Lydia, I think that they have got in deeper than they intended originally. Then, finally, they committed murder because they saw no alternative. It was either that or risk being identified by Barry Goff."

More quickly than Liz had expected, Lydia telephoned her: "I'm sorry, Liz; Superintendent Murphy has asked me to tell you to be patient for a few more days; he has run into resistance on the part of the 'Yard's' records department.

The super says that he's not sure whether the man in charge is being deliberately obstructive or is just behaving normally. He doesn't want to force the issue; that would only get the man's back up. However, he has promised that one way or another he will get you down here to have a look through retiree records."

Liz decided that she had best have a word with DCI Lawrence. Until she could look through records at the 'Yard' there wasn't much more that she could do in her investigation of the death of Barry Goff. Undoubtedly, the DCI would want her to lend a hand in the investigation of the drug-smuggling ring. That was proving to be a much larger operation than anyone had at first anticipated. The investigation had expanded to the point where it now involved various law-enforcement groups in six countries spread over four continents.

Liz wasn't altogether surprised when the DCI assigned her to a part of the operation that was concerned primarily with liaison with other London law-enforcement groups as well as keeping records up to date. He had said that it was because of her verbal skills. However, she was fairly sure that it was because she was a woman. In the briefing meetings on the case he had emphasised that officers involved in the investigation should exercise caution when approaching any of the individuals involved with the drug ring. He believed that most of them would not hesitate to use physical violence or even to kill as a first response to attempts to detain them.

After four days of mind-numbing monotony, Liz was very pleased when she answered her extension phone to be told that Detective Sergeant Lydia Mussett was on the line. Lydia said that Superintendent Murphy had at last got approval for a scrutiny of files kept on police officers who had been based at Scotland Yard and who had retired in the previous five years. Files on officers who had retired earlier than that no longer were kept at the 'Yard'. Consequently, if her search did not produce results, Superintendent Murphy had indicated that "they" would have to think again about whether or not to continue that line of enquiry.

* * *

Liz spent three days searching through the retiree records. During that time it had become obvious that none of the files through which she had looked were those of the two men Liz was seeking. She had discovered that fact after two days enduring the petulance of the officer in charge of the records department, Detective Sergeant Thomas Prendl. He had insisted that the space in the records department was very cramped; he had used that as an excuse to put her in a small annex room that had been empty when she had arrived. Fortunately, his assistant, Mrs Alison Jacobs, was as pleasant as the officer was surly. Missus Jacobs arranged to have a small table and chair placed in the room Liz would use. Liz felt that the woman had been embarrassed by the behaviour of her boss, and had gone out of her way to be helpful. Unfortunately, her pleasant behaviour had served only to make that of the officer even more objectionable; he kept insisting that Liz was wasting both his time and hers: "I've known most of the men whose details are in the files you're searching through. They're honest, decent men; they would not be involved in the crimes you're accusing them of." Liz tried to explain that she was not accusing anyone of anything; she was only doing a job.

Whilst she had been working at Scotland Yard, Liz had stayed with Lydia at her flat in West Hampstead. That had been most enjoyable. In fact, Liz had somewhat prolonged the time she took in her research in the records department just so she could extend her stay with Lydia for a third night. Liz preferred not to think about the fact that staying with her friend served as a reminder of the rather lonely life she led. She knew that Lydia was not prepared to do anything about Liz's loneliness or, for that matter, her own. It was Lydia's ambition to rise to the heights in the police service, and she had no intention of allowing anything to stand in the way of that ambition.

Although she was unhappy because her search through the records of recent retirees from the 'Yard' had produced no results Liz was looking forward to finishing the task. She had spent almost three days isolated in the small room, feeling guilty about any time she spent away from the task at hand. She had stopped having afternoon tea in the canteen because the sergeant in charge of the records office grumbled so much about it. He complained to her that the time she spent drinking tea just extended the length of time that he would have to put up with her presence.

The room in which she worked was very badly ventilated and illuminated. It was at one side of the main records office and served primarily as a storeroom for objects that had been used as evidence in various police enquiries. Sergeant Prendl had insisted that she work in the small room, using the excuse, "you'll only be in the way if you work in the main office." To make matters worse her period at the 'Yard' corresponded with a period of unusually warm weather in London. Consequently, the room was uncomfortably hot and humid. She attempted to compensate for the lack of ventilation by leaving the door of the room open.

As she worked on what she hoped would be her last day in the stuffy little room, Liz's attention was drawn away from the file through which she was looking by the voice of a man who had begun speaking in the next room. The voice seemed familiar. It took her a few moments to realise it, but she was certain that the voice was that of the man who had spoken to her in her bedroom the night the two men broke into her flat. The man was speaking to Mrs Jacobs. They seemed to know each other. He called her "Allie," but she didn't use his name. She told him that the officer in charge of the records room was away for the morning. The man and Mrs Jacobs spent the next few minutes in amicable conversation, whilst Liz stood by the open door of her room, listening.

The more she heard the voice the more certain she was that it was that of one of the men for whom she was looking. It was obvious from the conversation that the man was a relatively recent retiree from the 'Yard'. He was extolling the virtues of retirement to Mrs Jacobs, supporting that statement by telling her about a trip that he and his wife had taken to northern Spain from which they'd just returned. Liz had resisted the impulse to go into the main office and see what the man looked like. Were he one of the men for whom she was looking it was likely that he would recognise her at once, alerting him to the fact that something was amiss.

Liz went back to the work that she had been doing prior to the man's arrival; a short time later, she heard him as he departed from the records office. He told Mrs Jacobs that he had been very pleased to see her again; his final remarks were, "give Tom my best and tell him I'll pop in to see him again soon."

Liz realised that she had to discover the name of the man who had just spoken to Mrs Jacobs, so she tried to think of a way to find out without arousing the woman's curiosity. Removing a handkerchief from her handbag she left the small room, mopping her brow and indicating by gestures that she was very hot and 'sticky'. She said to Mrs Jacobs, "I couldn't help but overhear your conversation just now; with that retired police officer? He sounded like he was really enjoying his retirement." As Liz had hoped, Mrs Jacobs told her his name, "yes, that was Mike Middlebury. He was in charge of the records office for many years until his retirement a couple of years ago. He was my first boss. He's such a nice man, and he's still got a lot of friends at the 'Yard'. He comes in from time to time to see them and have a cup of tea in the canteen. He says that he is enjoying his retirement, but I can't help but think that he would rather be back here working. I don't know why the police have to retire people when they're so young."

At the end of her conversation with Mrs Jacobs Liz excused herself, saying "I've got just a few more files to look at and then I'll be out of your hair!" Missus Jacobs said, "oh don't listen to police sergeant Prendl; I don't know what his problem was, but he's not really the stuffed shirt that he acted like when you came in."

A short time later, Liz informed Mrs Jacobs that she had finished her work and that she would be leaving. As she walked away from the records office she knew that her next move would not improve her standing amongst her colleagues at New Scotland Yard. She had looked once again through the retiree files and had been unable to find one for a Michael Middlebury. She thought it most likely that it had been removed. The implications of that were serious.

She headed toward Detective Superintendent Murphy's office, hoping that he had not gone home, although it was late in the afternoon.

* * *

Much to her relief, Superintendent Murphy recognised at once the full implications of Liz's suspicions. In fact, he was prepared to be less cautious than she. Her caution had been founded on the fact that she had not actually seen Michael Middlebury. It was entirely possible that Middlebury had a voice resembling the man who spoke to her in her bedroom, but in fact, looked nothing like him. She had to agree with the superintendent that it was unlikely that the fact of the missing file was purely coincidental. The superintendent said that he considered the missing file to be worrying. It indicated the likelihood that at least one of the active Scotland Yard officers was involved in a conspiracy to pervert the course of justice.

His next words had frightened Liz, making her realise that she had not considered fully the consequences that might arise from her investigation. Superintendent Murphy had said that during the next few days, during which time he would make his investigations, he would insist that Liz make herself scarce. "Under no circumstances go back to your flat, Liz. If what we suspect is true is really true, there is a distinct possibility that whoever is involved may go after you. At least one of them has already committed murder, and quite obviously there are at least two people guilty of several serious assaults. Also, because of the reluctance of the assault victims to testify against their attackers, much of the evidence against the perpetrators will depend upon your findings."

"I'm afraid I'm rather sensitive on this point, Liz. It comes from my days in Ulster. Whilst I was working there, several times I saw police cases against terrorists, both loyalist and IRA, collapse completely because the only witnesses to the crimes were killed or simply disappeared. If you have someplace you can go that is not likely to be known to your police colleagues, I would go there. Failing that, perhaps I can get permission to put you under some kind of protective custody. The trouble with that is that it is hard to keep secrets from everyone here at Scotland Yard. God knows how many of my colleagues are involved in this thing. However, before we do any of that, we'll have to be certain that Middlebury is one of the men we're after. You go back to Mile End for a few days, and I shall try to locate some records for Middlebury. Failing that, we may have to pull him in and let you have a look at him. I'd prefer not to do that though 'cause it will risk alerting whoever are his accomplices, and that could make the future investigation less likely to succeed. I'll let you know as soon as I can, Liz."

Liz had only just settled to the task of going over the backlog of work on the drugs investigation that had piled up on her desk at the Mile End when she got a call from Superintendent Murphy. "I've had a chat with the Assistant Commander Belder, who's in charge of records at the 'Yard', Liz, and we both agree that it would be impossible to dig too deeply into the records without alerting Police Sergeant Prendl. If, as seems likely, Prendl is involved with Middlebury, that could prove to be disastrous. Therefore, I've decided that probably it would be best to approach the subject less directly. AC Belder doesn't know Middlebury; he took over the records operation after the man retired. However, he will make discrete enquiries and try to find someone who did know Middlebury. Then he will show that person the sketches that you had made and see if either of them looks like our man."

"In the meantime, though, I think it would be a good idea if you went away for a few days. I've already had a word with DCI Lawrence to clear it for you to take some time off. Have you thought where you might go?" Liz said that she had not thought that far ahead, but perhaps she could stay with her mum in Cambridge. Superintendent Murphy said that he did not think that that would be a good idea. "We must assume that any addresses that have been associated with you in the past could be visited by anyone having access to police records. You might not be safe staying with your family. Hang on, I've just had an idea. Last summer I took my family to a small hotel on the Devonshire coast. I was really impressed by just how isolated it was. It's a bad time of the year because they may be fully booked up, but you might give it a try if you're interested."

Liz knew that she more or less had to be interested if she couldn't stay with her mum. The only other place that she could think of going was Pat's place in Cambridge. However, she had spoken to Pat several days earlier and her friend had spent most of their conversation complaining about her husband. She and Roger were attempting a reconciliation, and it was not going well. Superintendent Murphy told Liz the name of the hotel in which he and his family stayed and the fact that it was located in a place called, Hope Cove in south Devonshire.

* * *

Chapter Twenty Five

Liz was uncertain whether or not she was doing the right thing by going to Devon. The hotel at which she had booked was certainly 'well off the beaten track.' She had taken the train from London to Totnes, hoping to take a taxi from there to the hotel. To her surprise, she found that most of the taxi drivers at the station were reluctant to take her to Hope Cove. Once she had managed to persuade a driver to take her she understood why must of those that she had asked had refused. The last part of the journey was spent on one-lane roads which had enormous hedgerows on either side. A driver had to rely on the courtesy of other drivers on the road to be allowed to progress very far.

Once she saw the hotel at which she had booked accommodation, Liz decided that the journey, even if it was slow and relatively expensive, was well worth it. She had got the booking only because of an extraordinary bit of luck. When she had rung up the hotel in an attempt to make a reservation, she was told that there was nothing available until well into the autumn. The only consolation the receptionist offered was to take her name and telephone number and to ring her in case the hotel had a cancellation.

Liz could not delay her plans, but in order not to seem impolite she told the receptionist her name and was preparing to give her telephone number when the woman to whom she was speaking said, "Elisabeth Andresen? You're not the Liz Andresen who was at King's College a few years ago, are you?" Liz said that she had gone to King's College and had been there a few years ago. The voice said, "what an amazing coincidence; I'm Fiona Speller; I was at King's at the same time; do you remember me?" Liz said, "of course

225

I remember you, Fiona. What have you been doing with yourself since your days at King's?" Fiona said, "let's not go into that now, Liz; let's get you sorted out with a room. Actually, I'm not supposed to do this, but I can get you into one of our single rooms. It's not very elegant, but it's very comfortable. We've just had a cancellation by a woman who comes here every year at this time to go on walks along the coast. Poor thing, she got knocked off her bike yesterday and rang us from her hospital bed. Her reservation was for only three nights, but we can sort something out if you want to stay longer."

After she had rung off, Liz thought about the time she had spent sharing a small flat with Fiona Speller. That had been during her final year at King's. She remembered Fiona as being very pleasant, but more interested in having a good time than in studying. At the time Liz had thought of Fiona as a spoiled brat. The flat in which the two of them had lived had been rented for Fiona by her father. The rent that she had charged Liz had been used by Fiona mainly for buying clothes. It was a cause of some slight friction between the two young women that Fiona had the lion's share of the space in the wardrobe that they shared. Liz had been fairly sure that Fiona's father was unaware that his daughter had a tenant and was earning extra money. Whenever the man was due to make a visit to her, Fiona had insisted that Liz should make herself scarce.

As Liz had thought about Fiona, a memory crowded into her mind that she had not remembered before that time. Liz had returned to the flat one evening after a choir rehearsal. Upon entering she became aware of noises that sounded like those that might be made by a distressed animal. Cautiously, she had peered into the front room of the flat where she had seen a sight which, at first, had shocked her.

Fiona's head had been buried between the legs of another woman; it was the other woman who had been making the noise. Quickly, Liz had let herself out of the flat and had gone down to the nearby Strand to a coffee shop, where she had stayed until she thought it might be safe to return. She had never mentioned the incident to Fiona, and such an event never had happened again as far as Liz had been aware. Liz knew that her flatmate often had drunk to excess, so perhaps alcohol had fuelled Fiona's behaviour that night.

When she arrived at the hotel in Hope Cove, Liz knew that she had been very lucky to be able to spend her time away from London at such an ideal place. The hotel was relatively small and set in its own grounds. It overlooked a small natural harbour that a coastal stream and wave action had carved into the Devonshire coastline. Her room was relatively small, and it did not have a balcony or a view of the sea, but it had proved to be charming nevertheless.

There was a middle-aged woman at the reception desk when Liz checked in. When she heard Liz's name she said, "just a minute, Miss Andresen. I promised Fiona that I would let her know as soon as you arrived." She left the desk and went through a door behind the place where she had been standing. A short time later a young woman with a familiar face came out of the room and went up to Liz, hugging her and exclaiming, "oh, Liz, it's so good to see you. We've got so much to talk about...we could spend your whole three days just talking!"

* * *

Twenty-four hours after her arrival, Liz had relaxed completely and, despite her initial misgivings, she was enjoying herself. Each evening, when she telephoned Superintendent Murphy, she did so with the hope that he would not tell her to return to London.

It had come as a surprise to Liz to discover that Fiona's parents were the owners of the hotel in which she was staying. The middle-aged woman who had been in reception when Liz checked in was Fiona's mum; she shared that duty with the dad. Liz now understood how the Spellers were able to afford to rent a flat in London for their daughter's use whilst she was at university. Apparently the same flat now was being used by Fiona's younger sister who was in her final year at University College, London. The younger sister was home for the summer and during that busy season shared with Fiona the duties of hotel telephone receptionist. The reason that Fiona could spend so much time with Liz was because the sister had agreed to stand in for her.

During her first full day Liz had gone sailing with her friend in a dinghy owned by Mr and Mrs Speller. Since Liz and Fiona were about the same size and shape, Liz was able to wear Fiona's wetsuit, whilst Fiona borrowed that of her younger sister. Fiona was a keen snorkeler and insisted that Liz should at least learn the rudiments. The young woman would bring the sailing dinghy close to exposed areas of the coastline near the hotel, anchor it, and then she and Liz would spend a few hours exploring the submerged areas of the rocky shore. Fiona knew and told Liz both the scientific and common names of all of the animals that they had encountered, which seemed to consist primarily of rather spectacular long-tentacled sea anemones, several tube worms, and, of course, the ubiquitous sea urchins.

It took Liz a little time to get used to the paraphernalia of snorkelling, especially the mask which kept becoming fogged by her breath. However, finally she got used to breathing through her mouth, which did not come naturally to her. Initially, Liz had planned to get in some walking, but Fiona's enthusiasm for sailing and snorkelling was infectious; she relaxed and allowed her newly-refound friend to make the plans.

Despite being with her for only a short time, Liz was finding that she was very much enjoying her friend's companionable personality. During their talks together Liz found that she was listening to a young woman who had matured considerably since her undergraduate days. Fiona told Liz that she thought it likely that her future lay with her parents' hotel. "I did history at King's, but I didn't really take it seriously. I reckon I was lucky to get the lower second that I did. I thought at first that I might like to teach and I even started on a PGCE. However my dad had a heart attack, so I came down here to help out. I don't know, Liz; I suppose I don't have much ambition, but somehow this place appeals to me. I don't think I'll mind spending the rest of my days here."

"There's a bloke in Kingsbridge. He runs the shop where we get all of our fish and shellfish, which he delivers to us. I know that he's kinda sweet on me even though he's almost old enough to be my father. I suppose if I decide to stay here, and if he asks me, I'll marry him. He's not married, and as far as I know he never has been."

"How about you, Liz? As I remember from our undergraduate days, you were never much for going out. Is there anyone serious in your life?" Liz felt that she had to be honest and tell Fiona that there was no one in her life. She could have added, but thought better of it, "in fact there's not likely to be anyone in my life. I am too busy enjoying doing what I do." When she had said that before usually it had been met with the words, "oh yeah, just wait until the right man comes along." Liz was certain that she wasn't waiting for the right man, but beyond that she didn't really know what she was waiting for. All that she had said was, "no, there's no one in my life right now." In response to that statement, Fiona had merely winked at her and said, "atta girl; take it from me, men are highly overrated!"

* * *

On her third night away from London when she telephoned Superintendent Murphy, Liz was told that she would have to either extend her stay in Devon or find another place to go. The superintendent told her, "there is a strong likelihood that ex-Sergeant Middlebury is the man in the sketch that you had made but obviously that resemblance is not really enough to detain him. Therefore, whilst he's still out there I don't want to take any chances that he might come after you."

"I have decided to put Middlebury under covert surveillance. That has just begun, so I don't know where it will lead, but I'm hoping that at the very least that will tell us who his accomplice is. Also, we are keeping an eye on Sergeant Prendl. I am pretty sure that Middlebury could not have got the information he had both on you and the animal-rights activists without some co-operation from Prendl. Anyway, Liz, I hope that you aren't feeling too isolated way out there in the West Country; it shouldn't be for too many more days. It's obvious when I speak to DCI Lawrence that he's not happy having you away for so long. However, I think he's accepted my argument that it can't be helped."

"As soon as we know enough to bring in Middlebury we shall need you to return. Then I will want you to do your damnedest to persuade at least one of Middlebury's assault victims to testify against him. Unfortunately, the amount of forensic evidence recovered from the scenes of the assaults and the one murder is minuscule. Therefore, I am sure that we will need the testimony of at least one victim to make any charges stick."

Before she had telephoned Superintendent Murphy Liz already had made contingency plans for extending her absence from London. In fact, it was Fiona who had suggested it. She said that she would be pleased if Liz would stay with her at the hotel: "you've seen my room, Liz; it's enormous. My mum and dad had it converted from a couple of the guest rooms when they first bought the hotel. They lived in it until I came along and then they needed more space so they bought a house in the village. I'm sure my parents will be pleased to have you stay; they've both remarked to me about what a nice person you are. As you've seen, my room has a small kitchenette, and you can fix food for yourself there or eat in the dining room, whichever you prefer. I keep stuff for a light breakfast in my room, but I take lunch and dinner in the dining room; you can do the same if you wish. I'll have to get back to work, of course, but that'll leave you free to go on some of those walks you were interested in."

After checking out of her room and paying her bill, Liz was helped by Fiona to move her clothing into the wardrobe of her room. Fiona had made space for Liz's clothing, but it was obvious that her habit of buying new frocks had not diminished since her undergraduate days. The room was clearly more than adequate for two people, which pleased Liz.

In the brief time during which she and Fiona had become reacquainted, Liz had become aware that her friend had an interest that she and Liz should become more than just friends. In thinking about what response she would make to a future overture by Fiona, Liz had decided that she would try to remain firm in a resolve not to engage in sex with someone whom she didn't love. Unfortunately, Liz had violated that resolve as often as she had invoked it. However, she felt that this time would be different. She and Fiona had enjoyed their time together, especially the sailing and the searching out of shoreline creatures whilst snorkelling. However, Liz was certain that her friendship with Fiona could not deepen into love. The two women really had very little in common. Liz hoped that she could convey her true feelings to Fiona without either hurting her or offending her.

A week later, Liz and Fiona parted company, with Fiona expressing the hope that the two of them might get together again, perhaps every few years or so. Liz was pleased that she had successfully resisted her friend's sexual advances the first time that they had been made. She realised that her resistance had been made easier by the fact that she had had nothing to drink on the night in question.

After ten days at Hope Cove, Liz got the order from Superintendent Murphy to return to London and to report directly to him at Scotland Yard. "We have taken both Middlebury and his accomplice, Robert Alder into custody, and Police Sergeant Prendl has been suspended from duty. All of them are denying everything, so I'm afraid that it will be up to you, now, Liz. Anyway, get back here as soon as you can. I've cleared it with DCI Lawrence, but you'd best drop in to see him on your way down here."

Once she had spoken to Superintendent Murphy, Liz tried to form in her mind what she would say to Fiona.

On their last night together, the two young women discussed the future. Fiona had confessed that she had been somewhat relieved when Liz had indicated her lack of interest in the two of them being more than just friends.

Fiona went on to explain the difficulties that she faced, saying, "the curious thing is, Liz, my mum knows the way I am. She said that when she was my age and younger she was the same way herself. However, she said, she wanted to have kids and to be a normal woman. She thinks that the only way to do that is to marry and settle down. Before having you here this summer, I had about decided that I wanted the same things as my mum. Then you came and I began to have doubts. So you see, Liz, you probably did me a favour by acting the way you did. My parents have talked about wanting either me or my sister to take over the running of the hotel in a few years time. My sister isn't really interested; it's not really her thing. She's doing Medicine at UCL and then wants to specialise after she finishes her MB. Probably I'll end up marrying my fishmonger, if that's what he wants. I know he really likes kids and he says he wants to get started pretty quick or else his kids with grow up thinking he's their granddad!"

Liz was pleased that Fiona had explained her position so clearly; it obviated the necessity for her to say anything. Just before she left the hotel, Fiona made Liz promise that she would visit Hope Cove again many times in the future where she would be welcome always.

* * *

Chapter Twenty Six

Superintendent Murphy showed Liz the videotape recordings the police had made during interviews of the men suspected of assaults on animal-rights activists and the murder of Barry Goff. At every opportunity during their interviews the men had denied strenuously that they had had any involvement with either the beatings or the death of Barry Goff. It had worried Superintendent Murphy that neither man had asked to have a solicitor present whilst they were questioned. In the superintendent's view that usually indicated that suspects considered that the police case against them was weak. He told Liz, "unfortunately, Middlebury and Alder are right; we haven't much to go on."

Once Liz had viewed the tapes and listened to the dialogue she told the superintendent that in her view there was little doubt that ex-Sergeant Middlebury was one of the men the police were seeking. He bore a distinct resemblance to Barry Goff's description of one of the men who attacked him except he was a little fuller in the face. Liz had confirmed whilst listening to the recording of Middlebury's voice that it had sounded very much like that of the man who had spoken to her at the time that she had been accosted. Also, Middlebury had mispronounced the word, interest, although not precisely in the same manner as did the man who had accosted Liz in the bedroom of her flat.

There was more doubt about the guilt of the second man the police had interviewed: the one named Alder. He had been detained because during the time that Middlebury had been kept under surveillance, he had met Alder in a pub three times; it was obvious that they were friends. Also, he bore a resemblance to one of the men whom Barry Goff had described, although the fit was not as good as was the case with Middlebury.

Superintendent Murphy had impressed upon Liz the necessity of moving quickly in attempting to persuade at least one of the animal-rights assault victims to help the police. Middlebury and Alder were being kept in custody, but the time during which the police could do that without bringing a charge was running out rapidly. Superintendent Murphy thought it unlikely that a magistrate would give the police an extension of time based on the evidence available up to that point.

Liz thought that it was possible that she could persuade Richard Cowling to help the police, especially since Middlebury and Alder were in custody. Unlike most of the assault victims to whom she'd spoken, he had seemed to be willing to be friendly toward her. However, the superintendent had made it clear that Liz should contact as many as possible of the assault victims. He thought it unlikely that an identification by Cowling of Middlebury and Alder as the men who had assaulted him would be sufficient evidence to charge the two suspects. However, he believed that the police would need at least two witnesses prepared to testify against the suspects once the case had got to court. He said that twice in his experience he had seen men walk free whom he considered to be guilty. In each case the defence barrister had used the existence of only a single victim willing to come forward out of many who might have done so as an indication of something suspicious. The barristers involved had managed to convince the jury that there was a strong possibility that their client was being victimised by the police.

Superintendent Murphy supplied Liz with the complete list of assault victims which included their home and work addresses. What she did not discover until later was the fact that from the moment she left Scotland Yard to interview the assault victims she became the focus of a team of plain-clothed policemen. The men had been charged with two tasks: they were to follow DC Andresen at all times when she was not at Scotland Yard or at the Mile End police station. During those times never were they to allow her to be aware of their presence.

* * *

Liz had thought of the superintendent as a mild-mannered man who, as long as she had known him, had displayed admirable caution. However, the personality that Liz perceived concealed a side to the character of the superintendent that had developed over the more-than-twenty years of his police career. He could be ruthless, if it served what he considered to be a worthwhile purpose. He held the opinion that there was as yet no proof that the two men held in police custody were the only ones that had been involved in the assaults and the murder of Barry Goff. If that view were correct, there was a strong possibility that Detective Constable Andresen would be in constant danger whilst she sought to question the assault victims. In fact, the superintendent hoped that that would be the case, and that Liz would act as bait to attract any other suspects. If he were wrong and Middlebury and Alder were the only parties involved in the crimes, that could produce an acceptable outcome also. If Liz could persuade one of the assault victims to help, that would give the police the time necessary for a full investigation. If not, and the two suspects had to be released, then Liz would return to her rôle as 'bait'.

It took Liz the better part of a day to contact Richard Cowling. Although he still worked for the company whose address he had given the police, he had taken on the job as a delivery driver. The company for which he worked rented out water coolers and kept them supplied continually with bottled water. It was the job of the delivery drivers to keep the rented coolers adequately stocked. By the nature of the job, Cowling's movements could not be predicted. However, his boss was able to supply Liz with a list of the names and addresses of clients upon whom Cowling was supposed to call on the day she attempted to contact him. Liz got an approximate schedule from the boss, deciding that she would go to premises to which Cowling would not be expected to reach until about lunchtime. She would wait for him there.

Liz thought it was a hopeful sign that Richard Cowling smiled pleasantly and said, "hi," when she approached him as he got out of his delivery van, going to the rear doors. It was obvious that he had recognised her. She started to ask if she could speak to him when he interrupted to say, "just a minute, officer; I have to drop off a bottle of water in that building across the street, but then I'll be able to talk to you 'cause I'll be on my lunch break" Liz waited by the van until Cowling returned. He said he usually went to a nearby pub for lunch when he got to the drop off about mid-day. "It's not bad food and it has a car park which makes things a lot easier. Parking in this part of London is murder; I'm surprised that I didn't collect a ticket just in the short time I've been parked here. Usually they're on to ya like buzzards. Follow me to the pub and we'll talk there."

Liz had decided that the best approach to Richard Cowling would be to attempt to assure him that the two men who were a danger to him were now detained by the police, and if only he would co-operate they would remain there. He began the conversation by telling her that he had

238

stopped being an animal-rights activist. He explained, "oh, it didn't have anything to do with being beaten up. It's just that after Barry was killed I began to wonder if it all was worth it. I saw that woman on television that night, and I never really thought about it that much before. I grew up in a house full of animals. I like animals, and I didn't want people to mistreat them. However, that lady didn't look like she mistreated animals; I liked the way she sat there with her cat in her lap while she talked to the bloke on the telly. Anyway, I've decided to give it all up. My best mate, George, don't agree with me, but he at least lets me make my own mind up."

After speaking to him for over an hour, Liz had managed to get Richard Cowling to talk about what had happened to him the night that he had been beaten by two men. That was a feat that none of the police interviewers had accomplished with any of the assault victims. Once Liz heard Richard Cowling's story, she understood why. "I was in my local with George when I seen these two blokes sittin' across from us. The only reason I noticed them was because every now and then they'd look at me an' George and I was wonderin' what's their problem. Anyway, that night we was goin' to make it an early night 'cause it was just before payday and both George and me was a bit low in the pocketbook. As we got up to leave, I noticed that the two blokes were drinking up in a hurry. They put down their glasses and began to go follow me and George into the car park. I walked with George to his car and then watched as he drove off. I noticed two men messing about over near one of the other cars, but I didn't think no more about it."

"I was just gettin' over to my car when these two geezers set upon me without warning. They grabbed me and pushed me into a space beside my car where no one was parked. One of them grabbed me and held my arms whilst the other began punching me in the stomach. I tried to bend over, but the one that was holding me was strong. I could see both of them plain as day. They weren't makin' no effort to keep me from seeing who they were."

"Finally, the bloke who was holdin' me let me go and I fell to the ground. Then either him or the other one began to kick me. I just covered my head with my arms trying to keep them from breaking my head open. Then they stopped and one of them started talkin' to me. He said something like, 'listen real good. You've just had the shit beat out of you 'cause you're an odious, little bastard, raising hell with people who are only trying to do you and your undeserving-bastard mates some good. So, from now on give it a rest; if you don't, you can expect more like this or even worse. And if you think that we won't know where to find you, don't worry, Richard Cowling, arrested once in 1987 for assaulting a police officer. We have good connections with the police. We know just where to find you and those who are just like you, including George Baird. And another thing, you miserable little shit; don't think for a minute that we won't know if you tell the police what happened to you tonight'."

Cowling continued, "the next thing I knew some woman was screaming, telling someone else to send for an ambulance. I tried to get up to go talk to the woman and tell her to shut up, but I couldn't do it. Well, you know the rest. When the ambulance came they insisted that I go with them to the hospital to be checked over. However, I never told nobody nothing. The only reason you lot got wind of it was because somebody at the hospital rang them or something. The young copper that interviewed me said that it was pretty obvious that I had been badly beaten, but it was my business if I didn't want to do anything about it."

Back at Scotland Yard Liz was relieved when Superintendent Murphy got the message that a Mr Roger Brown was asking for him at reception. Before leaving him at lunch time, Liz had got Richard Cowling to promise that he would call in at Scotland Yard just after leaving work that day. She would not have been surprised had he not done so. Despite the fact that he had told her that he realised that he should help, he wasn't certain who he could trust. For that reason Liz had told him to use the name, Roger Brown when calling in at the 'Yard'. She told him that it was unlikely that anyone would associate that name with anything to do with the investigation that she was pursuing.

* * *

Richard Cowling looked closely when a group of seven men were paraded onto a well-lit platform at one side of a room that was otherwise darkened. Two of the men who stood there attempting to shield their eyes from the bright lights Liz recognised as fellow police officers. She thought it likely that the others, bar Middlebury and Alder, also were policemen. Each man was asked a few questions by the police officer who had accompanied the group. Most had mumbled their replies. However, Middlebury had used the occasion as an opportunity to speak out against what he considered to be an outrageous violation of his rights. It was obvious that he knew exactly why he was there and he was seeking to intimidate whoever it was in the darkened portion of the room who was looking at him.

Liz watched Cowling's face as he scanned the line of men; he paused momentarily, when he reached Middlebury, but he made no reaction. None of the other men provoked a response from Cowling. Finally, he turned to Liz and said, "no; I don't see nobody there that I recognise. It's obvious that you lot have got the wrong men if you say that the men who beat me up are there." At that point Superintendent Murphy broke in, saying, "are you absolutely sure, Mr Cowling, ..." Cowling interrupted to say, "I bleedin' outa be sure, mate; I sat there looking at those men for at least an hour in the pub and then I saw them in the car park. Naw, I don't see nobody up there 'at I recognise."

Liz was certain that Cowling had recognised Middlebury and she was sure that the superintendent had seen that reaction also. However, it had surprised her when the superintendent made what in her opinion was a mistake. He got mad at Cowling, saying, "I ought to arrest you for wasting police time! I know as well as you do that number three in the line up was one of the men who beat you up; I'll bet number seven was in on it too. Take him back to my office, constable; I've got some things to attend to: releasing a probable murderer onto the street, and then I'll join you in a few minutes."

Liz and Richard Cowling walked to the superintendent's office in silence. She felt certain that any attempt on her part to persuade the man to change his mind would be futile. Her silence provoked him into a 'half-way' apology: "I was going to do it, really, constable, but when I saw that bastard standing there it brought back everything that happened to me that night. I'd like to help, but I can't. However, none of them other men that you showed me was involved. I'd never seen none of them before."

After waiting a few minutes, Superintendent Murphy arrived at his office. He had recovered his composure and appeared no longer to be angry with Cowling. Liz didn't know whether or not the superintendent was attempting to frighten Cowling, when he told him, "I'll be honest with you Cowling; I didn't believe you when you said that you did not recognise any of those men in the line up. However, I have now had them released. That means that they are now out there someplace and I have no doubt at all that sooner or later they will get in touch with you. I would not like to be in your shoes when that happens." Cowling protested once again, "you've got it all wrong. I ain't never seen none of them men before." The superintendent put up his hand and said, "alright, alright; you've told us that before. Let's just hope that you don't end up like your friend, Barry Goff."

As Liz made her way home that evening her mood was rather sombre. She felt as though she was right back at the beginning of her investigation. The only thing that she could do would be interview as many as possible of the other animal-activist victims of Middlebury and his associate. Superintendent Murphy had made it clear that he was certain that the Crown Prosecution Service would insist that the police obtain statements from at least two of the victims before they would proceed. He was of the opinion that Cowling could be brought 'round in due course.

* * *

Chapter Twenty Seven

The hiatus in the assaults on animal-rights activists that had been in force since the death of Barry Goff ended within a few days of the release of Middlebury and Alder from custody. Over a period of a week, two separate attacks had been made on men who were known to be animal-rights advocates.

As had been the case in most of the previous assaults, the police learned of the attacks only because they had been alerted by medical staff at the hospital Accident and Emergency Departments to which the men had been taken. One of the victims had been detained in hospital overnight and then released. The other was in hospital still. His injuries were more serious, having sustained three broken ribs and a partial collapse of a lung. Despite their injuries, neither man was willing to give a statement to the police. Both claimed that they had no idea who it was who had attacked them, and they were equally ignorant as to the reason for the attacks. Superintendent Murphy was not alone in his opinion that the latest assaults and the release of Middlebury and Alder were consequential events. He felt that it was almost as if the two men were thumbing their noses at the police.

Liz had managed to locate and attempt to interview fifteen of the animal-rights activists known to the police to have been assaulted. Only one of them, a Mrs Susan Rider, was willing to speak to Liz. She had indicated that she might be willing to help in the enquiry, but that she would have to have her safety guaranteed.

Prior to contacting the victims, Superintendent Murphy had obtained permission to offer such a guarantee to any of the victims who would be willing to help. Accordingly, a male police constable was assigned to provide protection for Mrs Rider. The PC was to stay close to her from early morning to early evening on weekdays only. Missus Rider said that she thought that her husband would be able to take over during the rest of the day and during the night.

When she spoke to Mrs Rider, Liz learned that the incident that had made the victim decide to co-operate with the police was a letter that she had received only the day before Liz had contacted her. She showed it to Liz, who obtained permission to keep it as evidence. The letter consisted of a photocopy of a single A4 sheet which contained a typewritten message and a copy of an article that obviously had been taken from a newspaper. The article described the finding of the body of Barry Goff in his flat. It said that the police were treating the death as suspicious. The typewritten message said only, "The fate of people who talk to the police."

Liz wondered if, perhaps, all of the assault victims had received the same message received by Mrs Rider. Otherwise, why would the sender bother photocopying the sheet. Unfortunately, none of the other assault victims whom she had attempted to contact had been willing to talk to Liz, so there would be no immediate answer to Liz's query.

Liz was disappointed, but not surprised when forensic examination of the photocopy and the envelope revealed fingerprints belonging to Mrs Rider and two unidentified persons. Undoubtedly Middlebury would have taken precautions when preparing and handling material he knew that the police would use as evidence. However, should the case progress to the point where Middlebury could be arrested, the photocopy and envelope might prove to be useful. Hopes that Mrs Rider might provide the breakthrough the enquiry needed were dashed when the lady was unable to identify positively either Middlebury or Alder as the men who had attacked her. After watching the videotaped recordings of the police interviews of the two men, Mrs Rider said that she thought that Middlebury looked like one of her attackers, but she couldn't be sure. She said that she was sure that Alder was not one of the men who had assaulted her.

Meanwhile, an enquiry set up by Superintendent Murphy to investigate who was responsible for the disappearance of certain files from the Scotland Yard records office had got nowhere. It was thought likely that the disappearance would, by necessity, involve Police Sergeant Thomas Prendl, the officer in immediate charge of the records office. However, it was possible, also, that his assistant was responsible. Nonetheless, in the absence of evidence, there was nothing that could be done.

Finally, after a short discussion with Liz and the Scotland Yard officers who had been involved, Superintendent Murphy took the decision to discontinue active investigation of the assaults on the animal-rights activists. Liz was surprised at the superintendent's decision. In her opinion the fact that a murder had occurred gave the enquiry considerable weight. However, the super seemed to be treating it as merely routine, which was not his usual habit.

When she returned to her duties at Mile End she confessed to herself a sense of relief. Almost immediately she became involved in an investigation on which palpable progress was being made.

* * *

Despite what he had declared in the final meeting with Liz and her Scotland Yard colleagues, Superintendent Murphy had no intention of ending the active investigation of which

Liz had been part. After she had left the 'Yard' to return to Mile End the superintendent had reinstituted the team of plain-clothed policemen who had kept Liz under surveillance previously. This time, however, he had arranged with Liz's boss at Mile End, DCI Lawrence, to keep the surveillance officers informed should Liz leave her place of work for any reason except that she was on police duties. The superintendent was convinced that sooner or later another attempt would be made to silence the constable.

Liz was totally unaware of the consternation that she had caused amongst the team of officers keeping her under surveillance when she left the Mile End station on a Friday evening and had taken the tube to Liverpool Street train station instead of her flat in Plaistow. That morning she had decided that it was time that she should make a visit to Cambridge. During recent telephone calls her mum had been more complaining than usual, accusing Liz of being a very neglectful daughter. So to avoid wasting time returning to her flat, Liz had taken a small suitcase in to work with her, ready to go at the end of the day to catch the train to Cambridge.

Liz had not thought that there was any necessity for informing any of her work colleagues of her plans for the weekend; as a consequence the police officer who was to follow her during the evening was caught off guard. Once the officer realised that she was catching a train out of London he had had to call for back-up assistance. He journeyed to Cambridge in the same train carriage as did Liz, but unlike her, he was completely unprepared to spend the weekend.

Liz arrived by taxi at Audrey's house, finding that although her mum was at home, she was planning to spend the evening in the pub. Liz didn't really fancy a pub evening, but it was patently obvious that her mum was going to insist. Her mum was an expert at making Liz feel guilty, and as far as Liz was concerned, going to the pub was the lesser of the two evils. She did manage to make a telephone call to Pat, hoping that her friend would be able to join her and her mum. However, Pat used the excuse that there was no one to look after her baby son. "I'm afraid being a mum has kind of curtailed my social life, Liz. You'll have to come here if you want to see me." Liz promised that she would visit Pat on the following Sunday and would bring a bottle of wine.

Some minutes after Liz had arrived at her mum's house, the officer who had been following her managed to put in an appearance. Unlike his quarry he had been unfamiliar with the procedure for queuing for a taxi at the entrance to the Cambridge train station. Consequently, Liz had 'got the jump' on him by several taxis and had arrived at her destination well before the police officer who was following her. The main worry of that man was that DC Andresen's destination in Cambridge was someplace other than her mother's house: the only address in Cambridge that had been given to him. He found himself a place within view of the house at which he could station himself to keep watch and to await the arrival of reinforcements from London.

When Superintendent Murphy had learned that Liz had gone to Cambridge he had decided to continue the surveillance operation even if it did mean a long car drive for one of the members of the surveillance team. He knew that the suspects whom the police were seeking were well aware of the location of the house where Liz's mother lived. Just in case emergency backup was needed, the superintendent had arranged with the Cambridge police to monitor the wavelength to which the police radios carried by the surveillance team had been tuned.

That evening, in the pub, Liz was unaware of it, but she and her mum were being observed surreptitiously by a young man who sat across the room from them. The next door neighbours, Rose and Fred Paltry, were there also. As usual, Fred was entertaining everyone by talking animatedly about his garden and his gardening. Liz was hoping that she could persuade her mother to go home at the same time as the Paltrys. That way, she hoped, Audrey would not get quite as inebriated as she did usually. The last time she had been with Audrey in the pub she had had to order a taxi to take them home. The woman had been incapable of walking the less than a quarter of a mile between the house and the place in which they had spent the evening. Following that, she had had difficulty getting her mum out of the car, into the house and up the stairs into her bedroom. It was her mother's apparent unwillingness to control her drinking that had caused Liz to be reluctant to come to Cambridge to visit her.

Fortunately, this evening, Audrey was persuaded to leave the pub well before she had reached an incapable state. Rose and Fred Paltry had provided the excuse by inviting everyone back to their house for coffee.

* * *

Liz had decided to return early to London from Cambridge. Pat had rung her on Sunday morning to say that she and Roger had had a disagreement and that things were "rather tense in the flat at the moment. I hate to do this to you, Liz, but I don't think it would be a good idea for you to be here just now. I'm ever so sorry." It was obvious to Liz that her friend was very badly upset because all traces of her usual sense of humour had vanished and their telephone conversation was very brief.

On the train journey to London her thoughts were occupied entirely with Pat and how her life had changed since she had got married and had a baby. More than once her friend had expressed regret that she had given in to pressure from her mum and Roger and had got married.

From Liverpool Street Liz went first to the Mile End police station where she spent a couple of hours reviewing some work that would be occupying her time during the upcoming week. She realised that her weekend had not been a pleasant experience when she barely resisted the temptation to make a snide remark to the station sergeant when he teased her by suggesting that she was being very eager, coming into work on a day off. After completing her work she went to the Mile End underground station to continue her journey home.

After she seated herself on the train she made a discovery that occupied her thoughts throughout the journey to Plaistow. Seated at the opposite end of the carriage was a man who she was certain had been on the train with her between Cambridge and Liverpool Street. In her mind that was too much of a coincidence, especially in view of her stopover at the Mile End police station. She thought that her suspicion was confirmed when, after staring at him for a time, he looked at her and then looked away very quickly.

The presence in the carriage of a man who probably was following her brought back all of Liz's memories of the night when the two men broke into her house. She was thankful that that incident had convinced her to buy a mobile phone. She reached into a side pocket of her handbag to assure herself that she had her 'phone with her. She did. However, when she switched it on she was dismayed to find that its battery was almost fully discharged. She hoped that the phone would work for at least the short time it would take for her to summon help. She was thankful that there was still daylight; that would allow her to keep an eye on the man who she thought was following her.

Liz allowed the man to go ahead of her out of the underground station at Plaistow. He seemed not to be concerned about her, walking off in the direction opposite to that leading to Liz's flat after he had left the station. Liz waited for a few minutes until he was out of sight, and than she started toward her home. She debated with herself whether or not she should ring the Mile End station, deciding finally that she wouldn't. She would walk home cautiously, and if she encountered anyone on the way, then she would use her mobile 'phone.

As she walked up to the front door of her flat Liz was saying to herself, "you silly git; here you were worrying for nothing. It's just your bloody imagination getting the better of you. Thank god you didn't ring the station; you really would look like a right ninny." Liz decided to celebrate being home by having a couple of glasses of wine and the remainder of a Lasagne that she had made a few days earlier and then had frozen. Then she would take a long, hot bath and make it an early night. Once in bed she had no plans to go immediately to sleep; she would indulge in an activity which, of late, at least, she had had to accomplish on her own. However, she refused to think about her loneliness; tonight was a night for self-indulgence.

Liz finished her activity relatively quickly she thought because it had been some days since she had indulged. She decided that she would lie there in the dark, thinking about her life until she was overtaken by sleep. Throughout her life that had been her habit. When she was younger she used the time to plan out what she was going to do the next day. Now she was more circumspect, attempting to plan out the future course she wished her life to take. Moments later she heard a noise which she thought was almost certainly that made by the loose tread on the staircase that led between the ground and first floors of her flat. Alerted, she listened carefully because she knew that there was also a loose floor board in the hallway just at the top of the stairs.

The intrusion of a second noise into the silence of the night caused her to become really frightened. She rolled over in bed and turned on the lamp that rested on a bed-side table. At that moment the door opened and two men came into her bedroom. They were dressed in protective coveralls of a type usually worn by so-called 'scene of crime' police officers. She could not see their faces, but the fact that a lighted room had not deterred them from entering told Liz what she really did not want to know. In the next few moments she would be fighting for her life.

Taking no time to think she removed herself from the bed and ran at one of the men whilst screaming as loud as she could. Everything she did was contrary to the training in self defence that she had been taught, but she was too frightened to follow a rational plan. One of the men grabbed her, pinning her arms. She tried to use her knees and teeth to defend herself, but his strength and the evasive actions he took rendered her efforts futile. All she could do was continue to scream. However, moments later, even that response fell silent; the second man applied a pillow to her face and together the two men held her down on the bed, smothering her. She could not alleviate the fear that overtook her; she knew that she was going to die and there was nothing that she could do to prevent that from happening.

* * *

Chapter Twenty Eight

Liz found herself rather bewildered by the events that occurred during her stay in hospital. Her memories of the night that she had been attacked had given her a profound feeling of relief that she was alive still. The only physical manifestation of the attack on her was extensive damage to her throat; there was considerable bruising and soreness there. One of the medics attending her said that in the attempt to strangle her, her assailant had nearly completely fractured the thyroid cartilage in her neck. He attempted to make a joke of that condition by saying, "that'll keep you quiet for a few days!" However, when his statement elicited no response from Liz, he added quickly: "but it shouldn't trouble you for very long."

Although her throat was uncomfortable, Liz was more concerned about her profound feeling of sadness. She remembered that before losing consciousness, when her efforts to fight back had been completely frustrated she had sworn at her assailants. However, those efforts had only added to her frustration. The sound of her voice had been reduced to no more than a whimper by a length of duct tape wrapped around her head a few times. Her anger at the time had been generated less by the fact that she knew that she was going to die, more by the fact that they were depriving her of any chance of saving herself. They were just too strong. Facing death as she had done had made her realise, once again, just how frail life could be.

During her first day after arriving at the A & E Department of the hospital, Liz was transferred to a ward from whence she was taken off from time to time to undergo testing. At the end of that day she was pronounced 'fit', but it was suggested to her that she should stay in hospital for a further day or so because there was some concern about her mental recovery from the ordeal. Liz could not seem to dispel a feeling of depression. She had refused the suggestion of the psychologist who spoke to her that at least for a brief period she should take anti-depressant medication.

Liz's depression was exacerbated by a visit from Detective Superintendent Murphy. The superintendent was accompanied by a police constable whom he introduced as PC George Holmes. The fact that the PC's face seemed familiar became apparent immediately. She thought to herself, "he was the man who rode down from Cambridge on the train with me. Also, he was on the tube train that night." Before she could ask why the PC was following her, the superintendent gave an explanation: he said that the constable had been one of the men in a team of officers who had kept her under surveillance for three weeks before she was attacked. On the night in question, once the two of you had arrived in Plaistow, PC Holmes radioed for another member of the team to join him. Police Sergeant Maris arrived a short time later by car. Then the two officers maintained surveillance parked a short distance from your flat. Some time later, they heard the screams that you made when you were attacked. It was fortunate that we'd placed listening devices all over your flat. They called for backup and then went to see what the problem was. They had not seen anyone enter your flat, but then they could only observe the front entrance. When they got into the flat they immediately encountered the two men who had attacked you. Their first priority was to subdue your two attackers, which they did. However, when they turned their attention to you it seemed obvious that they were too late: you were lying on your bed, limp as a rag doll. Sergeant Maris looked you over and felt your pulse concluding from his examination that they had arrived too late. However, PC Holmes asked if he could 'have a go'. I think you were very lucky, Liz, that George Holmes was there. Before he joined us he spent five years as a paramedic with St John Ambulance. Anyway, George, you tell Liz what you told me afterwards." Hesitantly, George said that he had learned by experience that the absence of breathing and a heartbeat did not necessarily indicate that a person was dead. "Quite often they are capable of being revived. However, if the person has gone for a long time without breathing it usually leads to brain damage. I wasn't sure how long you had been out when we entered your bedroom, but I figured it couldn't have been too long, and, anyway, there was nothing to lose. Therefore, I had a go, and, happily, you began to show signs of life after only a short spell of CPR on my part. You didn't regain consciousness right away, but your heartbeat and breathing became steady. It wasn't long after that that the ambulance arrived."

George Holmes spoke in such a gentle, self-deprecatory way that Liz felt a surge of emotion. She hugged him and kissed him on the cheek, saying, "thank you." Her actions embarrassed both her and her saviour, and prompted him to mumble a platitude: "well, I only did what anyone would have done in my place, Miss Andresen; sorry, I mean, Constable Andresen." Liz recovered enough to say, "well, apparently not; hadn't that colleague of yours concluded that I was dead? Anyway, I am very grateful to you, George." Liz was relieved when PC Holmes stepped back from her bedside indicating that their conversation was over.

What Superintendent Murphy had to say next had profoundly shocked Liz and answered a question that had been 'niggling' at the back of her mind. "Well, Liz, I suppose you are wondering how George and his colleagues knew what was happening to you that night? That was my fault, I'm afraid. Obviously, you weren't aware of it, but a group of coppers of which George was part had kept you under surveillance for most of the time in the three weeks prior to the attack on you. They were doing that under my orders, I'm afraid. I figured that the only way we would get Middlebury and whoever was working with him to show their hand was to tempt them with a baited trap. You were the bait, my dear."

Liz could not disguise her shocked feelings, prompting the superintendent to add quickly, "oh, we did everything in our power to make certain that you were safe, my dear. You didn't spend a moment away from your police duties during which you were not being watched by at least one member of the team. We even managed to cover you when you made your unannounced trip to your home in Cambridge. Each night when you were in your flat there was an un-marked police car parked not far away with two members of the surveillance team in it. Also, as I said before, we put listening devices all over your flat, so that the coppers in the car could hear it even if it was only a pin dropping. That's why they were able to get to you so quickly."

As Superintendent Murphy was speaking, Liz was barely listening. She wondered how she could have been so badly mistaken in her opinion of the man. Into the awkward si-lence that followed after he had finished, the superintendent injected words that he hoped would please Liz. "Anyway, Liz, we are all so happy that you appear to have made a full recovery. We'll leave you now and let you get some rest. However, before I go I wanted to tell you that I've arranged it with DCI Lawrence for you to take a short leave. Maybe that will give you some time to recover; you deserve it after all you've been through."

Just after the superintendent and PC Holmes left Liz's bedside, Lydia arrived; her appearance prompted Liz to burst into tears, provoking Lydia to hold her in a firm hug in an attempt to be comforting. Lydia said nothing as between sobs Liz voiced contemptuous feelings toward Superintendent Murphy: "how dare he treat me like an object; who does he think he is?"

Lydia surprised Liz by agreeing with her, saying that her boss's action had been contemptible, but fairly typical of him. "That Irish charm of his masks considerable ruthlessness, Liz. I think that it is unforgivable not letting you know about what he was doing. I thought all along that he had your agreement. C'mon, let's forget about old Murphy and think of how we're going to spend your short leave. I want you to come and stay with me. Unfortunately, I can't stay home during the day; I'm right in the middle of something at work. However, we can be together every night. What do you say to that?"

In response to the question, Liz hugged her friend, which was all of an answer that Lydia required. "Good; I have a couple of keys to your flat; that was one of the things I was to do today was give them to you. You weren't aware, obviously, but Murphy had your flat keys nicked from your handbag whilst you were at the 'Yard' and had duplicates made. The surveillance team used them to gain access to your flat so that they could plant the 'bugs' and, also, they were used for getting in the night you were attacked. I'll go right now to Plaistow and pack a bag for you with enough clothing to last you for three days at my place." Then, winking, Lydia said, "I won't bother packing your 'jamies!"

* * *

After three nights spent with Lydia Liz had got over her feelings of depression and had become anxious to get back to work. During each of the days she spent at Lydia's flat Liz engaged in an activity she called her "housewife therapy." She walked to nearby shops in Fortune Green, purchasing a bottle of white wine and the ingredients for the meal that she and Lydia would have that evening. Also, she just walked along at a leisurely pace and looked in shop windows.

Upon Lydia's arrival home in the late evening, the meal that she and Liz were to have had been prepared and was ready for cooking. Whilst that was taking place, the two women sat and talked, at the same time consuming the wine that Liz had bought. Then, after placing the supper dishes in the dishwasher, it was time for bed. The loosening of inhibitions by the wine consumption prompted sexual activities which, at times, became rather frantic.

During the talks that the two women had each evening, the subjects usually revolved around their experiences as women in a male-dominated occupation. Liz was not surprised to learn that Lydia had faced the same prejudice, as did she. However, her friend had refused to allow such incidents to depress her. She said that in a way she felt sorry for her male colleagues because they seemed to be trapped in some kind of "time warp." Most of them hadn't updated their view of the opposite sex from that prevailing in Victorian times. As far as Lydia was concerned the only thing that could be said in their defence was the fact that for most of them the male chauvinism was unconscious.

It was during their last night together, when Lydia was talking about her response to male chauvinism, namely, hard work, that she revealed to Liz, "I have heard whispers that it won't be long before I'll be made up to inspector. That's not bad, Liz; not many people, even men, can expect to go from constable to inspector in the short time I've been with the police! When it happens, I'll see what I can do to get you transferred to the 'Yard'. However, don't hold your breath on this Liz; it's all *sub rosa* at the moment."

After her stay with Lydia, Liz concluded that she was lucky to have such a friend. The stay had its down side also. She was unable to avoid the thought that she was a very lonely person, and how much different life would be if only she and Lydia could make their temporary arrangement permanent.

It was with regret that Liz bade Lydia goodbye. Lydia had to be in attendance at an important meeting at the 'Yard' so that she had to make an early departure. Liz decided to return to her flat and see what needed doing before resuming her duties at the Mile End station. She thought, "If they consider that I've overstayed my leave, tough!"

* * *

Liz's first assignment upon returning to work was to journey to New Scotland Yard to meet with Superintendent Murphy and the team who were continuing the enquiry into the assaults on animal-rights activists. It was obvious that Lydia had spoken to the superintendent about Liz's unhappiness with being used as bait without being consulted. Before the meeting he took her aside to speak to her privately. He apologised for putting her under risk. "It was the only thing I could think of doing, Liz. I didn't let you know because I thought that knowing would cause you to be looking over your shoulder all of the time. Fortunately, the plan worked and everything came out alright in the end."

"In your bedroom that night we captured two men. One of them was a person that we had suspected was part of the operation; that was Alder. Remember, he was the friend of Michael Middlebury. However, the other, Gregory Kline, was completely new to us. The evidence indicates that it was Kline who was trying to murder you. He said that the fact you went unconscious was an accident. I think it unlikely that he'll ever get anyone to believe him though. Our forensic medic has had a look at the report of the injuries you sustained. Also, he spoke to the A & E doctor who examined you immediately after you were brought into hospital. That man is in no doubt that you would not have sustained the injuries you did unless someone was definitely trying to strangle you."

"Surprisingly, Kline and Alder have admitted to taking part in assaulting animal-rights extremists. In fact, Kline has stated that he is proud of his rôle in that activity. However, both men have denied being involved in the murder of Barry Goff. Neither of them was able to give a satisfactory answer as to why you had been attacked. Kline said that you had ignored their previous warning, so they were there to teach you a lesson. Anyway, Liz, I've asked that Kline and Alder be taken into one of our interview rooms that has a two-way mirror. In a few minutes we'll go down there and you can have a good look at them. See if they are the men you saw near Barry Goff's flat on the night he was killed. If you can identify them, then I'll fill you in on what we know about the two men."

Liz was in no doubt that Gregory Kline was the man who had held open the door for her allowing her access to the building in which Barry Goff lived. However, she could not be certain about Alder, because her attention had been diverted by Kline's act of courtesy. Superintendent Murphy told Liz that it was less important that she was able to identify Alder because the most serious charge against him would be accessory to murder. However, her identification of Kline was helpful because it put him at the scene of a murder.

Back in his office, Superintendent Murphy asked Liz to be seated whilst he went to his desk, seated himself, and opened a file folder. "We now have a pretty good idea about the three men involved in the attacks on animal-rights activists." He handed her three photographs; she recognised the features of Michael Middlebury, Robert Alder and Gregory Kline. "You may wonder why Middlebury isn't in custody? Well, we've released him on his own cognisance because he has agreed to help us. I'm afraid that we had to threaten him with a charge of complicity in murder before he would agree to help. Anyway, I think Middlebury was involved mainly by feeding Kline information that he got through contacts with his former police colleagues. We are undecided whether or not charges will be brought against Police Sergeant Prendl. However, I think he can take as certain that his career in the Metropolitan Police is over."

"Kline is the really interesting character in the case. He's a scientist with a Ph.D. and a relatively long career doing scientific research. Presently, he works at Charing Cross Hospital. So far, he has been very unco-operative, but fortunately, an associate where he works has given us some details about his background."

"It seems that Kline's specialty is neurophysiology, which, I guess, is a fancy way of saying that he works on brains, 'cause that's what he does. Apparently, the animal he and his group use in their research is some kind of monkey which they keep in cages in their laboratory."

"According to the associate, Kline's troubles began a few years ago when he was working at Birmingham University.

His work there involved monkeys also, and he was continually harassed by local animal-rights activists. The final blow came when his laboratory was destroyed by a fire. Two people, who were working there on the night of the fire, were very badly injured. One of them was Kline's daughter. After several days lying unconscious in hospital, the daughter died. Although there was considerable evidence implicating a local extremist animal-rights group, the police never were able to charge anyone."

"The death of his daughter and, particularly, the reason for her death, caused Kline to have a nervous breakdown from which it took him three years to recover. Once he had recovered he wished to leave the Midlands. I gather that on the strength of his reputation, he got the post at Charing Cross that he now occupies. He became very distressed when, shortly after taking up his new job, he became the target of hate mail from animal-rights activists. He discussed the topic with Robert Alder, a retired policeman who lived in the flat next to his. Alder was sympathetic to Kline because several times during his active career he had had to police demonstrations by animal-rights activists. During their discussions the two men decided that they would strike back at the animal-rights activists. Both men felt that the extremists had had things their own way for far too long."

"It was Robert Alder who recruited Michael Middlebury. Although Alder had not served in the Met he knew Middlebury from the time both of them were on active duty. Consequently, the former police officer agreed to help. Middlebury used the friendship he had with a serving Met officer, Thomas Prendl, to obtain information about people who had been arrested because of unlawful activities connected with the animal-rights movement. For the most part, that was Middlebury's only contribution. He told me that he had become involved with breaking into your flat to give you a warning because he was worried about what Kline might do if he was involved. He told me that Alder had said that occasionally he, Alder, had been worried about Kline's behaviour. Alder had said that when Kline got very angry he seemed to lose his self control. He said that he'd seen that happen a couple of times when they were assaulting animal-rights activists."

* * *

Two months later Liz found herself on the way to New Scotland Yard. A few days earlier she had received a telephone call that had reminded her of something that had slipped her mind completely: the possibility that her friend, Lydia Mussett, would be promoted in the near future. Well, the future would be arriving soon. Lydia shortly would be known as Detective Inspector Lydia Mussett. Detective Superintendent Murphy had asked Liz to attend a small celebratory party to be held in a pub close to the 'Yard'. He assured her that the drinks would be on him, but he wouldn't object if Liz brought Lydia a bouquet or a box of chocolates.

Liz had smiled to herself as she listened to the speech that Superintendent Murphy made when everyone was assembled in the pub. As everyone expected, he was full of praise for Lydia. He described her rise from detective constable to soon-to-be inspector in only seven short years as an example of what could be achieved by hard work and dedication. Unfortunately, he seemed unaware that implicit in the words that he had chosen for his speech was the phrase, "for a woman." In other words, considering that Lydia Mussett was a woman she had done remarkably well.

Perhaps almost as well as a man might have done under the same circumstances.

Liz appreciated that probably she was supersensitive on the subject of male chauvinism, so she would wait until she had a chance to talk to Lydia to determine if she was just being silly or her interpretation of the superintendent's words was correct.

After praising Lydia, Superintendent Murphy explained that just that morning he had received the paperwork on the case against the men involved in the assaults on animal-rights activists. "It will be submitted to the Crown Prosecution Service shortly. I can tell you that Gregory Kline has been charged with the murder of Barry Goff and the attempted murder of Detective Constable Andresen. Richard Alder has been charged with being an accessory to murder. Much as we regret doing it, we felt that Michael Middlebury should take some responsibility for his rôle in the whole affair. He is being charged with perverting the course of justice. However, we decided not to bring any charges against Middlebury arising from his attack on DC Andresen. Police Sergeant Thomas Prendl, as some of you will be aware, has been forced to take early retirement because of his rôle in supplying Middlebury with information that he had no right to."

At that point he turned toward Liz and said, "speaking of DC Andresen, I have invited her to be with us today as a guest. I'm sure you are all aware that it is Liz who will be the lynchpin of the case against Kline. Her testimony will put him at the scene of the murder of Barry Goff. Also, of course, he was apprehended at the scene of the attempted murder of herself." The superintendent finished his speech by saying, "well, that's enough from me, but before I go, let's raise our glasses to Lydia and Liz."

Liz knew that Lydia had had something to drink prior to their first chance to speak to each other, but her friend's reaction to the query about the male chauvinistic tone of the superintendent's speech took her by surprise. Lydia had not interpreted Superintendent Murphy's remarks in the same way as had Liz; in fact, she accused Liz of being overly sensitive on the point. "I thought the super's remarks were very fair; I didn't see anything sexist in them at all. You'd better get a grip on yourself, Liz. If you continue to think that all men are plotting against you you're in for a rough time in the police." Lydia's remarks had stung Liz sufficiently that shortly thereafter she made her excuses and left the pub.

On the tube journey back to her flat thoughts of Lydia's remarks and her response to them occupied her mind. She wondered if, perhaps, she was indeed in the wrong.

* * *